THE RAGE

THE RAGE

Gene Kerrigan

WINDSOR
PARAGON

First published 2012
by Vintage
This Large Print edition published 2013
by AudioGO Ltd
by arrangement with
The Random House Group Ltd

Hardcover   ISBN: 978 1 4713 3676 8
Softcover   ISBN: 978 1 4713 3677 5

British Library Cataloguing in Publication Data available

Printed and bound in Great Britain by
MPG Books Group Limited

For Pat Brennan and Evelyn Bracken

The law was something to be manipulated for profit and power. The streets were dark with something more than night.

Raymond Chandler,
Trouble Is My Business

His fingers gripped the thick wooden rail, both hands clenching so hard that it felt like he might crush the wood to splinters. His breathing was shallow, the air sucked in and expelled in short puffs, hardly seeming to reach down as far as his lungs. His shoulders and chest were suddenly sweaty. It crossed his mind that something serious might be happening, something more than a panic attack. He was a big man, and fit, but he was a smoker, and at forty-seven he was carrying the consequences of a few failed New Year's resolutions. There was fear, and there was relief too. Let someone else, or no one else, deal with this—he'd have no choice but to let it all go. The tension of recent days would be swept away as his body shut down and everything evaporated in a smothering rush of mortality.

If that happened, Holly would feel the pain of it, then she'd accept his absence as just another fact of life. Like the creases around her eyes, regrettable but inevitable—and no big deal in the long run. And Grace and Dylan would feel the shock of the loss, but they were already shaping lives of their own. It was the way of things.

And without his protection Maura Coady would die. Sooner or later the lunatic would come out of the shadows and take a few minutes to crush out the small amount of life left to her.

It was towards the end of a warm April evening, a foretaste of summer. Detective Sergeant Bob Tidey was standing on the north bank of the River Liffey, on the boardwalk overhanging the dark water. Upriver, to his right, the sun left a golden

1

glow on the clouds above the Phoenix Park. Behind him, on the quays heading into the city centre, the sound and the smell of traffic.

A city going about its business, getting ready to wind up the day. Smug and oblivious.

Bob Tidey had been born here, grew up here and raised a family, he knew the city and loved it and served it and hated the way it could turn a blind eye. He was gripping the rail so hard his fingers hurt—his arms and shoulders pushed and pulled at the wooden rail, as though he was trying to shake it, to shake the entire boardwalk, to shake the whole fucking city. He pushed himself away from the rail.

The way things had gone, there was no good way out of this, no moral thing to do. The banker's murder, the Maura Coady situation—Tidey's last conversation with the brass had shut down the safe options.

He lit a cigarette and tried to still the shaking in his hands. He took a deep drag, let the smoke out slowly, then began to walk up along the boardwalk towards O'Connell Bridge.

No moral thing to do. But something had to be done.

Part 1
The Smoking Garden

1

Lying on his back, Emmet Sweetman opened his eyes.

Everything was familiar, but all wrong.

A dark raindrop—

Falling from the ceiling—

He was lying on the floor of his wide front hallway, the cold, hard marble beneath his back. All around him, the familiar dark green walls topped with the moulded cream cornices that bordered a high white ceiling. To his left, the antique walnut table where he dropped his keys when he came home each evening. He'd never seen the table like this, from below. Underneath, barely visible in the shadows, there was a scrawl in pink chalk—*VK21*.

Someone did that in the auction room, probably, where Colette bought it.

Falling slowly, from the ceiling, a dark raindrop—

All wrong—

He felt a desperate need for certainties. Time and place and other people, and where he was in relation to it all.

Dark out—

Late, now—

Lunch with—

Then—

In an instant, the day unfolded in his mind, moments emerging one from the other. Afternoon, long meeting—fat fella from the Revenue Commissioners, then more fucking lawyers—

Evening, late home, tired, the sound of his car

keys dropping onto the walnut table.

Colette—

There was—

On his way up the stairs to join her—

Doorbell—

'I'll get it.'

Now, watching the dark raindrop, falling so slowly it was still only halfway to the floor, he felt a rush of cold flooding through his body. It felt like his flesh had suddenly fused with the marble beneath him. His mind stretched towards something he didn't recognise, failed to connect—

Turning on the stairs, coming down again—

Two men on the doorstep—

The one on the left wore a hoodie, a scarf across the lower half of his face. The one on the right, his shadowed face under a baseball cap, had a midget double-barrelled shotgun and it all happened together.

The flash.

The impossibly loud bang.

The incredibly fast movement.

Lying on his back, Emmet Sweetman opened his eyes.

Dark raindrop, falling—

From skull to toes his body was icy cold.

Oh, Jesus—

The one in the hoodie was—

God, no—

Leaning forward, bending down. He looked into Emmet Sweetman's eyes—

Big black handgun.

No—

The dark raindrop—

Still falling from the ceiling—

6

Jesus, please—

2

The court opened for business in—Bob Tidey glanced at his watch—fifteen minutes. Lots of time for a smoke. He got out of the lift on the second floor of the Criminal Courts of Justice building, walked through the cafeteria and out into the Smoking Garden. There were four or five others stealing a last few puffs. Bob Tidey preferred the old Four Courts building, where smokers had to go out into the yard to enjoy their vice. The new building was an uninhibited display of affluence, but there was something indecent about splashing out so generously to facilitate a bad habit. The Smoking Garden had several tastefully designed wooden benches, where you could sit and have a puff and a coffee. It was decorated with plants and saplings and a lot of thought had gone into the design of the receptacles for stubbing out your cigarette. Despite all this, the area already seemed a little frayed about the edges—abandoned Coke cans and cardboard coffee cups, carelessly discarded butts.

Bob Tidey's disposable lighter should have been disposed of a couple of days back. He had to flick it several times before he got a tiny flame. He was leaning forward, hands cupped to light the Silk Cut, when his mobile rang.

Tidey let the flame die.

'Yeah?'

The voice was raspy, unmistakable.

'That thing we talked about, Mr Tidey—you said we could, you know, have a chat. See if there's anything can be done.'

'That'll depend, Trixie. The kid's got to open up, just to me, it won't go on the record. Get him to—'

'I told him. I think he's OK with that.'

'Good.'

'We need to talk, Mr Tidey.'

'Look, I'm at a meeting. I'll drop by when I can.'

'That'd be great.'

'No promises, OK?'

'Whatever you think—it's your game, Mr Tidey.'

It took several attempts to get the lighter working. Tidey took a long drag, sucking the shit out of the Silk Cut. Low tar was a scam, he reckoned—it meant he smoked twice as many. Ought to go back on the Rothmans.

The courts had eaten up a significant amount of Bob Tidey's working life over the past twenty-five years and ordinarily the courtroom routine was something he welcomed and enjoyed. For civilians, the courts were approached reluctantly, as defendants, litigants or witnesses. For the police, they were the goal to which months of hard work were devoted—where you got to bring your case into the winners' enclosure or watch it vanish down the toilet. Bob Tidey felt at home here.

The shiny new Criminal Courts of Justice lacked the historic heft of the old Four Courts, the higgledy-piggledy layout and countless nooks and crannies where quiet deals were done. Instead, it offered light and space, technology and comfort, all the bells and whistles that the legal community of a proud and prosperous little nation could desire. The building was conceived in the exuberant period when money was plentiful. There was so much of the stuff that the right kind of people earned big bonuses sitting around all day just thinking up new things to spend it on. The tables of the golden circles groaned with the weight of the feast. Their admirers piled into the property gambling game and sufficient crumbs fell to minimum-wage level to keep the skulls happy. Everyone knew the money-go-round would keep spinning as long as two or three bad things didn't happen simultaneously—then four or five bad things happened at once.

By the time the shiny new Criminal Courts of Justice building opened for business it had become clear that the plentiful supply of money was imaginary. At first it seemed almost a technical hitch, like someone needed to sort out a knotty little arithmetic problem. Then, house prices went through the floor, jobs evaporated, factories and businesses that had been around for decades folded overnight. There were hundreds of thousands of houses and flats empty, hundreds of unfinished estates in which no one lived or would ever want to live, all built with borrowed money to take advantage of tax breaks. The knowledge that all the backslapping and arrogance of the previous decade was nurtured in bullshit made the country blush like a teenager caught posing in front of a mirror.

Bob Tidey was in the law and order business, and whatever else went belly-up there'd always be hard men and chancers and a need for someone to put manners on them. He'd taken wage cuts, but he could live with that. These days his needs were few.

At first he missed the make-do atmosphere of

the Four Courts, now used solely for the lucrative civil law end of the business. But wherever the legal tournaments might be held, Tidey felt at home with the intricate preparation of cases, the tension, the post-trial comedown. Do the job right and it wasn't often the villains managed to slide out of the handcuffs. And on the rare occasion they did, he could bide his time. The thing about criminals, they usually give you a rematch.

This, though, was the first time he'd come to court in a role other than that of investigator. In a few minutes he'd be in a courtroom on the fourth floor, preparing to commit perjury.

Fuck it.

Made your bed, don't complain about lying on it.

Once you make a witness statement, in the aftermath of an alleged offence, that's that. Go on the stand and deviate from the written word and the defence barrister will spend the next half-hour dancing on your bones.

Tell me, Detective Sergeant, were you lying then or are you lying now?

Answering questions about that evening in Brerton's pub, after the hubbub died down, he'd kept it simple.

'I didn't see anything.'

'We'd better take a statement, anyway, just for the record.'

'No problem.'

I heard a commotion somewhere behind me and I tried to ignore it. I thought it was just someone being loud, the way it is in pubs sometimes. By the time I turned round it was all over.

End of story.

Nothing in that to help or harm either side.

That evening, when he turned round from where he was sitting at the bar of Brerton's, the batons were already swinging. Two gobshites ended up in handcuffs, followed by a trip to Beaumont A&E and a night in the cells at Turner's Lane.

Asking for it.

The gobshites, late teens, maybe twenty or so, were brave with drink. Loud, playing tough guys, throwing unfunny and insulting remarks around the pub, then laughing and staring down the regulars. A nervous young barman who asked them to cool it was told to fuck off. The gobshites laughed so hard they squeezed their eyes shut and rocked in their seats.

Bob Tidey was having a quick bite to eat, after a long, lunchless day, on his way back from a fruitless journey to see a potential witness in an insurance fraud. When two uniforms arrived at Brerton's, looking pissed off, like they'd had to interrupt a tea break, the gobshites quickly sobered up. Just what you need, when there's dozens of people chasing even minimum-wage jobs—a court appearance and a yob conviction on your record. They suddenly looked like the dim-witted boys they were. It should have ended there, with a warning, and an order to leave the pub. Instead, just as the gobshites moved towards the exit, their exaggerated swagger implying that leaving was their own idea, one of the uniforms crooked a finger, beckoned and called after them. 'Let's hear an apology to the customers, lads. And make it sincere.'

The two gobshites stood awkwardly, their faces a mixture of embarrassment, fear and anger.

'It's over,' one of them said.

The Garda raised an eyebrow. 'I'm not hearing anything that sounds like repentance.'

The other gobshite couldn't stop the anger pushing through the fear. 'Go fuck yourself.'

It was like the sound of a starting pistol, and the two policemen and the two gobshites went at it. Four young men doing what a certain kind of young man always longs to do—lock horns.

Bob Tidey took a sip of watery pub coffee. He heard the sound of baton connecting with soft tissue. He looked up and saw a spray of blood fly horizontally away from the mouth of the bigger of the two gobshites. He watched the other one cowering, one hand raised in front of his face, then he heard a scream and saw a baton knock the hand away, then a backhand blow from the same baton smacking the side of the gobshite's face.

It lasted twenty seconds tops. Tidey swallowed the last of his coffee, chewed what remained of his ham and cheese sandwich and left.

'Bob?'

The call came four hours later, when Tidey was at home, watching the highlights of a Champions League match that didn't have any highlights.

'Derek Ferry, Turner's Lane.'

'Derek, long time.'

They'd started in the force around the same time, worked at the same station for a few months.

'What it is, Bob, two of our lads picked up a couple of drunk and disorderlies this evening, down in Brerton's. One of the lads recognised you, went back to have a word and you were gone.'

'Finished my sandwich, nothing to hang about for.'

'What I was hoping—the two drunks—it turns

12

out one of them's the son of an adviser to the Minister for Commerce and Enterprise.'

'Bad luck.'

'The parents are making a fuss—they've sent a photographer down to take snaps of the bruises. Our lads are charging the two idiots with assaulting a Garda. Probably the best thing to do, in the circumstances.'

True enough. You leave bruises on the son of someone connected, there's going to be a fuss. Best thing to do is charge him with whatever's credible, and that puts the parents and their legal people on the back foot. Most likely, everyone agrees to back off and it's like nothing ever happened.

'I didn't see anything,' Tidey said.

'The lads were just wondering, if—'

'Sorry, Derek, I was sitting with my back to it all.'

Ferry hesitated just a moment, and when he spoke he managed to keep the disappointment out of his voice.

'We'd better take a statement, anyway, just for the record.'

'No problem.'

If this thing ended up in court Tidey wasn't inclined to be a police witness. He'd little appetite for hanging a conviction on a couple of drunken yobs who'd had the bad luck to bump into a couple of coppers equally eager to spray testosterone over everything in sight. On the other hand, to give evidence that confirmed the amateurism of the two uniforms was the route to professional isolation. In some circumstances it might be the right thing to do—but he'd no interest in sacrificing his career on the altar of justice for a couple of drunken fools.

13

It's a rule of life. When fools—in uniform or out—start a stupid fight, leave them to it. And when the two yobs were hit with a D&D charge it should have been a quick fine, over and out. But these yobs' parents brought in a team of legal heavyweights, and everyone was fearful of backing down, so months later it was about to squander court time.

Tidey's statement was so bland that his name wasn't on the original witness list. Then, the previous evening, he'd got the call that brought him down to the Criminal Courts of Justice.

Best to stick to the story in the statement. Get on the stand, get off it, get out of it.

He stubbed the butt of the Silk Cut, popped a Tic Tac into his mouth and went back inside.

'Sergeant Tidey?'

The tall barrister with the wrinkled face was waiting when Bob Tidey stepped out of the lift on the fourth floor. His first name was Richard, and his perpetually dour expression had earned him the nickname Mopey Dick. He was prosecuting the case in which Tidey was a witness. 'A word, if you please?' he said. He was holding a sheaf of papers in one hand.

Tidey nodded. Mopey Dick led the way to the glass barrier overlooking the massive circular atrium around which the building was designed. He took off his wig, stroked his thin grey hair and put the wig back on. He spent a few seconds carefully adjusting it, gazing down at the small figures milling about the ground-floor lobby. He looked up at Tidey, as a doctor might look at a patient for whom the results were ambiguous.

'We've got a problem. Or, to be more precise,

14

you've got a problem.'

3

Doesn't get much better than this.

Bopping down Henry Street, the warm mid-morning sun above and a free day ahead.

Feeling good.

There was a swagger to Vincent Naylor's walk. Ten days since he'd got out of prison.

The pedestrianised street wasn't too busy this morning. He caught an appraising glance from a woman with blonde hair and dangling earrings that were half the size of her face.

And looking good.

Vincent's hair was dark and curly. Everything decorating his tall, slim frame, from his Tag Heuer shades down to his charcoal Converse sneakers, he'd bought in the days immediately after he got out of the Joy. Treated himself to some fresh style—blue striped shirt from Thomas Pink, grey jacket from Pull and Bear, Sean John jeans.

He turned left into HMV.

Back to the scene of the crime.

He took off the shades and hooked them on the V of his shirt and went up the stairs two at a time up towards the DVD department. Hang a right at the dog-leg—

Half expecting to meet the Geek.

Little bollocks.

Most mornings he was up early and out, driving down to Clontarf for a run along the seafront—he got a rush from the mixture of freedom, the fresh air and the stretch of muscle and sinew. The body, Vincent often told his brother Noel, is the temple of the soul.

This morning, he'd skipped the run. Vincent was in HMV in search of a Tommy Tiernan DVD. Noel had recommended it. 'He'd make a cat laugh,' he'd said. Vincent was meeting some of his mates tonight at Noel's house in Coolock. Lift a few cans, a bite to eat, watch a DVD and have a laugh. Part of the fun of getting out of prison was the reunions.

'If you don't mind,' the Geek said in his prissy little voice.

That afternoon, fourteen months ago, Vincent Naylor had just arrived in HMV, moved past the new CDs and DVDs, headed for the stairs, in search of the *Columbo* box set. He'd seen it upstairs here a few days before, reduced to half nothing. His gran doted on Peter Falk. She'd seen most of the *Columbo* episodes but that didn't matter. Once she got her hands on the DVDs it'd take a crowbar to get her away from the telly.

'Left side of the stairs,' the Geek said. 'It's the rule.'

What fucking rule?

Geek written all over him. Collarless shirt, black waistcoat and jeans, he's wearing a little Pete Doherty hat and he's got shades, and—no kidding—the shades are perched on the brim of the hat, which must have seemed cool when he was looking at himself in the mirror this morning.

They met midpoint on the stairs, just before Vincent reached the dog-leg up to the right, and if the Geek had kept his stupid mouth shut everything would have been fine. Vincent was on

16

the right-hand side, fingers skimming the metal handrail. He hadn't even seen the little bollocks and if the fool hadn't made a thing of it Vincent might have stepped around him, all things being equal, though probably not.

'What's your problem?' he asked the Geek.

The Geek just stood there inside his smug little face, looking down at Vincent, throwing a glance towards the security guy up near the front door, knowing he was safe within sight of the bouncer. His face, though, gave him away. Little shade of red creeping across his cheeks.

Vincent Naylor stared him out, tilted his head to one side, looked right into the creep's eyes, moved his face forward no more than two or three inches. And the Geek blinked. He let out a small, dismissive noise and he stepped away from the handrail, walked around Vincent, and Vincent turned and watched him go. He knew the little bollocks would look back, so he put a smile on his face and waited, and when the Geek turned and looked back and saw Vincent standing there, it must have been the scornful smile that gave the Geek a dose of the stupids. His face flared as he turned away and headed for the exit.

Probably feeling he was safe enough now, the Geek looked back at Vincent and shouted, loud enough so everyone at ground-floor level could hear, even above the pounding of some stupid hip-hop shit, *'Scumbag! Skanger!'*

Vincent came down off the stairs in one jump. The Geek was suddenly moving, accelerating out the door, into the street, turning right and heading up towards the Spire.

The security guy held up a hand and said, 'Take

17

it easy,' but Vincent was past him, leaning forward, legs pumping.

The Geek was twenty yards ahead, running through the thin crowd of shoppers like his legs were made of flower stalks. Vincent knew the Geek's mangy little heart was in his scrawny little throat, and his stupid little brain was fluttering like a sparrow in the shadow of a hawk. Vincent's fury vanished, and he grinned. He accelerated, enjoying the ease with which he could narrow the gap between them. The Geek was barely past the junction with Moore Street.

When Vincent caught up with him he gave a little push on his shoulder and the Geek went stumbling forward, his knees hitting the ground, then his hands, then his face, his HMV bag hitting the bricks with a noise like something was coming apart inside. His Pete Doherty hat was on the ground and Vincent gave a little whoop as he stood on the Geek's shades,

'What's your hurry, smart-arse?'

He kicked the little bollocks in the ribs. The Geek rolled to one side and flattened his right hand on the ground, to lever himself up to one knee. His scream was girlish when Vincent stood on his fingers. Vincent's next kick broke the Geek's nose and that was when a gum-chewing security man from some shop or other pushed Vincent aside and said, 'That's enough.' There was a second security man off to Vincent's left and he raised a hand and said, 'Back off.'

Vincent nodded and said, 'Sure,' and drew back his foot and kicked the Geek in the ribs one last time, hard. Then he turned, ready to do a fade, and found a copper six feet away and closing fast.

18

Someone stuck out a foot and when Vincent turned and ran he tripped and went down.

He looked up at the Garda and—like he was showing off a magic trick—the fucker was suddenly hefting a baton. The Garda said, 'Give me an excuse.'

Six months later, Vincent's solicitor put down his fountain pen, leaned back in his big chair and said, 'Your best bet—you were provoked by his remarks, you felt that you and your family had been deeply insulted and you don't know what came over you.'

'I'm not pleading guilty,' Vincent said, and the solicitor shook his head.

'Twelve months,' the judge said when it got to court, and Vincent was out in eight.

Now, upstairs in HMV, Vincent looked at the *Columbo* box set. Cheaper than ever. No point buying it, though—his gran had shuffled off three months before Vincent got out. When that happened he applied for compassionate parole but—seeing it was just two days after he spat in the face of a screw who'd been asking for it—there was no fucking point.

He searched the comedy DVDs and had a look at the Tommy Tiernan. Seemed OK. For just a moment he found himself casually scoping the place. Just the one spotty loser at the cash register. There was a wide, deep pocket inside Vincent's jacket.

Daft.

He went to the register and paid up.

Only losers risk a stretch for the price of a DVD.

Sooner or later, Vincent Naylor knew, he'd be back in jail. It was part of the game. You play the odds and most of the time, if you're good enough, you'll go free and clear with a profit. Sooner or later the odds run out and that's the dues you pay. But that thing with the Geek, no more shit like that. No percentage in it. The months in the Joy had cooled his blood, given him time to think it all through.

Doing the Geek was fun, but the reward wasn't worth the risk. No more emotional shit—all business from here on. Vincent Naylor knew that with all the care in the world he couldn't stop his luck from running out some day. But before then he'd play it smart. No petty shit, no reckless moves. All business. Business is business and fun is fun. And if you do the first one right, you'll have lots of time for the other.

Spitting in the screw's face—that was a bit of a relapse. Vincent cursed himself for a day or two, but what the fuck, he wasn't a saint.

The way Vincent saw it, there are two kinds of work. The routine stuff—that's good for walking-around money. A few hundred here, a few hundred there—jobs that are safe and easy. Then there's the real thing—maybe not more than a couple of jobs like that in a year. The upside is they cough up the kind of money that takes a while to spend, and that's worth the increased risk of a stretch in the Joy. The next time Vincent Naylor went to jail it would be for something worthwhile.

4

The defence barrister looked over the top of his glasses at Bob Tidey. 'That *is* you, isn't it,

Detective Sergeant?' He was pointing at a large flat-screen television, one of several visible to the judge, the jury and the witness. The picture on the screen was frozen, the image of poor quality.

Tidey said, 'It appears to be.'

'And in this image, you're looking—where?'

'What we're looking at here,' Tidey said, 'is just a snapshot, one instant in a fast-moving event—'

'Quite the contrary, Detective Sergeant,' the defence barrister said. 'It's a video, not a snapshot, and it makes a nonsense of your sworn evidence, does it not?' He raised a small remote control. 'Let's see that again, shall we?'

Outside the courtroom, Mopey Dick hadn't used any sugar to sweeten the medicine. 'They've got a video—just a few seconds—of the incident in Brerton's. Someone got it on their mobile.' He took off his wig again, draped it over his hand, shook his head. 'There's very little to see—a couple of batons swinging. In the normal scheme of things this wouldn't either help or hurt our case.'

'But?'

'The video moves about a bit, and for a second or two it shows you sitting at the bar, looking towards the action. Then it swings back and the two policemen can clearly be seen striking the two defendants.'

He held up a sheet of paper.

'*I heard a commotion somewhere behind me,*' that's what you said. '*By the time I turned round it was all over.*'

Bob Tidey used thumb and forefinger to squeeze his lower lip. 'How come this is a big deal now?'

'They had no intention of calling your evidence.

No point—you didn't see the incident, according to your statement. Yesterday, one of the defence lawyers was doing preparatory work on the video. The whole thing lasts about twelve seconds, the shot of you lasts one-point-seven seconds—one of his colleagues saw it and identified you.'

'Proves nothing.'

'Your statement says something the court will know was untrue—you did, in fact, see what happened.'

'Still proves nothing, one way or the other.'

Mopey Dick sniffed. 'It isn't always about what you can prove.'

They went into the court and a minute after Bob Tidey took the stand the defence barrister was reading aloud Tidey's short statement.

'Those are your words, Detective Sergeant, to the investigating officers, your colleagues?'

'Yes.'

'You were the senior officer present?'

'I was off duty, I was in the pub to get something to eat.'

'You were the senior Garda officer present?'

'Yes.'

The barrister made a big thing out of nodding. He looked around the court, took a deep breath and held up the single sheet of paper. The theatrics signalled to the jury that something significant was on the way.

'And, tell me, if you would, Detective Sergeant Tidey—here, in this court, having sworn a solemn oath—do you stand by that statement?'

'I told the investigating members what I remembered, and I stand by that.'

The barrister looked up at the bench. 'I think

22

now would be a good time, Judge.' The court clerk switched on the television and handed the remote to the lawyer.

After the short video clip was run for a second and a third time, with the picture frozen at the appropriate moment, the defence barrister said, 'What this proves, Detective Sergeant, is that you clearly witnessed the events that are the subject of this case. Short though the video segment may be, it clearly shows you facing the action.'

'That evening was—'

'And I put it to you that we can conclude from this that—for some reason—you sought to avoid giving true evidence of what you saw. So, you lied and said you saw nothing, is that right?'

'Not true.'

'And the first thing you did on taking the witness stand today was to claim—on a solemn oath—that the statement you made about not seeing this incident was the truth, the whole truth and nothing but the truth.'

'The whole thing—'

'What are you hiding, Detective Sergeant?'

'The whole thing happened in seconds—I wasn't timing it, I wasn't taking notes about exactly when I turned round—'

'You saw what happened or you didn't. What were your two colleagues up to that was so—so *criminal*, perhaps, that you lied on oath in order to conceal it?'

'I saw nothing, and that's what I said.'

'What I want to know is whether you conspired with the other officers—officers using their batons in such a flagrantly irresponsible manner—in order to deceive this court about the truth of this incident.'

'I conspired with no one.'

'When the senior officer on the scene tells a lie on oath, it surely follows that a conscientious jury must have a reasonable doubt about any and all aspects of the police case.'

'My statement—'

'Thank you, Detective Sergeant.'

The defence barrister sat down.

Mopey Dick stood up and asked Bob Tidey a few questions, designed to emphasise the irrelevance of his role in the case. His heart didn't seem to be in it.

5

Leaving HMV, glad to be back in the warm sun, Vincent put his shades on and strolled back up Henry Street towards the Spire. He was thinking about Noel's big job—the hundredth time he'd gone over it, looking at everything from every angle, narrowing the odds of anything going wrong. Vincent had done some big shit in his time, but always as part of someone's else's crew. This was the first big one where Vincent was in charge, with his own people, doing it for more than wages.

'You're kidding me,' he'd said to Noel, when his brother brought him the story shortly before he got out of the Joy.

'Pissed, and mouthing out of him in the back seat.'

Noel's friend Tommo collected a fare at the taxi rank at the top of Grafton Street. Nuts Corner.

Three o'clock in the morning, and the guy's plastered, yapping about his job—driving a security van. 'All that money in the back of the van,' Tommo tells Noel. 'Every time he goes to work he doesn't know if he's gonna get his head broken. And what's he get at the end of the month?—peanuts. Not bad enough the pay's shit—he's just had a wage cut, he's paying shitty levies the government takes to bail out the fucking banks. And here he is, with maybe three hours' sleep ahead of him, then he's up to deliver another vanload of cash from one shower of rich bastards to another.'

All Tommo does is say, *Man, you're right, that's crap*. And he remembers all the details and when the fare staggers into his house—out in Ballybrack—Tommo makes a note of the address.

'Tommo wants a couple of grand—wants nothing to do with the job.'

By the time Vincent got out it was all there, the target and the modus. All it needed was a bit of tweaking from Vincent. Sometimes Noel forgot the obvious stuff, like scorching your back-trail so the police don't have prints or traces to put under a microscope.

As Vincent reached Moore Street he paused. He'd intended buying a few steaks from FX Buckley's, cook something classy for the lads tonight, but the warm day made him feel like a stroll. He'd get the food later.

Continuing up Henry Street he thought again of the Geek. It was somewhere up here the little bollocks went down. Remembering him in court, giving evidence, a permanent tilt to his nose where Vincent's boot connected.

25

As he turned into O'Connell Street Vincent's eyes were flashed by a reflection of sunlight from a passing bus. He stopped and just stood there, breathing deeply. The sun made everything in the city look cleaner, fresher. So fucking *good* to be out, and what a terrific morning. A morning made for a laid-back stroll.

Never know what might turn up.

*   *   *

The original idea was to have the press conference at Garda headquarters, but the media wasn't happy with that. 'No pizzazz,' one crime correspondent explained to Assistant Commissioner Colin O'Keefe. 'We need better optics than a couple of brass coppers sitting behind a table.'

O'Keefe, although alone in his office and on the phone, was careful to keep the irritation off his face. These fuckers could read your mood long-distance. This was one of those cases where media cooperation was useful, and if that meant kissing the hacks' arses, so be it.

'How about we do it at the murder scene?' The hack sounded more hopeful than demanding.

O'Keefe took just a moment, then he said, 'Good idea. I'll set it up for this afternoon.'

'This morning would be better,' the hack said.

The fucker had to have the last word. O'Keefe kept his tone even. 'That's fine.'

Every inch of the Emmet Sweetman murder scene had long been searched and cleared, but O'Keefe had the uniforms throw up a few lengths of scene-of-crime tape, to give the area the CSI atmosphere that helped feed the hacks' fantasies

26

about themselves. He'd organised a handful of uniforms, to stand around looking thoughtful. In exchange for presenting a reassuring image of the police at work, the hacks got to hang about the murder scene, trying out their favourite theories of the case. Detective Chief Superintendent Malachy Hogg from the National Bureau of Criminal Investigation, in operational control of the murder inquiry, was along to add some weight.

There were a few minutes of informal queries and responses—mostly O'Keefe and Hogg answering amateur detective questions and saying positive things about the investigation, without giving away any detail. The main point of the exercise was the photo opportunity and the declaration that the investigation was making steady progress.

'Assistant Commissioner?' The reporter was from the *Irish Times*, puffy-faced, with an air of boredom. 'Are you aware of an academic report showing that gun killings in Ireland are currently—'

'To be frank, I'm too busy investigating crime to indulge in negative academic chit-chat about it.' O'Keefe put on his sweetest smile.

'Researchers at Aberdeen University—'

'Next question.'

'Proportionately, the figures show that gun homicide in Ireland is five times the rate in England and Wales.'

'Next question.'

Another hack obliged. 'Would you say, Assistant Commissioner that the police are leaving no stone unturned in this investigation?'

For a moment, O'Keefe thought the hack was

taking the piss, but the bovine expression was too earnest to be faked. 'No stone unturned', he said.

When the hacks couldn't think of any more questions, O'Keefe and Hogg stood outside the front door of the Sweetman house, chatting while the snappers got their pictures. It had a touch of drama—the investigators standing where the killers had stood when Emmet Sweetman opened his front door for the last time.

'I have real work to do elsewhere,' Hogg said.

'Think of it as penance for your sins.'

'The minister leaning on you?'

'Every few hours, phone calls from his secretary, asking for updates. This bullshit, it takes a few minutes and it helps kill the notion that it's open season on wealthy scumbags.'

Since the Sweetman murder, one bank had a breeze block thrown through a window and two had Molotov cocktails thrown at their front doors. In separate incidents, three mid-level bankers had been assaulted by members of the public and the son of a leading property developer was kicked senseless after leaving a nightclub. Most worrying of all, the former chief executive of another bank returned from a business trip to Chicago to find two bullet holes in the front window of his mansion. The media had agreed to a police request to play down such incidents. If bloodying the noses of bankers and developers became fashionable, things could very quickly get out of control in a target-rich environment. Today's photo opportunity kept the media onside. It also put the word out that the police were taking the Sweetman murder so seriously that two senior officers got out from behind their desks and came personally to the murder scene.

Looking at the hacks, thirty feet away behind a length of blue-and-white tape, Hogg murmured, 'Next time we do this, I must remember to bring a magnifying glass, get down on all fours and check the ground for clues.'

One of the hacks called out, 'Any chance of a look inside?'

O'Keefe put on a regretful expression. 'Not possible, I'm afraid, lads—operational reasons.' He turned back to Hogg. 'Ballistic results?'

'There's a backlog, but I'm assured they're imminent.'

Two minutes later, duty done, O'Keefe was getting into his car. A young reporter he didn't recognise hurried over, determined to get a few exclusive words—a little guy with a suit and over-gelled hair. He had the look of someone who took a lot of time polishing his appearance, but wasn't very good at it.

'Anthony Prendergast, *Daily Record*.'

'How can I help you, Anthony?'

'An in-depth interview, any time, any place.'

'Why should I piss off your colleagues?'

'I write it up, submit it to you so you can be assured the quotes are accurate, then—'

'Not a chance.'

Anthony smiled. 'No harm asking—if you're not in, you can't win.'

'True enough, son.'

As O'Keefe gently eased the car away, he gave the media pack a wave. Normally, he'd be sitting in the back of an official car, with a driver up front. These days of public service cuts and pay levies, the privileges of rank were best not advertised.

Oh, now, that's promising.

Vincent Naylor didn't break stride, didn't gawk into the shoe shop, just kept moving. These days, you can't scratch your balls without being picked up on a CCTV camera.

That could be taken care of, no bother.

In a camping supplies shop, Vincent found a plastic rain jacket wrapped up into a compact plastic bag—bright red. Just the job.

Twenty-two fucking euro. A plastic raincoat in a cutesy plastic bag—*you've got to be fucking kidding me.*

All that shit about prices falling through the floor . . .

There was room for the raincoat, stuffed down his jeans, under the back of his jacket—for a moment, Vincent considered it.

Not worth the risk.

At the cash register, his shades pushed up into his hair, Vincent paid the beardie behind the counter and said, 'Bit pricey, for a plastic mac. Celtic Tiger prices, right?'

'It's a first-rate product, sir, and I—'

'Rip-off merchants.'

He dumped the cutesy plastic bag in a litter bin and kept the raincoat in the deep inside pocket of his jacket, with the Tommy Tiernan DVD. As he sauntered down a lane close to the target shop, he stopped in the doorway of an Asian food shop and adjusted his shades. He took out the raincoat, put it on, zipped it up and pulled the hood over his head. He hated hoodies, hoods of any kind—made him feel like a horse in blinkers. But there was no better shield from CCTV cameras.

Quick glance inside. No customers.

First thing, once he got into the shoe shop, he clocked the inside of the door, looking for a latch or a bolt he could slip, lock the door behind him. *Nothing doing.*

Not to worry—this time of morning, this kind of snooty shop, customers would be thin on the ground.

He turned towards the shop assistant, her expression slightly amused as she took in the rainwear, the shades. It took a moment, then she seemed to shrink into herself as it hit her what was happening.

*   *   *

The thing was, they were wearing gloves. Both of them. Without that detail, Maura Coady mightn't have given them a second thought.

Getting out of the dark green car. Gloves, in this weather. Cream-coloured, thin, stretchy plastic gloves. Like a surgeon wears.

If just one of the two men was wearing plastic gloves it could be he had a problem with his skin. Both men—

None of your business, Maura.

When Maura Coady moved to this house in North Strand, two years back, the excitement of finally living alone, of having a space to which no one else in the world had a right, filled her with exhilaration. She didn't have a television, a detachment from the outer world that she

31

inherited from the long decades in the convent. But she had a window—and the view through the net curtain provided sufficient drama. The window looked directly out onto the street, no garden, the pavement just inches away. The routine was mostly humdrum, workaday, but there were moments. She'd be crossing the room, about to do some chore, when she'd notice someone wheeling a trolley back from the Spar on the corner. She'd stand and watch them pass, imagine their lives for a few moments—not out of curiosity or envy, just enjoying the fleeting indulgence. Then she'd get on with whatever she was about.

Other times, there were kids down the corner, messing—nothing rough, just youngsters enjoying a bit of horseplay, and that would hold her attention. Sometimes it brought back memories of her pupils, decades ago. Very occasionally, there would be a trivial argument—a parent and a child, a couple of adults—never anything serious. There was always something happening, small and all as it might be. She sometimes felt guilty, like she was a bit of a sneaky-peeker, but she easily forgave herself. It was just a small interest in how people lived their lives.

Now, she watched Phil Heneghan carefully stand up. He'd been kneeling at the front of his house across the road, using a pencil to clear dirt out of the holes in the ventilation block. He'd be over later today, offering to do one chore or another, as he did several times a week. The need to fight a rearguard action against household disaster was a regular thing with Phil. 'If the vent gets blocked, you're asking for trouble. Lord knows what kinds of mould starts growing under the floorboards and next thing you know you're smelling dry rot.'

Phil and his wife Jacinta were even older than Maura, cresting eighty. They looked after the little house as though they were newly-weds tending a first love nest. 'When the Tolka burst its banks—it was a long time ago, but the houses, you can still see the waterline in places. Boats, they had—they came down this street in little boats, it was so bad. Things like that, they leave their mark, even decades later.'

Phil went into his house now, and came out a moment later with a yellow duster and a tin of something. He began to work patiently on the brass knocker, bringing up the shine.

What happened was the oddest thing ever. The gloves, then the driver locking the car, his friend going to the front of the car, the driver to the back, and they both hunkered down and began working on something. She could see only the one at the back, and just the top of the other man's head. Within seconds they stood up and walked away, down the street, past the Spar shop, then across onto the main road. And a day later the car was still sitting there outside Maura's house.

This wasn't right.

Ought to do something.

And maybe make a fuss over nothing. The old woman making a commotion over something that ordinary people—real people with real lives— would take for granted.

Two men park a car—maybe they didn't know the area, they weren't sure where the place was they were visiting, so they park somewhere, go off on foot to find the place they're looking for. And there's a reason, some reason, why they're too busy

33

to come back. Perhaps they drove away when she was asleep, came back before she got up, parked in the same spot.

Much as she wanted to believe that, it didn't seem likely.

But it was wrong to simply presume they were up to something sinful.

No good comes of jumping to conclusions.

It was like the newspaper story she read about people who saw a Muslim man praying before he got on an airplane and they created a commotion, got the flight delayed and the Muslim taken off, so he missed his flight while they made sure he wasn't a hijacker. Thirty years back, people in England heard an Irish accent, the first thing they thought of was maybe this is a bomber. She knew a priest— this was half a lifetime ago—who was pulled in by the police when he got off the boat at Holyhead, held for two days. No good comes of thinking the worst of people.

Why couldn't two men arriving in the same car have some reason that required them both to wear plastic gloves?

Maura Coady had been standing at the window for the best part of an hour this morning, hoping the men would come back, drive away. She shouldn't let another day pass without doing something. If the men had stolen the car, they could come back at any time, drive it away, maybe paint it, sell it—whoever owned it would never see it again.

She forced herself to move away from the window. She stood at the kitchen sink for ten minutes, washing up. Then she made a cup of tea, sat at the kitchen table and opened her book.

When she finished the tea she washed the cup and left it on the drainer. She went back to the front room. The dark green car was still there.

*   *   *

The jury was removed from the courtroom while the defence put forward a motion to have the assault case thrown out. As the babble continued, Detective Sergeant Bob Tidey wanted to let his mind drift, but professional habits are demanding. Stay on top of the facts even through the boring bits and you're ready for anything. He found himself parsing the defence lawyer's argument, anticipating the prosecution's responses. The conventions of the courtroom insisted on such jousts, in which arguments assumed a logic of their own, anchored in legal precedents and obscure judgements. Sometimes the whole thing separated completely from the facts of the case and drifted off into the upper atmosphere of legal reasoning. With each sentence, the case drifted further from the truth—that two arrogant idiots took a walloping from two overbearing policemen. Courtroom custom demanded that they all pretend that this was about matters of great legal significance.

'In that case,' the judge said, glancing at the clock at the back of the court, 'I'll adjourn until tomorrow morning, at which point I'll rule on the application.'

'You won't need me—tomorrow morning?' Tidey asked Mopey Dick.

The lawyer made a face. 'I really think—given the way this has gone—it might be best, just in

35

case, if you make yourself available.'

Tidey nodded. Another day on the front line in the war on crime.

7

The assistant in the shoe shop said, 'Please,' and Vincent Naylor said, 'Money.'

It was a small shop, little more than a brightly lit rectangle. Cream walls, chrome and crystal retail decorations, walnut chairs and footstools. Tasteful lighting illuminated carefully positioned glass shelves on which a sparse assortment of women's shoes was stylishly displayed. Vincent knew nothing about women's shoes, but he'd bet the stuff in here came with cute little labels that jacked the price up big time. He'd bet the people who owned this place never said they owned a shoe shop—they'd call it a footwear boutique. They wouldn't have customers, they'd have clientele. And they'd charge through the nose for the freedom of shopping away from the riff-raff. Shop like this, not up to paying top rents, but discreetly advertised and close enough to Grafton Street so the right people would be able to find it. Not a lot of trade, but every sale would be at a tidy price.

For Vincent, the problem with a place like this was that most purchases would involve credit cards. Still, there was bound to be a bit of cash on the premises. And, to get his hands on it, just this tasty little bird to go through.

He gestured towards the back of the shop, where a cash register stood on a curved waist-high counter.

'Get the money.'

Vincent made his voice come out low, harsh, like he was barely holding himself together. He could see the tremor in her hands. *Jesus, she was something.*

Maybe a couple of years younger than Vincent, which would make her about twenty-four, something like that. A cool face with barely a hint of make-up, a permanently stuck-up kind of face. Short blonde hair drew attention to her long, slim neck. Loose silky dress, a lot of blue in it, coming down to just above her knees. Neat tits, not much showing. He liked that. Bare legs, going right up there. He could feel his hands sliding up the backs of her thighs. Pressing against her, her knees opening—

Which would be really stupid. A bit of money goes missing from a city centre shop—with all the things going on in the world, what's the chances the cops will give a crap about that? Bend little missy over the counter and make a bit of a mess on her—and do it within a spit of Grafton Street— that's when they haul out the heavy gang and start pumping up the overtime.

'Money,' he said again.

'Please—'

Vincent was standing with his hooded face turned sideways on to the dinky little CCTV camera, high up on a side wall. He pointed towards the cash register. The woman backed away, until she was standing next to the counter. Vincent made his voice loud, abrupt. *'Give it!'* The woman made a high-pitched *Ah* sound, her hand jerked in fear. It hit a small brown pencil cup and knocked it

37

over, spilling a couple of biros and a long scissors to the floor.

She hurriedly opened the register and took out a thin wad of banknotes, left them down on the counter. She fiddled in the drawer and took out a handful of coins. Vincent shook his head.

'Any more notes in there?' he said.

The woman shook her head.

'I check that and you're lying,' Vincent said, 'you'll never want to look in a mirror again.'

'No, there's—that's all.' She spoke quickly, her voice thin. She backed away as Vincent went to the counter and picked up the money. Three fifties, a lot more twenties and tens.

Vincent pointed at a door set into the back wall. 'What's in there?'

'Shoes.'

'You've got a handbag, a purse?'

She nodded.

'In there?'

Another nod.

'Show me.'

'Please,' she said.

'Show me.'

Her legs were quivering, her hands too, as she went to the door and opened it.

'No delay, get in there.'

As he followed her in he glanced back, out through the shop window. People passing, no sign of any interest. He closed the door behind him.

The walls of the back room were lined with shelves holding layers of shoeboxes. There was a short counter against a side wall, with a sink, an electric kettle and some mugs and glasses. The woman picked up her brown leather handbag and

38

offered it to him.

'Take out the purse, get out the money.'

She did as he said, putting several notes—at least two fifties—beside the kettle.

'Hand it to me.'

It took her a moment to work up to it, then she picked up the money and extended it towards him. He stayed where he was and after a few seconds she stepped closer, hand outstretched with her offering. He stared at her face, forced her to make eye contact. Then he let her see that he was lowering his gaze to her breasts, to her hips and her legs, just for a moment, then back up. As he took the money with one hand, he reached out with the other, his palm cupping her hand. It felt soft, warm and promising, and it trembled.

Jesus, it would be just—

Not on.

Anything like that and this becomes more than an easy cash pickup and maybe he's missed something along the way and it leads the cops to his door and he's looking at serious time.

'You see this?' he said. He gestured towards his face.

She nodded.

'You see this face?'

For a moment she was puzzled, then it clicked and she said, 'No, I didn't see your face.'

'I could find you.'

'Please.'

He let some silence run and watched her tremble.

'Ten minutes before you call anyone.'

'Yes.'

'I'll know.'

Her voice was barely there. 'Yes.'

As he let go of her hand, his fingers brushed hers and he forced eye contact again. He held that for a moment, then he smiled. He turned and left the back room. Again, nothing happening outside on the street. He left the shop immediately, turned right and hurried away. Walking up a narrow lane, out of sight of any CCTV cameras, he took off the rain jacket, rolled it up and stuffed it into his inside pocket.

His hand touched the Tommy Tiernan DVD and he remembered tonight's get-together with his mates. Something to look forward to.

8

William Dixon, known to his friends as Trixie, was feeding a succession of red-and-white jerseys into an industrial-strength washing machine. The walls of the small room were breeze blocks, almost all of the floor was covered with dusty, scuffed brown linoleum, layers of dirt worn into it. There was an old bicycle lying against a large, rusted tool chest, a ladder attached to hooks high on a wall. Shelves were laden with cardboard boxes, tins and tools and half-full jars, coils of wire and pieces of metal that might once have had a function. The room was cluttered in the way a room gets when it has no purpose except to hold all the things that don't fit anywhere else.

'This is a minimum-wage gig,' Trixie said to Detective Sergeant Bob Tidey. 'And I was trying to work out, the other day, what kind of money I earned when I was thieving. I reckon—allowing for the value of money all those years ago—I probably take home more, doing this.' He coughed. 'Mug's game.'

Mostly Trixie's history was shop burglaries, small change—only twice did he make the papers, each time no more than half a paragraph in the District Court reports. The *Herald* promoted him to the front page—this was twenty years back—after Trixie shimmied up a drainpipe and into the front bedroom of a burning house. THE HERO, the headline said over a picture of William 'Trixie' Dixon in a hospital bed. On his way home, after an unsuccessful expedition to liberate a few boxes of cigarettes from a local Centra, he saw smoke coming from an open window. After he roused a neighbour to call the fire brigade, he rang the doorbell of the burning house and began shouting. When there was no response, he went up the drainpipe, in through the window and came back out and down the drainpipe, a baby tucked inside his zipped jacket. A neighbour collected the kid, then Trixie went back up and did it again, this time sliding and groping his way to ground level, using both feet and one hand, the other arm clutching a two-year-old. By then, the brigade had arrived and they took the parents out. Trixie ended up with scorched lungs and a cough that occasionally still troubled him.

A uniformed Bob Tidey was one of the first Gardai on the scene, as Trixie was lifted into an ambulance. Tidey went to Beaumont Hospital later, where a nurse showed him the roll of housebreaking tools she'd found in a long inside pocket of Trixie's jacket.

'Isn't there somewhere we could lose these?' Tidey said. The nurse looked at him for a moment, then she took the tools away.

The Glencara GAA club, where Trixie had played as an under-21, stepped in when he was back on his feet and still fragile. A variety of things that would otherwise have been done by volunteers were cobbled together into a paying job. Looking after the hurling and football gear, a bit of bartending in the clubhouse, a bit of stewarding on match day.

When Trixie's son Christy's image turned up on a CCTV tape after a warehouse break-in, a couple of uniforms were sent to pick him up. Christy didn't make a fuss. It was only when the uniforms began searching his flat that he got nervous, and when one of them came out of the bedroom carrying a .38 Ruger wrapped in a T-shirt, Christy came close to crying. He sat on the arm of his shabby two-seater sofa, his hands covering his face, and said, 'Oh fuck,' over and over.

Bob Tidey was involved in questioning Christy when he was brought to the station. When Christy's father approached Tidey to put in a good word, Tidey's Superintendent agreed there was no harm in that. 'The son's going to jail, no doubt about that, but he's a pathetic little fucker.'

Trixie Dixon slammed the door of the washing machine. After he fiddled with the controls for a moment the thing made a noise like a 747 hurtling down a runway. Trixie and Tidey went outside. On the pitch, a dozen young hurlers were warming up, pucking a ball about, one lad crouched in a goalmouth, his hurley at the ready, a Spartan holding the pass.

Trixie said, 'Will he be OK?'

'He'll do time.'

'I know that, but there's time and there's time.'

'Possession of a loaded gun—and no explanation. These days, gangs all over the headlines—judges don't like to be seen to be soft on that kind of thing.'

'You know that's not Christy.'

Bob Tidey let it lie for a moment, then he said, 'He tell you who the piece belonged to?'

'You know I can't say.'

'Off the record—and you know I won't fuck you over.'

Trixie began walking along the side of the pitch, watching the kids slashing at the ball, listening to them shout encouragement and derision at one another. The only others around, apart from the hurlers, were three old guys standing on the far touchline, shouting occasional advice. Trixie and Tidey had almost reached the halfway line before Trixie stopped and said, 'Roly Blount.'

Tidey winced. 'That's bad.'

Roly was one of Frank Tucker's nearest and dearest. Working from his base in the west of the city, Tucker had established outposts on both sides of the river, everything from armed robbery and protection to drugs and smuggled cigarettes. Anything that might be a danger to him or his outfit was simply removed. Christy Dixon had no option but to take the weight for the gun possession.

Trixie said nothing. After a while, they turned and walked back towards the clubhouse. Bob Tidey said, 'There's no happy ending to this, but let's see what we can see, right?'

9

Carrying meat and vegetables bought in Moore Street, Vincent Naylor emerged from his local Spar with a carton of milk. The small cluster of shops—Spar, hairdresser's, coffee shop, pharmacy—was set apart from the main retail area, on the other side of an almost empty car park. That was a shopper's paradise. You could buy all you needed to build and furnish a house, stock the fridge, turn the garden into a botanic wonder and get your hair coloured for the house-warming party. Everything was spread out, all the shops huge, the paved areas twice the size they needed to be. Designed for relaxed shopping. The place had everything, including lots of *To Let* signs.

It was a long walk across a flat space towards the MacClenaghan building. Just six floors, but all the emptiness around it gave the impression of a majestic tower. The MacClenaghan was to be the first of a set of four apartment blocks—the only one completed. The hoarding around the intended site of the other blocks was shabby and broken, the foundations half finished. The flats in the MacClenaghan came furnished, fitted out with standard low-grade stuff—aimed at workers anxious to get on the property ladder, with not much left over after paying the mortgage. Then, just as the MacClenaghan went up, the property ladder turned to dust.

Vincent was breathing normally when he reached his fourth-floor apartment. The door was ajar, the lock broken. The lift had been disabled but Noel arranged for an electrician mate to hook up the apartment, so the sockets worked, the fridge and the shower. He bought a kettle and a microwave.

Vincent stashed the food, made an instant coffee and sat by the window. Taking his time, he counted the money he'd stolen. He liked this bit, not sure exactly how much it would amount to, but knowing it was a good handful—it was like opening a gift on his birthday.

It came to three hundred and eighty. Not bad.

Sitting here, a coffee within reach, some handy money, nice view—Vincent didn't see how life could have worked out better, all things considered.

Vincent was the only one living in the block.

'No point paying rent,' Noel said. Two days before Vincent got out of the Joy, Noel broke the lock. Fourth floor—a good choice. Too far up for casual snoopers. He also paid a visit to a couple of junkies squatting in a flat two floors down. No electricity, no fridge or heater. That kind of thing wouldn't do—a junkie gets cold and lights a fire in the middle of the living-room floor and dozes off. Vincent might go to sleep one night and never wake up.

'It's our flat—we've done things, fixed it up,' the woman said.

Noel looked around—it was like someone had dumped the contents of a wheelie bin on the floor, then spread it around a bit.

'Tell you what,' Noel said. He held out a twenty-euro note.

'No fucking way,' the woman said. Her partner reached out and took the money, folded it and tucked it inside his shabby shoe. The woman stared

45

a moment, then turned her back and looked out the window.

Vincent filled a closet with clothes and he was more or less ready to rock. Noel offered to get him a telly, but Vincent said it was all shit—he had his iPod. Noel got him a speaker dock so he could listen without earphones.

There was a balcony outside the window—just about deep enough for a potted plant. At night, Vincent liked to stand out there, looking across towards the Edwardstown housing estate, music playing loudly behind him. A six-floor building, sticking up into the sky, all shiny and new, at the edge of the low-rise estate. Gave him a Lord of the Manor feeling.

He didn't use the lights at night, just candles—with the curtains closed. You never knew when a weary developer might come by to look up at his property and mourn the death of his ambitions. Besides, the flicker from the candles added to the magic of the place.

Three hundred and eighty euros—fair enough, for a few minutes' work. It would do for walking-around money. All going well in the days to come, what he'd have was more like sitting-down-and-putting-your-feet-up money.

*　　*　　*

When Vincent Naylor got out of jail, Noel took him to see a man named Shay Harrison. Vincent gave him a big smile. 'What's the story, Shay?'

The security guy looked defeated. He'd mouthed off in the back of Tommo's taxi, complaining about his job, Tommo provided his address, and it took

Noel just days to suss out the basics. Married, four kids, a house in Ballybrack, an eight-year-old Fiat and a girlfriend several years younger than his wife.

They took him late at night, after he'd left his girlfriend's flat. Liam Delaney and Kevin Broe brought him to a garage out in Stillorgan, owned by a cousin of Liam's. Shay did his best to behave like the tough guy he was paid to be, but that stopped after a couple of hours with his hands tied behind his back.

Shay was a big man, muscle still holding under a layer of flab. He'd spent a lot of time working on a delicately trimmed hairy decoration on his chin— probably figured it would make his face look thinner. By the time Vincent and Noel got there the beard was flecked with beads of sweat.

No marks on the face, Vincent had told Liam and Kevin. He goes to work with marks on his face, it's all over. It took no more than half a dozen punches to his stomach and kidneys before Shay was ready to cough. They gave him a few more, just because.

'Tell him where you work, Shay.'

'Protectica. I deliver cash.'

Vincent said, 'Of course you do, old son.'

Vincent decided there was no need for any more physical stuff, just a threat followed by something Shay could use to claw back some pride.

The threat was very basic. 'You probably know the best way out of this is to stay calm and do what we say. And probably you're thinking that once you get out of here you make a phone call and when we make our move the cops are all over us. Or, after the job, the cops show you a line-up and you point

47

a finger and we spend the next twenty Christmases in the Joy. Am I right, Shay?'

Shay said nothing, but his face said that was about right.

'All I'm going to tell you, Shay, is we've got another place like this—much more isolated. You could scream your eyeballs out and no one would hear you, OK? We've got a machine there—they call it a wood chopper, you know the kind of thing I mean? One of those machines the gardeners use in the parks, to grind up branches and shit—a wood chopper.'

'It's called a wood chipper,' Noel said.

'It's pretty old, to be honest, a bit rusty, but that's not your problem. Your problem, Shay, is making sure you don't say a word to anyone about any of this—ever. Not even when this is over and the cops are sniffing around everyone who works for Protectica. Say a word, one word—even if they've picked me up and I'm safely locked away in the Joy—that's where you go, into the wood chopper, an inch at a time.'

'I said I'll do whatever you want.'

'My guess is you'll pass out by the time it gets to your ankles—that's what happened, the couple of times we did it before. What I'm saying—by the time the machine gets to your balls the chances are you'll be unconscious, so that won't be so bad.'

Vincent gave Shay a moment to take that in, then he offered him a chance to see this in a positive light.

'What you earn—I don't know what you take home, but I'd say you could do with a bit of loose change, am I right?'

Shay said nothing.

'It's not like you'd ever steal it, we know that. But if some money showed up in the post—no account, no paper trail—I mean, that's bound to come in handy. I'm not talking about a fortune, nothing that will change your life, get the cops excited. Your eldest girl—weddings don't come cheap. She's engaged, right? The older boy is already in Manchester—the way the job scene is these days, the other one might need to join him.'

Noel said, 'The kid could maybe use a little help, rent and shit, for the first month or two.'

'It's not like it's your money in the van, is it?' Vincent said. 'And those fuckers—the way they piss on people like us, it's not like you owe them anything, is it?'

It got so Shay saw a big, big downside to pissing off Vincent—and a small benefit if he cooperated. And it helped that doing the sensible thing stuck a finger in the eye of the fat bastards who treated him like he ought to be grateful for a toytown wage.

'But—look, I'm not on my own in the van, there's two others. And there's all sorts of—'

'Not to worry, Shay—we need you for information. The van we hit, it won't be yours, OK? No one's going to connect you with this.'

Vincent cupped his hand behind Shay's head and pulled him close. He spoke very quietly. 'No more chat, my friend. Which is it to be, play or pay?'

When Shay began talking, with long answers to every question, they had to slow him down while Noel took notes.

10

Holly raised her head from the pillow, to see the time on the bedside clock.

'Pushing midnight,' she said. 'You'd better go.'

Bob Tidey looked at his watch. 'Twenty past eleven.'

'She'll be home soon,' Holly said.

'Jesus—we're all adults.'

'Still.'

He badly wanted to just lie here, to let himself drift off to sleep. All the tensions and worries of the day had been drained, his head was heavy and his whole body was melting into the bed.

'Please, Bob.'

'The fact that we've had sex has probably dawned on her—I mean, her very existence might be a clue.'

She didn't reply and he knew there was no point arguing.

He sat up and felt the tiredness pulling him back towards the pillow. By the time he got dressed he was fully awake and resenting it. He took out his packet of Silk Cut and Holly said, 'Not up here, please. She'll smell the smoke. Downstairs.'

By the time Holly got dressed and came down to the kitchen, Bob Tidey had made two mugs of coffee and his cigarette was half smoked.

'You working in the morning?'

Tidey nodded. 'Back to court. You?'

Holly shook her head. 'I'm down to two days a week. And they've let another six people go.'

'You OK for money?'

'I'm getting by.'

'Just say—'

'I know. Thanks.'

'Anyway.'

Ten minutes later, when they heard the front door opening, she smiled and made a face at him. 'Told you so.'

Grace was chirpy, pleased to see him.

'Hi, Dad, still chasing villains?'

'Anyone double-parks in my territory's in big trouble.'

It was the kind of walking-on-eggshells atmosphere that came from everyone being careful to be considerate. After a while Tidey kissed them both goodnight and prepared to go home.

In the four years after Tidey and his wife split up he visited the house once every couple of months. He saw Grace and her brother Dylan as often as they had the time to spare—both in their late teens then, they were usually busy. By and by, they both moved out. In those four years, Tidey didn't have anything with anyone else that lasted more than a couple of weeks. He had no idea of Holly's life. One night, melancholy and a little drunk, she called and asked Tidey to drop by.

'Are we OK?' he said, before he left the house that night.

'We'll never be OK.'

'I'll never be forgiven?'

She looked up. 'I needed someone to hold me tonight. And I needed a fuck, without the usual hassle. And I still like you, still want you. And, no, you'll never be forgiven.'

Since then—one or the other making the call or sending a text—they occasionally gave each other comfort, usually at Holly's house in Killester, sometimes at Tidey's apartment in Glasnevin. He accepted her rule that he never stay overnight, he never tried to make things more than they were, knowing she would tell him something like she'd told him that first night. 'We had what I thought we wanted, and it wasn't enough for you.'

Holly's squeamishness about the kids discovering the semi-regular relationship hadn't mattered too much. Dylan was in London, working for button money in a sound studio, still trying to re-form the band that was going to leave U2 in its dust. Grace was office manager with a firm of architects and had a flat on the Southside. Then, almost overnight, no one wanted to build anything in Dublin, and Grace was made redundant and moved back with her mother to save on rent.

Tonight, as she opened the front door to let him out, Holly leaned over and kissed him on the cheek and Tidey looked her in the eye. She gave him an off-the-peg smile. Nothing had changed.

Tidey smiled back and nodded. He heard the door close as he moved down the path towards the front gate.

It is what it is.

11

When his mobile rang, Vincent Naylor had just come back to bed from taking a leak. Still mostly asleep, wobbly, not yet on top of his drinking after eight months' forced abstinence, it took him a moment to recall where he'd left the phone.

He rolled off the bed, looking for the jeans he'd thrown somewhere. Moving in the darkness, the jaunty ringtone relentless, he glanced back at the bed where Michelle was still asleep. As he picked up and discarded items of clothing, one foot touched something on the floor near the end of the bed and he bent and found the jeans. When he picked them up the mobile fell out of a pocket. The volume of the ringtone shot up—no way that wouldn't wake her. Vincent picked up the phone, looked at the screen and in the second before his thumb jabbed at the answer button he noticed two things—the screen said it was 3.27 and it announced the caller as *Unknown*.

'Yeah?'

'Vincent Naylor?'

He kept his voice low. 'Who wants to know?' He moved across the room, out and along the landing to the bathroom.

'Vincent?'

'Who is this?'

'Albert Bannerman.'

'Albert? Long time, mate. And a funny time to be calling.'

'Vincent, it's about Noel. He's here, my place.'

Vincent was suddenly aware of the amount he'd drunk throughout the evening. After the meal, a string of Southern Comforts through the Tommy Tiernan DVD and beyond. When his friends left, Vincent took a taxi from Noel's house to Michelle's place, and he'd had a couple of beers here.

Albert Bannerman?

Vincent used to do a little work for Bannerman—back in his teens. They never

53

knocked heads.

'What's happened?' Vincent kept his voice calm. When the reunion broke up at Noel's house, Vincent assumed his brother was ready for nothing more than sleeping it off.

'He's all right, I've got him locked up, he's OK.'

'What the fuck do you mean, you've got him locked up?'

'Vincent, he came here with a knife.'

Fuck.

'What did—how is he now?'

'He's OK. I swear. Thing is, he's noisy. Best thing, you come here—I can't talk him out of this, you've got to do that. I'll explain what happened when you get here.'

'You're at home?'

'Same place as ever. I'll be waiting at the front door.'

Michelle's voice, from the landing. 'Vincent, you OK?'

'I'll be there as fast as I can,' he told Bannerman.

Michelle looked worried when he came out of the bathroom. He told her it was just a family thing, he had to go collect Noel.

'Is something wrong?'

'I'll manage. Go back to bed, love.'

In prison, Vincent had planned to spend his first month of freedom shagging a new woman every day of the week and two on Sundays. The first night out, at a party in Noel's house, he'd met Michelle Flood. In Mountjoy, Vincent had hung out with her older brother, Damien, who was doing four years for aggravated assault. She had the looks, but there was a lot more going on underneath the gloss. They'd been together all but

54

one night since he'd got out. It felt like he knew her better than people he'd known for years.

'What's happened to Noel?' she said.

'I don't know it all yet. Tell you in the morning.'

He wasn't up to driving. Get pulled in by a bluebottle, set the breathalyser on fire. They'd love that.

Kevin Broe or Liam Delaney?

He put on the bedroom light and began pulling on his clothes. When he made up his mind he tapped the phone and waited a long while. When Liam answered, Vincent said, 'Are you sober?'

'I'm OK.'

'Sober? I need a lift, some backup.'

'Yeah, I'm fine.'

'You know Michelle's place?'

'No.'

Vincent gave him the address. 'Call me when you get to the bottom of the street. Soon as you can. And bring stuff.'

'How many?'

'One for you, one for me.'

*　　　*　　　*

Liam Delaney said, 'I'll keep the Israeli automatic, if that's OK.' They were sitting in his Toyota Camry down the street from Michelle's house. Liam Delaney knew more than anyone needed to know about guns, and was seldom done talking about it. 'Nine mil, eighteen rounds in one magazine,' he said. 'The Israelis, they like a lot of firepower.' Liam used a finger to remove a small oil mark on the side of the gun barrel. Thin and small, he had the intense expression of someone in

55

a permanent hurry.

Vincent Naylor took the other gun, a revolver with a shiny steel body, a short barrel and a black rubber grip. 'Twenty-two calibre, eight rounds,' Liam said. Vincent didn't care what he used, as long as it made a bang and punched a hole in whatever he was pointing at. He'd carried a gun on a job not much more than half a dozen times. Just twice he used a gun on someone. First time, he took care of a smart-arse who was making trouble for Mickey Kavanagh, a player who gave Vincent occasional work. Just walked up behind the guy, gave it to him behind the left ear, one shot. Vincent was walking away before the loser hit the ground.

Mickey was generous, but the money was neither here nor there. What counted was that Vincent proved to himself he could do it. It was a line— once you crossed it for the first time it brought you out of the herd. It marked you as someone who made moves, not just a skull who lived in someone else's world. The thing that surprised Vincent most was that it wasn't such a big deal. He didn't feel any urge to do it again, but he knew he could if he needed to.

The other shooting was a reputation thing—a gobshite who was bad-mouthing Vincent to people who took that kind of thing seriously. The surgeons got most of the bullet fragments out of his kneecap and now he walked with a limp you'd hardly notice. Word gets around, people know you're not to be fucked with, you don't have to prove it too often.

'Could be Bannerman's setting me up,' Vincent told Liam.

'Did you ring Noel?'

56

'No answer.'

'What's Noel doing, screwing around with someone like Bannerman?'

'No idea—but that could be bullshit. Could be Bannerman picked him up somewhere, took him there—as bait.'

'Why?'

'How the fuck do I know? I stepped on someone's toes, maybe. Could be he's doing someone a favour. Could be that—or Noel really did turn up on his doorstep with a knife, could be that too.'

'Why would Noel—'

'You coming with me?'

'Of course I'm fucking coming with you.' Liam looked down at his Israeli automatic. 'How do you want to do this?'

12

Liam Delaney drove the Camry to the Glencara estate and parked two streets away from Albert Bannerman's house. When they got out of the car, Liam took the far side of the street, trailing Vincent Naylor by about ten yards.

'Tactics,' Vincent explained. 'If we stay together, we make a handy target. This way—you've got my back covered, and anyone comes for you they're wide open to me.'

Liam thought this was a load of bollocks, but he didn't say so. Vincent was like that sometimes, like when he said it didn't matter what gun you took on a job. For Liam, a gun was a tool, and you don't

57

take a wrench to a carpentry job. Vincent not bothering to know that kind of stuff, that was one of his weaknesses. But he made up for it in other departments. Vincent had guts, he was loyal. They'd known each other since their teens—when they both worked for Mickey Kavanagh. They'd worked together on small jobs of their own and Liam reckoned it was the right time for Vincent to take things to another level. The Protectica job would do that. Vincent had the head for that kind of thing—and the balls to take it by the scruff.

Always assuming they walked away from this Bannerman shit.

Liam reckoned if this was a set-up, if someone wanted Vincent popped, it wouldn't happen close to Bannerman's home—Albert wouldn't want to piss on his own doorstep. Most likely, it would happen afterwards. They'd get some bullshit from Bannerman, then it would happen on the way back to the car. Or not.

There was an edge to this kind of thing—not like doing a job, where it's all about preparing and about following the plan. Tonight, Liam found himself stepping lightly, arms loose, every nerve alert. He was surprised by the feeling, by the lack of fear—it was a kind of high.

Albert Bannerman's place was a corner house, at the end of the street. It was pretty much the average corner house on a council-built estate, except it had a large extension attached to the side. The council had sold off the houses decades back and most of them were tarted up one way or another, but Albert Bannerman's had almost doubled in size.

Alone among the houses on the street, all the

visible windows were alive with light. Bannerman himself was standing at the open front door, wearing a leather jacket, his hands in his pockets.

Bannerman was in his late thirties. He'd shaved his head as soon as his hair began to thin. Along with his thick neck and barrel chest, it gave him the look of a man who wasn't often told things he didn't want to hear. He ran a solid operation—stolen cars and smuggled cigarettes, mostly, with a sideline in protection. He and a friend from Dundrum were the money behind four Southside brothels.

Liam Delaney stopped across the road, stood there with the Israeli automatic in his hand, held down by his thigh. Vincent stopped a couple of yards from Bannerman's garden gate. Stood there with his gun hand in his pocket.

Albert took his hands out of his pockets and walked slowly down the front path, to stand by the metal gate.

'I've got two of my people inside—no weapons, none of us. Noel's around the back, in the garden shed. He's stopped making a racket.' Bannerman jerked his head, indicating the house behind him, 'Let's talk inside.'

Vincent Naylor stood where he was. 'What's this about?'

'Like I said, Noel's quietened down. Could be, though, that some of the neighbours got upset about the noise—could be someone called the cops.'

'You locked up my brother.'

'All I'm saying—it's possible the cops will send a car to nose around. You or your mate, you don't want to be caught out here carrying something you shouldn't be.'

'I'm going nowhere until—'

In the hallway of the house, a woman appeared. She was wearing a thick white dressing gown. Her arms folded across her chest, dyed blonde hair, a smug expression on her thin face. Liam Delaney didn't recognise her.

'Shit,' Vincent Naylor said.

Albert Bannerman looked behind him and said, 'Get the fuck inside.' The woman stood there, chewing gum. Bannerman turned back to Vincent and said, 'I didn't know.'

Vincent turned and crossed the road to Liam Delaney. He handed Liam the revolver and said, 'Wait for me in the car.'

'You sure?'

'It's OK.'

As Liam turned away, Bannerman was leading Vincent into the house.

*   *   *

'She's been with me about six weeks, now,' Albert Bannerman said. 'I'd no idea—not that I would have done anything different. I mean, you meet a woman, these things happen, and people get over it. They broke up—how long since?'

They were standing alone in Bannerman's kitchen.

'What happened tonight?'

'We were at a wedding, this afternoon, Lorraine and me. Friend of mine got hitched, down in Kildare. Ended up, on the way home—we dropped into Cisco's. You know it?'

'Noel hangs out there.'

'I didn't know that.'

'She did.'

'It wasn't—'

'Whose idea was it? To drop in there?'

'That's not the point.'

'That bitch.'

'Take it easy.'

'She likes games, always did.'

They said nothing for a while. Then Vincent said, 'I'll go talk to Noel.' Bannerman opened the back door and Vincent went out.

*　　　*　　　*

The garden was lit by a bright security light. Two of Bannerman's people were standing on the patio. The garden shed was off to one side, about twenty feet from the back door. It had a small barred window on the side, the glass broken. One of Bannerman's people nodded as Vincent passed him, approaching the shed.

'Noel, it's me.'

Vincent hunkered down beside the door. The wood was old, weather-beaten, the door held fast by a strong hasp and padlock.

'Vincent—' Noel's voice was slurred—'this is none of your business.'

'You're my business, brother. You OK in there— you OK to come out?'

'This is my fight, Vincent.'

'There's no fight, Noel.'

'He's a dead man. No way he's not.'

'You need to stop talking like that. You need to come out here. You and me, we leave here together—Liam Delaney's down the road, he's got a car, we go home, we talk it out.'

There was a long silence, then Noel said, 'Just let them get on with it, you mean?'

'Coming here with a knife, brother—that's not the brightest thing you've done all day.'

More silence. Vincent Naylor moved closer, until his cheek was touching the rough wood of the shed. He put his lips close to the door and when he spoke his voice was too soft for anyone but Noel to hear. 'Don't let's screw things up now, brother— we've things to do.'

Silence.

'You hear me? You've put too much work into this job to throw it away over something like this.'

He waited, and when there was no reply he said, 'We talk this out, you and me—and if you can't live with that, then I stand back and you do what you've got to do.'

This time the silence went on for a couple of minutes.

'Noel?'

'Give me a minute.'

Vincent stood up and walked over to Bannerman's men. 'Tell Albert to keep that bitch upstairs—and it's best if he stays up there, too.' The taller one nodded to the other, and the second man went into the house.

Behind Vincent, there was a double knock from inside the shed. Noel's voice sounded like nothing unusual had happened. 'OK, Vincent, let me out of here.'

Bannerman's man took his hand out of his pocket and gave Vincent a key.

13

The judge said there were things he'd like to say about both parties in this case. 'However, charity suggests I adopt the course recommended by my sainted grandmother—and hold my breath to cool my porridge.' He paused a moment, just long enough to allow the two barristers to emit token sycophantic chuckles.

On arriving at the court, Bob Tidey got the word from prosecuting barrister Mopey Dick. 'The DPP's doing a nolly.'

'It figures.'

The case had formally resumed, just long enough for Mopey Dick to rise and inform the judge that the Director of Public Prosecution had reviewed the case overnight. 'And he has, Judge, decided to take a certain course.'

The phone lines would have been burning, as the police and the lawyers for the two idiots negotiated a way out. The charges of assault were withdrawn—the lawyers for the two idiots would have told them that although the odds were now against a conviction, anything can go wrong in a criminal case and they ought to cut their losses. Nothing would be said in open court, but the lawyers would have privately agreed that the DPP's *nolle prosequi* would be matched by the yobs' parents dropping the civil suit.

'I find it impossible to terminate these proceedings without a word about the police evidence.' The judge favoured a languid delivery. 'Of the two policemen who arrested the accused—

perhaps it's best to draw a veil, though I trust their superior officers will discuss the matter with them.'

He looked down at Bob Tidey, sitting in the well of the court.

'Detective Sergeant Tidey, your evidence neither condemned nor exonerated the accused, yet it was clearly—how should I put this?—it was clearly lacking in frankness. Put simply—it flew in the face of the visual evidence we saw with our own eyes.'

Knowing he would probably appear in future cases before the same judge, Tidey kept his face expressionless. In the judge's world, all the lines between right and wrong are clear, all the choices are made on the basis of legal scripture.

'I can easily imagine circumstances in which I might feel moved to take this matter further. In the event, a public reprimand seems sufficient penance. Count your blessings, Detective Sergeant Tidey.'

* * *

When his phone rang, Assistant Commissioner Colin O'Keefe ignored the dagger glances from across the table. He took his time checking and saw the call was from Detective Chief Superintendent Malachy Hogg.

'Yeah?'

O'Keefe was seated towards the bottom of a long, highly polished table, on the second floor of the Department of Justice. Of the seven others at the table, two were from his staff, there to take notes and provide backup. Three were senior departmental place-fillers and one was a harmless old relic working out the last months to his pension. The only one that mattered was the department's Director General of Strategic Provision, Robertson Wynn.

'You got my email?' Hogg asked.

'I'm in a meeting—Mr Wynn has some suggestions.'

Every two weeks, O'Keefe found himself in this room, reporting on and demanding approval of the detailed consequences of the budget cuts the Department of Justice required. It was a process he insisted on, and he preferred to drag it out, on the theory that if he made it insufferable for the buggers they might shift some cuts elsewhere next year.

Hogg said, 'The email's got the Ballistics report on the Sweetman murder. It changes things.'

'Ring you back shortly.'

O'Keefe found the email on his HTC, opened it and opened the two-page attachment. As expected, the handgun round that went through Sweetman's head and flattened against the marble floor was beyond matching. The other bullet had entered Sweetman's cheek and was found nestled inside his neck. There were some rifling marks on the bullet, but it hit a bone somewhere on its travels, the slug was distorted, killing any chance of a match. Ballistics got nothing useful from the shotgun pellets—nothing a blind man couldn't see from glancing at the body.

It took O'Keefe a moment to see the significance of the two-sentence paragraph second from the end. Markings on the two shells recovered at the scene had been linked to one previous known killing.

Oliver Snead.

He scanned the single sentence that summarised the bare details of the Snead murder. He vaguely recognised the name and he spent a moment mentally trawling the countless cases he'd absorbed over the years, retrieving a small cluster of facts he'd retained about the Snead murder.

'Assistant Commissioner . . .'

O'Keefe looked towards Robertson Wynn, then ignored him.

The Snead murder was eighteen months back, or thereabouts. Two gunmen—Snead was with friends, a winter drinking party on waste ground in front of the block of flats where he lived with his grandfather. The Hive. He owed someone money, a drugs thing.

As memory filled out the details, O'Keefe paused for just a moment, then he opened the contacts list in his mobile and scrolled down through the names.

*   *   *

Outside the court, Sergeant Derek Ferry offered Bob Tidey a cigarette. 'Sorry you got dragged into this petty shit.'

Tidey lit Ferry's cigarette. 'Things happen.' He thumbed the lighter again and there was just a bare flicker of flame. He sucked it into his own cigarette.

He found a shop and bought a packet of Rothmans and two disposable lighters. Leaving the shop, his mobile rang. The screen said Colin O'Keefe.

Jesus, that was quick.

In the years since he partnered O'Keefe on a

66

couple of high-profile cases, the two had kept in touch. The friendship remained, but now that O'Keefe had reached the heights of Assistant Commissioner the contact was only occasional. Either Colin wanted to sympathise about the judge's reprimand, or he wanted to know if Tidey had been fucking about.

'Bob—it's Colin. You got much on your plate?'

Tidey took a moment to think. 'Some court work, paperwork, and a few witness depositions scheduled to start tomorrow—'

'Take a day to wrap it all up—two at the most. I can get you help with the witnesses.'

'It'll take longer than—'

'Malachy Hogg's running the inquiry from Castlepoint—touch base with him, do your best to sideline the other stuff and get stuck in.'

'What's this—'

'Oliver Snead.'

Tidey said nothing for a moment. Then he said, 'Go on.'

'We've connected that case to a recent shooting.'

'Good.'

'This other shooting—it's way beyond Oliver Snead's league. Something doesn't make sense.'

There was silence for a moment, then Bob Tidey said, 'Go ahead, surprise me.'

14

Michelle Flood had just forty minutes for lunch, so Vincent Naylor met her in the Abbey Street food hall, five minutes' walk from the hairdresser's where she worked. Over sandwiches he told her why he'd had to leave during the night, all about Noel and the shed and the bitch who used to live with him.

Michelle smiled. 'Lorraine—Paris Hilton without the inheritance. I know her sister.'

Long dark hair, big blue eyes and a smile that would melt granite. Even wearing the dark blue top and grey trousers that came with her part-time hairdressing job, Michelle looked like something from a magazine.

This thing between them went deep very quickly. At first Vincent worried about how and when—and if—he should let her know this was serious for him. Then it dawned that he knew it was serious for her, and she hadn't said a word.

'The bitch lived with Noel for over a year,' Vincent said. 'Cracked about her, he was. Total basket case when she dumped him.'

'She's a cow. An over-the-hill cow. Everyone knows that. How is he now?'

Vincent just said, 'Fine, he's OK,' but he still wasn't sure how last night's trouble would work out.

*   *   *

It had been pushing five in the morning when Liam Delaney dropped them off at Noel's house. Noel was drained.

'I'll get you a coffee.'

Noel shook his head, shuffled towards his bedroom. Vincent helped him take off his jacket, shoes and jeans, then Noel curled up. Vincent stared at the bruise on Noel's right cheek.

68

'What happened your face?'

Noel shook his head again.

'We'll talk tomorrow?'

Noel didn't open his eyes, just nodded. Vincent spent what was left of the night on Noel's couch.

At thirty-two, Noel was six years older than Vincent, with two stretches in the Joy while Vincent was still at school. From the off, Noel was able to do anything with a car. Open it up with a coat hanger, jump the leads, race it, slide it, spin it 180 with a touch of the handbrake, sideswipe it off lamp posts and parked cars if that's what he felt like doing. Back then, Noel's idea of a pleasant evening was to steal something fast and noisily drive around the estate until some busybody called the cops. When the bluebottles showed up, blue lights spinning, Noel waited, revving the engine until the cops thought they had him. Then, when they were close enough to see his smile, he'd give them the finger and floor the metal and the chase was on.

They never caught him behind a wheel. Instead, they collared him one night coming out of the rear exit of a chemist shop, his pockets full of cheap highs. That's when they beat the shite out of him. At first, he gave as good as he got, which was a mistake. He was on a drip in the Mater for ten days before he woke up to face charges of burglary, assaulting two policemen and resisting arrest.

These days, Noel had a bit too much flesh on him, too much grey in his hair and too little bounce in his stride. The lines around his eyes looked like the work of decades.

When Vincent heard Noel stirring this morning he started cracking eggs. By the time his brother

69

was up Vincent had a couple of mushroom omelettes ready. As they sat down across the kitchen table from each other Noel said, 'I know.'

Vincent paused, fork halfway to his mouth.

'You know what?'

'I was a prick last night. No need for a pep talk.'

'As long as you're all right now.'

'It was just—I was at Cisco's, they walk in and the minute it happened I could see what was going on. The bitch was making some sort of point. No other reason to bring Bannerman there. Not his kind of place. And after they'd gone—Jesus, them waltzing off—that bitch, throwing me away like I was something she wiped her arse with.'

'Noel—'

'It was drink, it was daft, I know that. It was a stupid, stupid thing to do. Could have screwed up everything. He's a cunt, Bannerman is, and she's worse.'

'That's—'

'I know, I know, and I'm not gonna do anything—OK.' He spoke now as though talking to himself. 'Every day it hurts, and every day it makes it worse that that bitch is out there enjoying herself.'

Vincent said, 'What happened your face?'

'What's the matter with it?'

'You've got a bruise—just there?'

Noel touched his face where Vincent pointed. 'No idea—the way it was, things got a bit frisky last night, Bannerman's boys.'

'Bastards.'

'Nah. They were doing their job, keeping me off the cunt.'

After a minute, Noel said he was right, wasn't

he? The Tommy Tiernan DVD—it was a good choice for last night, right?

Later, when Noel was having a shower, Vincent rang Albert Bannerman and said, 'Hope everything's OK—no strain, right?'

'Not from this end.'

'Let's talk, maybe tomorrow?'

Albert said that would be fine.

*   *   *

The Abbey Street food hall was awash with the smells of Turkish, Italian, Mexican and Chinese food. Vincent was wondering if he maybe shouldn't bin his sandwich and find something more tasty.

Michelle looked at her watch. 'I've got to get back.'

They'd walked a few yards up Abbey Street when Vincent said, 'OK for tonight?'

Michelle stopped and faced him. 'You and Noel, there's something happening?'

'How do you mean?'

'Bits of phone calls, things you said. There's something coming up?'

'That isn't—it's business, it isn't—'

'I don't want details.' Her eyes were big and round and he could stare into them for the rest of his life and it wouldn't be long enough. 'I just need to know if you're going to suddenly disappear for ten years.'

He grinned. 'You can't get rid of me that easily.'

Her face remained serious. She waited until a noisy Luas train thundered past, bell clanging. 'It matters to me. For the first time in a long time, it matters.'

'Anything I do,' Vincent said, 'if I take a risk it's for a reason.'

She had a way of leaning into him that made talking redundant, and she did it now. They embraced, Vincent closed his eyes. 'I'll be OK,' he said. 'I promise.'

'Tonight,' she said.

He said, 'Tonight.'

15

James Snead shook Bob Tidey's hand, and accepted the bottle of whiskey. 'You're welcome, you and Mr Jameson.'

James had long insisted that he wasn't an alcoholic. 'Those poor sods,' he once told Tidey, 'it's something in the body, they don't have a choice. Me, I choose to drink too much. I know what it does to me and that's OK.'

He led the way into his fourth-floor apartment. Bob Tidey closed the front door and followed.

James Snead was in his sixties, a former construction worker, tall and grey, muscular with a thickening middle. Face wrinkled around the eyes, thin red capillaries criss-crossing his nose. In another life he'd been a widower rearing a daughter alone, seldom going beyond his habit of two pints on a Friday evening. Then his daughter died with a needle in her arm. She left a baby son, and James reared him past his teens, until one day someone put two bullets in Oliver Snead's chest and one in his head. Shortly after that, James Snead decided that he'd been sensible for long enough. 'A world this ugly, I'd rather look away.'

The best part of two decades back, Tidey was the young uniform who found the body of James's daughter. The two kept in touch and when Oliver was murdered Tidey was part of the investigation. One night they shared a bottle and in a matter-of-fact tone James told him there wasn't much left he wanted to do or see. 'It's all repetition, now. It's hard to give a damn. Any day looks better when it's topped off by a few drinks, and if that brings me closer to lights out—that's a fair trade.' Given the circumstances, Tidey couldn't bring himself to argue the point.

James twisted the cap on the bottle of Jameson. 'Not often I manage to rise to a good whiskey these days, but after a couple of drinks it's hard to tell the difference.'

The flat smelled of Chinese takeaway.

Tidey said, 'You're eating properly, of course?'

'I'm a martyr to my five-a-day.'

James brought two glasses and poured. The block of flats was noisy, people talking loudly, music from more than one direction. Tidey sipped at the whiskey, James offered a silent toast and drank.

'I've a bit of news,' Tidey said.

James leaned back in his chair. 'You and Charlie Bird.'

'There was a murder—I've just been assigned. A man over on the Southside—two thugs came to his door with guns.'

James's interest seemed polite, less than wholehearted.

'One of the guns they used, it turns out it's the gun that killed Oliver.'

73

James lifted the glass again to his lips. He said nothing.

'What I'm hoping is, if we find whoever did this murder it might lead to whoever killed Oliver.'

James looked at the whiskey lining the bottom of his glass. 'That's good, I suppose.'

'I promised to keep you informed, for what it's worth.'

'If I had him within reach I'd have to be dug out of him. I imagined it many a time, but that's not going to happen.' He savoured some more Jameson. 'And, knowing it was this little shit who pulled the trigger, as opposed to some other little shit—that doesn't matter at all.'

He sat a moment, as though wondering if it was worth trying to explain. 'Oliver's death—it's not about the little shits who did it. It's about what Oliver lost. All the time he didn't have, the things he didn't get to do. Switched off like a light, and no sense to it. Nothing will fill that hole. I know you're doing your best, but knowing the name of the creep who killed him, that won't do it, not even if he goes to jail. There's nothing positive to be got out of any of this—it's all shit.'

*   *   *

James was leaning back in an armchair, his long legs straight out in front, the bottle within reach, the glass sitting in the palm of his upturned hand.

'You take it seriously, this policing lark?'

'You were a good builder, or so you've told me. People ought to take pride in their work.'

'Runs in the family, does it?'

'My father was a die operator in a plastics

74

extrusion factory—small place, non-union. Only time you got to open your mouth was to say "yes, sir". What he said to me—you get the habit of bowing and scraping, it becomes part of your nature. Don't get the habit, he said.'

'Why the police?'

'It was the 1980s,' Tidey said. 'I was just out of school, you know the state the country was in—queues at the American Embassy, kids begging for visas. So, a job's a job.'

'I don't believe that.'

'That was part of it. I had notions, in those days—I was young, I wanted to do something that meant something. If I wasn't an atheist I might have joined the Legion of Mary and delivered meals on wheels. What I did was hook up with the Simon Community—soup runs, that kind of thing. One day, I walked into my local station and asked how I could become a Garda. Know what I really liked about the job?'

'The overtime?'

'When trouble happens, most people turn and run. It's the people who run towards the trouble—medics, firefighters, the police—they're the ones I wanted to be with.'

James nodded. 'I can see the attraction in that. But there were times—on the picket lines—trying to protect the little we had, our backs were to the wall, and sometimes it got a bit technicolour. Your lot—the batons would come out, or they'd link arms and come at us like a tank. A lot of those fuckers were enthusiastic about their work.'

'Wherever there are uniforms, you'll find little corporals—people who get their kicks barking orders. But there's all sorts in the force.'

'No doubt—but back in the day, it was the little corporals I always seemed to come across.'

*   *   *

They were well into the bottle when Bob Tidey went to the flat's claustrophobic kitchen. He found some Cheddar in the fridge and half a sliced pan and made a couple of sandwiches. James accepted his and said, 'You still living the bachelor life?'

'Wouldn't have it any other way.'

'The women are flocking, no doubt?'

Tidey grunted. 'Have to beat them off with a stick.'

'Life's grand when it's grand, right enough.'

Tidey leaned forward, his voice gentle. 'You've given up, then, body and soul? Or does anything matter?'

'I'm mildly curious about how they're going to fix this mess—broken banks, queues for food parcels,' James said. 'When I was young, I waved my fist around. The workers' flag is deepest red, all that shit. Trade unions are out of fashion now, but everything we ever got we had to fight for it—money, hours, conditions. Today, it's like everyone's grateful to be a unit of labour, to be plugged in or pulled out according to their master's will.'

Tidey said, 'People are scared. They just want this to be over, whatever it takes.'

'After all the bullshit about the fight for freedom, about throwing off the foreign yoke—they gave the country away. The politicians fell in love with the smart fellas—gave them any law they wanted. The smart fellas made speeches and gave

76

interviews about how smart they were, and the journalists kissed their arses. And in the end it was the smart fellas broke the country in pieces, without any help at all from the red brigades.' There was no humour in his laugh.

'They'll figure something out,' Tidey said.

'They surely will. They always do.'

James poured more Jameson, topping up his own glass to near the brim.

'When's the last time you arrested one of those bastards, and all they've done?'

'Not lately.'

'Not ever.'

'Not unless I catch him, on live television—on the halfway line at Croke Park—fucking a chicken.'

James smiled. 'With the Artane Band standing behind him, playing "A Nation Once Again".'

'That would help.'

James carefully raised the brimming glass to his lips. 'Even then, the hard neck on those fellas— he'd claim the chicken led him on.'

*   *   *

If she let another day end without doing something
. . .

Pushing thought aside, Maura Coady reached for the phone.

'Yeah?'

'Mr Tidey? It's Maura, Maura Coady.'

He said nothing and she felt a slight disappointment that he didn't remember the name. But he was a policeman, and policemen must meet hundreds of people—and this was well

77

over a year ago.

'The Teresa O'Brien—'

'Of course—Maura, it's been a while.'

He sounded tired, his words a little slurred.

'There's something, I'm not sure—when I say it, it doesn't sound—'

'What's the problem?'

'There's a car, parked outside my house—I've wanted to call you for—look, I know it sounds silly, but they were wearing gloves, plastic gloves.'

'Who?'

'The men. There were two of them.'

'Look, Maura, I'm—it's getting late, and I'm on my way home—it isn't—look, I'll give you a call first thing in the morning, OK?'

'Of course, of course, it may be nothing.'

'Good to hear from you—I ought to drop around, come see you.'

'Of course.'

'First thing in the morning.'

*   *   *

When Tidey came back from the toilet, James's eyes were closed, his head back, his hand still holding his half-empty glass. Tidey took the glass away. He brought a blanket from the bedroom and draped it over the sleeping figure. Before he left he switched on the kitchen light, so James could get his bearings if he woke during the night. Then he switched off the main light and went in search of a taxi.

78

16

Noel Naylor's footsteps echoed in the stairwell. He was halfway towards Vincent's squat on the fourth floor when he met Michelle Flood coming down.

She smiled and grimaced. 'Late for work.'

'Need a lift?'

'My car's downstairs, thanks. Vincent's in the shower.'

Noel had coffee ready when Vincent emerged from the bathroom.

'Met herself on the stairs—this is looking serious.'

'Could be. She's—you know—' Vincent shrugged.

'Good for you. Hope it works out. Meanwhile—' Noel offered a folded piece of paper. Vincent opened it and saw a name and an address.

'Thanks, but I don't think so.'

'If it was me—'

'I broke his nose, he gave evidence against me, I went away for eight months—it balances out.'

'He's got it coming.'

Vincent folded the piece of paper, left it on the kitchen counter. 'You're probably right, but these things—do you know Michelle's brother, Damien?'

'Not personally—I've heard of him.'

'Their younger brother, Conor—he was done for shoplifting from an off-licence. Damien dropped in to see the shopkeeper, told him to withdraw the complaint. The shopkeeper told him to fuck off, so Damien put him on his back in Beaumont for two weeks. Michelle gave him an alibi, said he was with her that evening—but the cops had it on CCTV. When I went into the Joy, Damien was already there nearly two years. When I left, he still had a year to do.'

'I see your point, but—'

'The kid, Conor—he got probation for the shoplifting. It's a mug's game, taking these things personally.'

'It's your call—I just thought you should have the option.'

Vincent cupped the back of his brother's neck, his voice warm. 'I appreciate that—thanks. But we've got a big job to do. From here on, no emotional shit, just business.'

Noel picked up the folded piece of paper. 'Your call—besides, it's a long road. Put it in your wallet—maybe you'll change your mind.'

Vincent smiled. 'Not out of the question.'

* * *

When he went into the courtroom, Bob Tidey looked towards the back row and saw Trixie Dixon. A couple of rows ahead, he recognised Roly Blount, Frank Tucker's chief enforcer. Here to see that Christy Dixon behaved like the patsy he was. Tidey turned away without acknowledging Trixie.

There would be a number of cases processed this morning—this was a filtering court, cases sorted like mail for sundry destinations, remands and postponements as well as sentencing in cases already pleaded. Lawyers and witnesses chatted while they waited for the judge to emerge from his chambers. You could tell the defendants—they were the ones with the nervous, pale faces.

Everyone else was going home when the show was over.

Cases moved quickly and it was no time before the court clerk intoned, 'The DPP versus Christopher Dixon, for sentencing.'

The judge was one of those smart, decisive guys—no bluster, no quips, no throwing shapes. He was here to get a job done. Bob Tidey liked that kind of judge.

'I understand the defendant was cooperative, Detective Sergeant?'

'He admitted the break-in, Judge,' Tidey said, 'and when we found the gun, he immediately admitted possession.'

'His counsel says he was holding onto it for someone?'

'I believe that's true, Judge.'

'Have there been any further arrests in this matter?'

'Mr Dixon said he didn't know the name of the person who asked him to hide the gun. I believe that's true, Judge. I also believe that Mr Dixon believed—and I think he was right—that he had little choice but to do as he was told.'

'Has he made any effort to help the police lay hands on the owner of the gun?'

'Judge, we asked him the questions and I believe he answered them as truthfully as he could. I believe he knew the gun owner to be a dangerous person—knew him by sight and by reputation but not by name.'

'Have the police been able to establish if the gun was previously used in criminal activity?'

'No, Judge—Technical did the usual tests, but it's not a match to any crime for which we have

81

records. We made inquiries of PSNI, but there's no match in the North either.'

The judge nodded. The court was silent for a while as he made a note. There were judges on whom Bob Tidey's message would be lost, but this wasn't one of them. *This young gobshite is being as straight as he can be without getting a bullet in the head.* The judge finally looked up at Christy.

'Mr Dixon—I appreciate your dilemma. You felt yourself under a measure of duress, from someone you believe to be dangerous. But that does not justify your action—taking possession of a lethal weapon, a weapon that might, but for happenstance, have been used in some appalling criminal enterprise. Two years on the break-in, final year suspended. Three years on the gun-possession charge, final year suspended.'

Christy's counsel was on his feet. 'To run concurrently, Judge?'

'Yes.'

Three years, total, one suspended. Christy would be out in maybe sixteen months if he behaved himself, which he probably would. Trixie Dixon was still sitting at the back. He nodded his gratitude to Tidey. Roly Blount had already left.

17

Mickey Kavanagh looked at his watch again. Frank Tucker was twenty minutes late. Nothing unusual—Frank was always late. The mid-morning sun was warm, the sky blue—Mickey relaxed, lit another smoke. After a couple of minutes, Frank's

Saab stopped at the corner of Le Fanu Road. Mickey threw away his cigarette and climbed into the back.

Tucker nodded his hello and the driver, a big man named Sullivan, took them off down Ballyfermot Road.

'It's about Junior Kelly,' Kavanagh said.

Tucker said, 'Not here.'

They drove in silence and a few minutes later they were on their way through the Phoenix Park. The Saab stopped close to the Papal Cross and Tucker and Kavanagh got out. They strolled across the open landscape, towards the mound below the cross.

'I have the car swept every day,' Tucker said. 'My house, the pub—we've never found anything, but the technology they've got, you can't be sure. The fuckers are all over me. It's not a problem, long as we're careful.'

Kavanagh was looking up at the massive cross. 'My mother still talks about bringing us all up here thirty years ago, when the Pope came. Pretty much everyone in the city, a million people—all waving at His Holiness.'

Tucker smiled. 'No Holy Joes in my family.'

'She was pregnant with me. She named me after Father Michael Cleary.' Kavanagh snorted. 'Prancing around up there beside the Pope, him and Bishop Casey, directing the show. Casey knew well that Mick Cleary had a two-year-old son, but Cleary didn't know the Bishop had his own son tucked away in the States.'

'The good old days—saints and scholars and a randy clergy.'

'My ma was properly pissed after it all came out.'

When they were standing below the cross, Frank Tucker said, 'You've got a problem?'

'It's Junior Kelly.'

'What's the story?'

'He feels he's not appreciated.'

'He's a wanker.'

'It's turned serious. He's been talking to Chapman's people.'

'Is this pub gossip or is it solid?'

'Chapman sent one of his tools to see me last night, told me Junior came to see him twice.'

'With a view to what?'

'Junior thinks you and Chapman will end up butting heads. This way, he crosses over and sets you up, Chapman comes out on top—and Junior's got himself into a snug place.'

'You sure of this?'

'Played me a tape—it's Junior's voice.'

'And Chapman is pissing him away?'

'Must have his reasons.'

Tucker stood a while, looking down at the grass, gently prodding it with the toe of his shoe. Then he looked up. 'It's a peace offering. Chapman turns Junior over—he's telling us he could have done the dirty, but he didn't.'

'Trust him?'

Tucker shrugged.

'What about Junior?'

'He made his choice.'

'I'll send Danny and Luke.'

Tucker stood close to Mickey Kavanagh. 'I want you to do this yourself. Tell him what's coming, make him kneel, make him wait. When he's done pissing and crying, tell him Frank Tucker sends his regards.'

'Done.'

Hands in his pockets, Tucker looked up at the Papal cross and after a few seconds he said, 'Send Danny and Luke to take care of Chapman.'

'You sure?'

'Maybe he's being cute—maybe not. This game, you guess wrong and—'

'Still, I mean—'

'You leave a loose end, maybe it trips you up. He goes.'

*   *   *

'Gonna be a great summer,' Vincent Naylor said.

Albert Bannerman made a see-sawing hand gesture—maybe, maybe not. They were sitting at a table outside Grogan's pub. Somewhere up the lane that led to Grafton Street, three kids were whining a barely recognisable Oasis song over a couple of off-tune guitars.

'It was like this last year,' Albert said. 'April, May, the sun is splitting the bricks. What happened? August, rains all day and the country is flooded. Everything's upside down with this country.'

'Grab some rays while it's here.'

Albert's Guinness had a couple of inches left in the glass. Vincent Naylor was still just halfway through his Southern Comfort. Drinking in the afternoon wasn't his usual style, but this kind of meeting, some people can read a meaning into ordering a Coke.

'The country's fucked,' Albert said. 'The big boys got too greedy, ran everything off a cliff.'

Vincent Naylor nodded. When he thought about

85

it, though, the big boys might have got greedy, but when the shekels are there to be picked up, what else are you gonna do? Name of the game, right?

'Off a cliff. You know Jimmy Wrigley?'

Vincent shook his head.

'Does a bit of work for me, time to time. Last week, he was picking up a Lancia, outside some fella's house—Mount Merrion, I think, late in the evening, almost had the door open. Fella comes out of the house, stops and looks at Jimmy. Jimmy's frozen, knows he should be running like fuck, but he's just standing there and the fella starts laughing. Throws his head back—Jimmy said the guy was half hysterical—hooting like a fucking monkey. Fella puts his hand in his pocket, takes out his car keys and throws them to Jimmy. Take it, he says, off you go. They're taking the house, he says, the judge gave me two weeks to move out. They've taken the credit cards. They've even taken the fucking Ten Year Ticket for Lansdowne Road. They're coming for the car tomorrow. Fuck 'em, he says—you might as well have it.'

Albert grinned. 'Jimmy says, fair play to you, sir, and the fella starts laughing again. Like I say—upside down, it is. This country's fucked.'

Vincent took a sip of his Southern Comfort. He wondered if he maybe went down and gave the three little gobshites a tenner they'd take their Oasis shit somewhere up the road.

Albert Bannerman finished off his pint and took a long drag from his cigarette. 'Noel's OK, then?'

Vincent nodded. 'He's fine.'

Albert skimmed the flat of his palm back across his shaven head. 'What I don't want is this starts some kind of—you know, push and pull, you and me. This town, too many little niggles turn into feuds, you end up with the Hundred Years War.'

Vincent was shaking his head. 'Everyone did what they had to do—Noel, you, me—that's the way I see it.'

Albert nodded agreement.

Vincent said, 'Except that bitch.'

'Lorraine says she didn't know he'd be there. At Cisco's.'

'You believe her?'

'Maybe she was hoping he'd be there—that's what she's like. She was—' He made a gesture with his cigarette hand, like it was something he didn't want to put into words.

'She was showing you off?'

'One way of putting it.'

'Noel's soft,' Vincent said. 'Head over heels he was, from the start—a year of having his strings pulled. It had to end in tears. Bitch stomped all over him.'

Albert said, 'It happens.'

'Wasn't enough to walk out—had to do it in front of a couple of his mates.'

'He should've smacked her.'

'Noel's not like that. What I'm saying—I'm not trying to mark your card, you and her is your business. I'm just explaining.'

'Fair enough,' Albert said. 'And locking him up in the shed, it wasn't like I had a choice—other circumstances, someone comes to my house with a knife—' He made the same hand gesture.

'Everyone did what they had to do.'

'I could see he was out of his head.'

'Noel's a good guy.'

They said nothing for a while, then Albert

pointed at Vincent's glass. 'Go again?'

'My shout.'

When Vincent came back out with the drinks, Albert said, 'You got anything going at the minute?'

'Nah—things are slow. You?'

Bannerman took a sip of his pint. 'Pretty quiet. You still working for Mickey Kavanagh?'

'Mickey's a big shot these days—got his own scene with Frank Tucker.'

'You at a loose end?'

'Is that an offer?'

'Some of the kids I've had working for me—all muscle, from ear to ear. Someone who knows the score—if there's something we could hook up on—' The hand again.

'Could be awkward—Noel and all.'

Albert made a face. 'Lorraine and me—I've got a wife, four kids, they're living out in Tallaght, everything's cool. Lorraine's what she is, but these things, they've got a natural lifespan—no one believes in fairy tales.'

'No reason, then—if the right job comes along.'

'This country's fucked, but there's always work for them that's willing, is what I say.'

18

'What kind of car?' Bob Tidey asked.

'It's green,' Maura Coady said.

'You don't know what make?'

'No.' She sounded apologetic.

'Can you see the number plate?'

88

'Not from here.'

He was about to ask her to go outside and have a look, but he could hear the timidity in her voice. Besides, he felt contrite, having put off calling her this morning, enveloped in organising witness depositions. It was late afternoon before he got round to it. Once he'd listened to the details, it dawned that perhaps this wasn't the waste of time he'd first assumed.

'Look, it's best if I drop down there and see for myself.'

Before he rang the bell of her house he'd scribbled down the reg number of the green car and made a phone call.

'Maura, you're looking great.' Which she was, for seventy-whatever. Her white hair still cut short, a healthy sheen to her thin face. When she smiled, the slightly protruding front teeth gave her the air of a mischievous old maiden aunt. Her blue cardigan seemed a size too large for her narrow shoulders, but there was a lot of vigour in her slim frame. She had the look of someone who'd led a life that made workouts and diets redundant.

'Can I get you something, Mr Tidey?'

His phone rang and he made an *I'm fine* gesture with one hand.

The dark green car out front was a VW Bora. Command and Control told him the reg plate belonged to a Toyota.

'Is everything all right?'

'Not to worry,' he told Maura. 'I'll just get a couple of lads to have a look at it.'

It was getting dark by the time the motor specialists arrived. They opened the driver's door and poked about inside, then popped the boot.

Tidey stayed at the window of the unlit living room of Maura's house. No need for a crowd out there.

Even with his back to Maura Coady, Tidey could sense her fear. He turned and she was standing near the living room door, her features barely visible in the weak light reflected from a street lamp, her arms crossed as though holding herself together. 'It's OK, believe me, there's nothing to worry about.'

'This is awful.' Her voice was barely strong enough to cross the few feet between them. 'Awful.'

'Nothing special,' the motor guys reported. 'Plates changed, full tank, no sign of an accelerant. But it's not out there for no reason.'

Tidey called his Chief Superintendent at Cavendish Avenue, who was at home, breathing heavily as though he'd been shifting furniture. The Chief Super put in a request to the Special Detective Unit. It was an hour before a member of the Emergency Response Unit visited the house. Maura Coady paled when she saw the butt of the automatic pistol, holstered high on the man's right hip and peeking out from under his padded sleeveless jacket.

The man—a Sergeant Dowd—organised surveillance teams. A hundred yards to the right of Maura's house, just this side of the Spar shop, a white Ford Ducato van pulled up to the kerb. There was another white Ducato, already parked to the left of Maura's house, at the other end of the street.

Dowd told Bob Tidey there was no doubt the VW Bora was a secondary, and thanked Maura for her public spirit.

When Dowd left, Maura asked Bob Tidey, 'How long will the vans stay there? What if no one comes for the car?'

'It's not often we get a chance like this—a getaway car at the ready.'

'Getaway—from what?'

'No idea. But if there's a robbery—say a bank, a post office, whatever, maybe a planned killing—the primary getaway car might have forensic traces to connect the criminals to the crime, so they drive it a shortish distance and they burn it. They have a secondary car nearby, not connected to the crime, to take them the rest of the way clear. Even if it's a stolen motor, which this one probably is, all you can be done for is stealing a car.'

'So, there's definitely going to be a crime?'

'All the signs of it.'

Her crossed arms tightened. 'This is frightening.'

Bob Tidey said, 'Those people in the vans, they're the best. Whoever's behind this, it looks like a professional job—they'll know enough not to be foolish.'

'Should I move out until this is over?'

'Not necessary.'

Tidey had raised the same question with Sergeant Dowd. Evacuating the entire street, perhaps for days, the ERU officer concluded, just wasn't an option. 'Not perfect, but what in this life is?'

Maura seemed OK as Tidey prepared to leave. 'Nothing's likely to happen tonight,' Tidey said. At the door, he said, 'I'll drop back when I can—this is a good thing you've done.'

'You think they might be preparing to kill someone?'

'It's a real possibility.'
'It's for the best, then—if it saves a life.'
'It's for the best,' Tidey said.

19

Noel Naylor told the balls joke. The one he'd been cracking for years, whenever he and Vincent played snooker. The one about how you make a snooker table laugh. It happened the same way every time. With Noel bent over the table, his left hand making a perfect bridge, his right hand drawing back the cue—he'd pause, his head still, his eyes looking sideways at Vincent.

'Did I ever tell you how to make a snooker table laugh?'

And Vincent always laughed. For a while they'd chorus the punchline together—'You tickle its balls.' Then it got that there was no need for the punchline. Just the deadpan question, delivered as though for the first time, was enough to set Vincent off.

They'd had a quick bite in the diner downstairs, then up to the second floor of the leisure complex for a game. Having sunk a red, Noel missed the blue and straightened up. 'Got a new one—how can you tell when you've walked into a lesbian bar?' He didn't wait for an answer. 'Even the snooker table doesn't have any balls.'

Vincent laughed, then he said, 'I prefer the old reliable—but keep trying.'

Noel was in the mood, now. 'You hear about the time the FBI and Scotland Yard and the Irish cops had a competition?'

'No, and I don't want to.'

'What they had to do—they release a rabbit in a forest and the first one to track it down and arrest it is the winner. The Brits spend weeks watching every rabbit hole in the forest until a Brazilian electrician comes along and they shoot him dead.'

Vincent was eyeing a red at the far end of the table. 'You're just trying to put me off.'

Noel grinned. 'The FBI—they call in air support and bomb the fuck out of the forest, even the frogs are toast.'

Vincent took his time chalking his cue, then he stood and waited, knowing there was no stopping Noel.

'And who wins the competition?' Noel said. 'After half an hour the Irish cops come out of the forest with a fox in handcuffs. Blood running down his face, bruises all over. And he's shouting, "All right, all right, I'm a rabbit, I'm a rabbit!"'

Vincent laughed, but he still preferred the old snooker balls joke.

Twenty minutes later they were opening the boot of Noel's car, outside Vincent's squat at the MacClenaghan building. Vincent looked at the large green jerrycan and said, 'You planning to set the city on fire?'

'I wasn't sure how many cars we're using. Three, four?'

'Doesn't matter. We just need to torch two—the Lexus and the Megane, that's all.' He checked the side of the jerrycan. 'Twenty litres? You're going to have fun carrying that to the fourth floor.'

'Bollocks.'

They took turns carrying the jerrycan to the flat.

93

Vincent opened the window, to let the fumes disperse, then he held a funnel steady in the mouth of a large plastic Coke bottle, while Noel hoisted the jerrycan.

They filled four two-litre Coke bottles. Then they cleaned up and went for a couple of pints. Vincent always had a bit of a bash, the night before a job.

*   *   *

That was the thing about Vincent—he was positive. It might be he had his own opinions on these things, but he thought before he spoke, he didn't just mouth off. He could have called Lorraine dirty names, he could have said Noel was best off with the bitch gone. Instead, Vincent said, 'Happens to us all—things don't click, things that ought to, and people get hurt and there's nothing to be done about it.'

Noel Naylor sometimes got upset about Lorraine—but he was glad Vincent showed her respect. The way Vincent talked about it, it made what happened seem like an adult thing, a thing to accept and get over. Instead of feeling like a pathetic teenager, which is what Noel sometimes felt like when he thought of how the bitch screwed him over.

Funny the way it worked out. Was a time when Vincent was a kid and Noel had to look out for him, show him how things worked. Now, there were things Vincent knew best, times when he seemed like the big brother. Noel liked that, the give and the take.

'We make a good team,' Noel said.

'Laurel and Hardy?' Vincent said.

94

'Bollocks,' Noel grinned.

Vincent gestured to the barman, pointed at the almost empty pint glasses. When the fresh drinks arrived, Vincent raised his glass, looked his brother in the eye and said, 'Tomorrow.'

Noel nodded. 'Tomorrow.'

Part 2

The Job

20

Behind the wheel of his yellow Suzuki Alto, Turlough McGuigan glanced at his watch. He lived fifteen minutes away from the depot and he was halfway there. He had a reputation for getting into work early, staying a week ahead on the schedules and rosters. It was an attitude that had made the difference when it came to the rivalry for the job of depot manager. Turlough's ambitions didn't stop there.

Ahead, a red Renault Megane backed too quickly out of a laneway, but Turlough was onto it. Back in the old days, before he became depot manager, he spent six years on the road. He'd come across so many motoring morons that he took a course in defensive driving, the rewards of which were still with him. He'd clocked the Megane as soon as it showed its tail out of the laneway, and he'd factored in the possibility that the driver was a Jeremy.

Turlough slowed the Suzuki to a stop and when the passenger in the Megane gestured apologetically Turlough returned a gracious *be my guest* wave.

The Megane's door opened and the passenger got out—a tall, skinny guy with a moustache, wearing a bright orange T-shirt and knee-length khaki shorts with more pockets than a snooker table. Lucky bastards had the day off, probably on their way to a round of golf before finding a cold beer and a sunny spot.

The skinny guy in the shorts was headed for the

passenger door of Turlough's Suzuki. Still moving, he bent, smiled, looked at Turlough over the top of his round shades and said something. Turlough shrugged, put a hand to his ear. The man in the khaki shorts opened the door, got into the car and reached into Turlough's crotch.

'Stay calm, Turlough,' he said. When Turlough looked down he saw the man was holding a small black revolver in a latex-gloved hand.

Ahead, the red Megane was now out of the laneway and moving on up the street.

'Follow him.'

'Listen, man—'

'We can end this right here—all I've got's a wasted morning.' The man's moustache seemed slightly out of proportion to his face. He leaned closer. 'But you'll have to explain to your nice wifey how come your balls got shot off.'

*   *   *

The narrow road lifted and turned gradually to the right, the houses on each side masked by walls and bushes. Castlepoint was the kind of neighbourhood where the average house was impressive and the upper range imposing. The houses of the truly wealthy were hidden behind tall trees and high walls.

Detective Sergeant Bob Tidey was early for his conference at Castlepoint Garda Station. Although the Emmet Sweetman murder had been national news, he'd paid little attention to it, apart from the occasional radio news headline. After Colin O'Keefe's call, Tidey googled the murder and he wasn't much wiser, apart from the

100

information that Sweetman had lived at a house on the south end of Briar Road, on the outskirts of Castlepoint. This morning, he'd kill time while getting a feel for the neighbourhood, the access routes to the Sweetman house, the layout surrounding the murder scene.

He came to a straight stretch of road and slowed down. He stopped at a solid wooden gate, above which he could see the grey slated roof of a large, detached house. The brass plate on the gatepost said 'Sweetman's Retreat'. That's the way—spend a fortune on an exclusive hideaway, then stick up a sign advertising your whereabouts to any predators.

Tidey got out of the car, climbed onto the bonnet and looked over the gate. The land surrounding the house—best part of an acre—was bordered by a wall with a scalloped stone facing. No skimping on the finish. The road was sufficiently secluded to provide cover for intruders—it would be the work of a moment to exit a car and scale the wall. Enough trees and bushes on the far side of the wall to provide privacy while you prepared to clip your target.

Not much more to see, bit of a wasted trip, but better than twiddling his thumbs at Castlepoint Garda Station. He glanced at his watch. If he took the coast road back to Castlepoint village he'd catch some nice views and still be in lots of time for the conference.

21

Vincent Naylor took the gun out of the depot manager's crotch. 'Just keep behaving—this will be over before you know it.'

'I've no control over the money.'

'I know that, Turlough. You let me worry about that.'

'It isn't—'

'Watch the road and shut the fuck up.'

After a couple of minutes, the Megane veered into the car park beside a pub called Murnaghan's.

'Pull in behind him, Turlough.'

The depot manager did as he was told.

Vincent rested a hand on the depot manager's arm and spoke softly. 'You won't switch off that engine, will you, Turlough? If you do, the first thing háppens is an alarm goes off at Protectica headquarters. The second thing happens is you get shot in the face.'

The depot manager stared at Vincent.

'I know everything there is to know, Turlough—I know about overshoots, burners and blinders, carriers and maces, I know podmen, passwords and procedures—there's no end to the things I know.'

'Then you know I can't get my hands on the money?'

'I bet you could, Turlough, if you had to. But that's not the job we've got for you this morning. All you've got to do is make a phone call.' He tapped the manager's breast pocket. 'Use your own phone.'

'Who do I call?'

'You call the depot, you tell them you've a message for Mr Fry.' The depot manager's lips moved involuntarily. 'Yeah, Turlough, we know all that stuff. You're on your way to work and you're not going to make it. You had to pull over, you've got a dose of something and you have to take the day off. You're heading home. You tell them that.'

The manager took out his phone. He used the back of his hand to rub his lips.

'One last thing, Turlough—we know all the code words. You mention a Mr Crown or a Mr Wilde—you fuck around at all—this whole show is over.' Vincent made a face, like someone coming to terms with disappointment. 'Then they find you sitting here with the back of your head all over the inside of your car. Next time we do this, the guy who takes your place knows we're not kidding.'

The depot manager nodded, his face pale. He tapped a couple of buttons, then raised the phone to his ear.

*　　　*　　　*

At Castlepoint Garda Station, Detective Chief Superintendent Malachy Hogg shook Bob Tidey's hand and said, 'No point sitting down—conference is due to start in a couple of minutes.'

Tidey had never worked with Hogg, but knew him by reputation. Ambitious, a ladder-climber, but a solid enough policeman. Hogg said, 'We're down the corridor,' and led the way out of his temporary office. Walking behind Hogg, Tidey noted that the rumours were true. He dyed his hair.

'Colin rates you highly,' Hogg said.

'We worked together, back in the day. He rose to the top, I'm still knocking on doors. I think he feels sorry for me.'

Hogg's smile was rueful. 'We could do with another experienced hand on this case, but if there's one thing we didn't need it was a whole new line of inquiry.'

Tidey said, 'How big's the team?'

'At its core, handpicked by Colin, seven of the best detectives we have. Well, perhaps six. But that's OK—every investigation needs someone to make phone calls, coffee and witless remarks. Plus the usual filers and statement takers.'

Hogg gestured towards a door. 'In here. Listen and learn—you'll get a thorough briefing later.'

The room wasn't made for nine people, and it felt cramped. Hogg stood, the rest of the detectives found seats or the edges of desks. Tidey sat on the side of one of the desks, next to a fat, red-faced detective.

The case conference was mostly a run through the Jobs Book, noting assignments completed, none of them apparently fruitful. An analysis of questionnaire results, a background report on the husband of some woman who was apparently romantically involved with the victim. A lot of disconnected facts that didn't make much sense out of context. Tidey spent some time trying to work out which of the detectives was the Homer Simpson. They all sounded like they knew what they are doing. Hogg kept things moving, prodding detectives where they were too sketchy, cutting across them when they rambled. It was a daily base-touching exercise, ticking off a handful of tasks from what was obviously a long list.

'This is Detective Sergeant Bob Tidey, Cavendish Avenue. He's here this morning on the instructions of Assistant Commissioner O'Keefe.' Hogg made a take-the-floor gesture. 'Tell them why you're here, Detective Sergeant.'

Bob Tidey opened his notebook. 'The best part of eighteen months ago, a young man named Oliver Snead was murdered in Glencara—a hit job, in front of the block of flats where he lived. Oliver lost some drugs he was supposed to deliver—small-time stuff, but enough to piss someone off. He was trying to pay them back, but not fast enough. Two bullets in the chest, one in the head. We recovered the cartridges. And according to the ballistic report on the Emmet Sweetman killing, Technical got a match—same striations, same gun.' Tidey checked his notebook. 'The bullet was a .45 ACP, most probably fired from a Browning M1911—it's a fairly common weapon.'

The only woman on the team, sitting close to the door, said, 'Any suspects?' Bob Tidey had worked with her briefly a couple of years back. He shook his head. 'I knew the kid—knew his grandfather—I put a lot of time into that case. I eventually got a name—Gerry FitzGerald, a known hood. A tout picked up a whisper, but not enough to bring to court.'

'You pulled him in?'

'Name, rank and serial number.'

Hogg said, 'What matters is this—how come a forty-two-year-old millionaire banker and property speculator, a man at the heart of the property bubble, a man who was murdered in the doorway of his Southside mansion, got shot dead with the

105

same weapon that killed a minor mule on the Northside Dublin drug scene? It opens up a new line of inquiry—in a case that already has more than enough.'

The police officer's ideal murder case isn't one that involves clues and alibis, obscure poisons and convoluted motives. The ideal murder is one in which the victim is known to have pissed someone off and when the police arrive that someone is standing over the body with a bloody axe in his hand. With a bit of luck, several people witnessed what happened and someone has already uploaded a thirty-second video of the killing onto YouTube. Anything much more complicated was a pain in the arse.

The fat, red-faced detective next to Tidey said, 'Maybe someone sold someone else a gun? Simple as that.'

'Possible,' Hogg said. 'It's an orderly world, though. We have our lowlife gangsters—scams and hold-ups, smuggling, drugs, sex trade and protection rackets, all the mucky stuff. And we have our highlife gangsters—who do their thieving through layers of companies, hidden bank accounts, bribes, forgeries and offshore cut-outs. How does the gun get from one side of the city to another? From one category of crime to another? From one social class to another? A money grudge involving a ghetto kid, and a millionaire fraudster?'

One of the detectives said, 'I'm still betting on some IRA types. They shoot drug dealers—and there'd be almost as much kudos these days in shooting bankers.'

Hogg said, 'The Branch's touts haven't heard a word. Could be some new faction, of course.'

106

The fat detective said, 'How does this kid—this Snead killing—how does it change things operationally, sir?'

'Bob Tidey will concentrate on possible connections between the two murders. The rest of you will continue working through the existing lines of inquiry. Anything that might relate to the mucky side of the business, you let Bob know. If some business-school gangsters have begun calling in gunmen instead of lawyers—no one knows where that kind of thing leads.'

22

Vincent Naylor smiled and said, 'That was very good.' He took the phone out of Turlough McGuigan's limp hand. 'You nearly had me convinced you're having a sick day.'

Vincent waved at the Megane. Moments later, Noel got out of the car and climbed into the rear of the Suzuki. He too wore round sunglasses and a moustache. A floppy white hat hid his hair.

Noel spoke to Vincent, but smiled at the depot manager. 'He being sensible?'

'Turlough's a good boy.'

Noel said, 'Take off your shirt, Turlough.'

'What?'

'Put this on.' Noel dropped a dark purple sweatshirt into the depot manager's lap. 'And hurry.'

'What the fuck?'

Vincent said, 'You know why, Turlough, you know why.' The depot manager shook his head.

'We know everything, Turlough,' Vincent said. 'Passwords, codes, schedules, names, addresses, how everything's done—after this I could set up my own security business, the kind of stuff we know.'

His trembling fingers made the buttons difficult, but the depot manager took off his white shirt and gave it to Vincent. He pulled on the purple sweatshirt.

'Good man,' Vincent said.

Vincent handed the shirt to Noel, who clapped Turlough on the back and said, 'Time to go, man.'

Vincent said, 'We get out, now, Turlough, you and me. And we take the Megane.' A minute later, Vincent and the depot manager were sitting in the front of the Megane, as Noel pulled away in the Suzuki, Turlough's white shirt on the passenger seat beside him.

Over most of the previous decade, every cash-in-transit robbery was followed by security companies promising tougher procedures, and embarrassed Ministers for Justice threatening drastic regulation. The companies got a makeover. Tighter protocols, more sophisticated technology, consultants brought in to game-play the business until they'd accounted for just about every possible scenario.

'Going to be tougher than ever,' Vincent told Noel, 'specially after that Bank of Ireland guy.' Just as the recession hit, and the banks slid towards insolvency, a Bank of Ireland employee's family was taken and he ended up walking out of the vaults with seven million, which was the ransom for their return. 'Anyone with a key to the money— there's going to be so much technology all over

108

him and his family. Anything that big, it's too chancy.'

Noel looked disappointed. 'It's worth a try, that kind of money.'

'I'm not saying we can't do it. Long as we don't get too greedy—long as we do it fast enough, keep it small enough, we can take a bundle and we'll be home safe before they know it's gone.'

When Turlough McGuigan called in sick, the information would have been passed on to Protectica base, where the signal from the GPS chip in his Suzuki would show that his car had stopped on his way to work, the stop coinciding with the phone call. After the call, the GPS screen would show the car heading back to McGuigan's home, and the signal from the GPS chip implanted in McGuigan's shirt collar would confirm to HQ that the depot manager was in his car.

'What do you want me to do?'

Vincent Naylor leaned towards McGuigan and spoke quietly. 'No hysterics, now—OK? And no playing the hero.'

Vincent took a mobile phone from a pocket of his shorts and tapped the keys half a dozen times, then he found what he wanted and held the screen up so McGuigan could see.

It took a moment, then the depot manager was breathing fast and hard and it looked like he was about to be sick.

*　　　*　　　*

As the case conference broke up, Detective Chief Superintendent Malachy Hogg crooked a finger at the woman detective. 'Rose, a job for you.'

109

She shuffled her files and gave him a *Gee, thanks I was hoping I could cram some more work into my day* smile. As she approached, Hogg turned to Bob Tidey—'Detective Garda Rose Cheney, Macken Road.'

'We've met,' Cheney said.

'The Boyce arrest,' Tidey said.

Hogg said, 'All the better, then. Bob needs a backgrounder, and I want you to help him look at possible links between the murders.'

'No problem, sir.' She looked at Tidey and inclined her head towards the door.

Walking down the corridor, Tidey said, 'Sorry to be a bother—I imagine you've enough on your plate.'

'Not to worry.'

'Maybe we better find a quiet corner, so you can fill me in.'

'Better still—why don't I dump these files and meet you out front, take you to have a look at the murder scene? It's mostly cleaned up now, but you'll get the picture.'

'I had a look at the outside of the house—not a lot of help. A look inside can't hurt.'

'I'll drive.'

*   *   *

'Take this, Turlough. Hold onto it.' Vincent held out the mobile. The depot manager took the phone like it was an infected thing.

'Any time you want, Turlough, you tap open the photo album and you look at the picture.'

The photo in the mobile was something Turlough McGuigan never wanted to see again. It

110

showed his wife. She was wearing the same top she'd had on when Turlough had left for work less than an hour earlier. White, with red piping around the neckline and the ends of the short sleeves. There was a man standing beside Deirdre, a man in a Superman T-shirt, wearing a baseball hat and round shades. The man had an arm around Deirdre's shoulders, his hand coming down, casually cupping her right breast. Deirdre looked out from the picture, her face pale, terror flaring in her eyes.

'I've got no access to money,' Turlough McGuigan said. 'If I try to pick up money, there's no way—'

'We don't expect you to bring us any money.'

McGuigan stared at Vincent. 'What's it for, then? Why you doing this to me—to her?'

'One thing you should know—my people went into the house five minutes after you left. She hadn't time to take the kids to school—they're there, too.'

'*Fuck you.*'

'That's what I'd say, in your position, Turlough—you're entitled. But, just so you know—any pissing about on your part, it's over. My people don't hear from me—they have their orders.'

'I've told you—I've no access—'

'You and me, we're going to go have a coffee.'

Vincent Naylor started the engine and eased the car out of the pub car park. He glanced at his watch.

On schedule.

23

Through the half-closed venetian blinds at the living-room window of Turlough McGuigan's home, Liam Delaney watched the street outside. Nothing stirring.

Kevin Broe was standing at the sliding doors that led into the dining room, in his Superman T-shirt. Delaney and Broe were both wearing baseball hats and shades.

Deirdre McGuigan was sitting on the sofa. PlayStation sounds and the laughter of her two small boys drifted down from their bedroom above.

'Shouldn't be long,' Liam said.

The woman looked up, her expression a mixture of fear and disgust.

'What are you doing with my husband?'

'He's OK.'

'Get him to ring me, so I know he's OK.'

'He's OK.'

'I need to—'

Liam Delaney held up his hands to stop her. 'Look—the way this is, what's best is if you just keep quiet, do as we say. That way it's all over quickly, things get back to normal.'

'Things will never be normal.'

'Another hour—no more than that, maybe even—'

'When you work for a security company, and something like this happens—even when you're totally innocent, things are never the same. Even if he keeps his job, things won't—the police will—the company—'

'That won't—'

'Jesus, he's worked so hard, he's—' She lowered her head, waited a moment, and when she looked up again at Liam Delaney she was straining to keep her voice at a level pitch. 'What happens next?'

'Your husband's seen the photo by now—'

'Doing this, to a family—that picture—you're *disgusting*, all of you.'

'Count yourself lucky.' Over by the window, Kevin Broe was smiling. 'I know of jobs where people needed serious convincing—bank staff, security guys.' He bent forward towards Deirdre McGuigan, his smile fixed in place. 'Quickest way to do that is pick someone, a wife or a girlfriend, and give her a hammering. After that, no one gets lippy.' He seemed almost disappointed. 'Nothing like that here.' He made a cup of his right hand, as though weighing something. 'You got your tit felt up, no big deal, and—who's to say—' He kissed the palm of his hand—'maybe you enjoyed it?'

'Go fuck yourself.'

Kevin was still smiling. He held his thumb and forefinger an inch apart. 'Just a *little* bit, no?'

Liam Delaney said, 'Here he is.'

'Turlough?' The woman stood, turned towards the window.

Kevin Broe said, 'Sit the fuck down.' Deirdre McGuigan sat down.

Turlough McGuigan's Suzuki was parked outside. Noel Naylor was getting out.

By the time Noel got to the front door, Liam Delaney had it open. Noel handed over the depot manager's white shirt, nodded and turned to leave.

113

'Everything going OK?' Liam said.

Noel half turned and held up a thumb, then continued down the front path.

Kevin Broe moved towards the door, paused and turned to Deirdre McGuigan. 'Got to go, baby. Love ya and leave ya.' He blew her a kiss. Passing Liam Delaney he smiled and said, 'You get all the fun jobs.' He followed Noel Naylor down the street and around the corner to a black Lexus.

In the living room, Delaney was talking to Deirdre McGuigan.

'You need to listen to me, OK?'

'I need to hear from my husband.'

'Your husband's called in sick. He's OK, he's cooperating with us. This is your husband's shirt. That way, his company will believe he's home—the tracker device, you know? Same reason my friends have left his Suzuki parked outside.'

'Where is he?' Her voice sounded a couple of rungs below hysterical. Delaney leaned forward and tried to make his voice a lot calmer than he felt.

'Pay attention. This is important for you and your husband. They'll ring, the company—soon as they know he's home, they'll want to talk to him. It'll be a routine check. You tell them Turlough's gone to bed, soon as he came in the door. You got that? He's gone to bed, he's out of it.'

She nodded. Her hands were on her thighs, rubbing invisible creases out of her skirt.

'Soon as he's feeling better, he'll give them a ring, OK?'

'OK.'

'You can do that?'

The phone rang.

114

Delaney said, 'They don't hang around. You OK for this?'

Deirdre McGuigan didn't reply. When she picked up the phone the only sign of her distress was her pale face. 'Hello, yes?'

After a moment she said, 'He just got here, yes—listen, can I get him to give you a ring in a while?' Her voice was concerned, but self-assured. 'He's in bits—came in a minute ago, pale and sweaty, went right to bed.' Her head was back, her eyes closing as she concentrated on her task. 'Mind you, this morning, I knew he was a bit off colour, but he said he'd shake it off.'

Liam Delaney, sitting in the armchair next to the fireplace, realised he'd been holding his breath. For the first time since he came to the house, he allowed himself a moment of relaxation.

This is going to work.

24

Detective Garda Rose Cheney said, 'He died just short of ten o'clock in the evening. Shotgun blast in the chest—lifted him off his feet, threw him there. Just where you're standing.'

Although the white marble floor had been cleaned since the murder, instinct or squeamishness made Bob Tidey take a step back.

'Anyone else in the house?'

'He'd just arrived home. Wife was upstairs, on the phone to her brother. Sweetman came in, closed the front door, left his briefcase over there.' Her heels clicked on the white marble floor.

'Dropped his keys on the table here. According to the wife, she heard him come in, maybe thirty seconds later she heard the doorbell, then the shotgun.'

'She see anything?'

'She came halfway down the stairs, in time to see the two gents leaving—pretty messed up about it, as you might imagine. Hadn't a lot to offer.'

'She's not here?'

'Staying with her parents—Mount Merrion.'

'Kids?'

'Three—the youngest is seven, oldest is twelve. The granny's looking after them.'

Cheney passed over a bulky A4 envelope. 'Have a look at the snaps.'

Tidey took the album of crime scene photographs and tucked it under one arm. 'I assume they've got CCTV front and back?'

'Nothing useful,' Cheney said. 'Smudgy images of two men, wearing the usual gear. The angle—you don't see the shotgun blast. One of them takes a few steps into the hallway—that's the one put the two bullets into his head. Then they left.'

'He just opened the door when the bell rang?'

'Nothing unusual. Aged forty-two, still a bit of a lad. Golf, poker, big rugby fan—he and his mates often dropped in on one another unannounced.'

'The house next door—it's got cameras covering the grounds. Any chance they caught something relevant?'

'We've checked every house on the road, and the CCTV on all the approach roads. Nothing.'

Tidey was looking up. 'Jesus, what's that? Blood?'

Directly above, a pattern of darkened, dried

116

blood speckled the white ceiling.

Cheney said, 'The shotgun tore into his chest, knocked him off his feet. The body goes back, the blood flies out. Some of the blood—' Cheney pointed up at the ceiling—'the blast was so strong, his body jerking back, some of the blood flew all the way up and hit the ceiling. Then, after a few seconds—Technical says—droplets came down from the ceiling. Left little sunbursts on the floor.'

'A shotgun blast, then two in the head?'

'Someone was taking no chances.'

Tidey opened the photo album and found a head-and-shoulders shot. The bullets had torn lumps out of Sweetman's flesh, and the neck and face were veiled in the blood thrown up from the chest wound. He flicked towards the back of the album and found a studio shot of Sweetman. Handsome features, expensively groomed, oozing confidence. Not the kind of man to ever imagine someone might open him up and spill him all over his own hallway.

*   *   *

Vincent Naylor said to Turlough McGuigan, 'My friends have arrived.' The Protectica depot manager looked across the coffee shop to where Noel and Kevin were ordering something to drink. Noel was still in his shorts and T-shirt and false moustache, Kevin was wearing jeans and sweatshirt and a baseball hat.

'What are we waiting for?'

Vincent looked at his watch. 'Another ten minutes—then we're in business.'

'What do you want me to do?'

117

'You're not thinking, Turlough. Where are we?'

'What do you mean—we're in Doonbeg.'

'And where in Doonbeg?'

'The shopping centre.'

'And what happens this morning in Doonbeg shopping centre—twenty past eleven, give or take five minutes?'

It took McGuigan a few seconds to get it.

'That's not on.'

'Well—'

'There's no way—they're not going to—'

'The mobile I gave you, there are some pictures.'

McGuigan flinched, shook his head.

'Not that one, Turlough, unless you need to refresh your memory. Give it to me.'

Vincent tapped the phone until the screen showed a photo of the outside of a house. He thumbed a button, and again, another house, then a third.

'Mick Shine, Paudie McFadden, Davey Minogue. You know them, Turlough, though you mightn't recognise their homes.'

'There isn't—'

'You have a job to do, Turlough.' Vincent thumbed the button once more and the picture on the mobile screen changed and Turlough looked away from the image of his wife's terrified face.

*　　　*　　　*

Rose Cheney opened a pair of double doors, leading into a living room big enough for tennis doubles. There were oil paintings on the walls, with big, gold-coloured frames and subjects out of the nineteenth century—a bewigged man sitting stiffly

118

on horseback, a hunt in full cry, a garden party, women in pale dresses and flowered hats ranged around a marble fountain.

Cheney said, 'Some house, huh?'

Tidey nodded. 'The wages of sin.'

'Four million, he paid for it, four years ago. Four-point-four, to be precise, which was considered a bargain for this neighbourhood. Today, if anyone was buying—which they're not—you'd get a million and three-quarters, probably less.'

'I've seen better taste in Phibsboro bedsits.'

Cheney smiled. 'I've been in a few of these places—this isn't the worst. Some of them, they look like Barbie grew up and became a footballer's wife. No limit to the budget, all spent on a twelve-year-old's notion of taste. One thing they've all got on display—and there it is.' She stopped at a table flanked by two wingback chairs. The table held a large chess set, the base a couple of inches thick, edged with steel, the squares of the board in dark grey and light grey wood. 'Monster chess sets—they've all got them.'

Tidey picked up a black knight. It was intricately carved to resemble a Roman legionnaire. 'Someone loves his hobby.'

'Handmade pieces, inlaid boards, they cost more than the biggest LCD telly. And—ask them—hardly any of them can play the game. If the new Irish aristocracy had an emblem, that's it—a swanky, overpriced version of a game they can't play.'

'What do we know about Sweetman? Any threats, any real suspects?'

'No threats we know of—a whole sea of possibilities, nothing solid. Lines of inquiry—' she began ticking them off on her fingers—'husbands he pissed off, business partners he cheated, bank shareholders he swindled. Take a walk through Dublin 4, throw a stick, chances are you'll hit someone with a reason to shove a shotgun in his face. Most of them, they wouldn't know which end of a shotgun to point—but, someone did.'

'Paramilitaries?'

'Killing a corrupt banker—you could see the patriotic side of that, if you did your thinking with your trigger finger. But Hogg says Special Branch has every second patriot on the payroll—not a whisper.'

'What's the score with pissed-off husbands?'

'He didn't make a big secret of screwing around. Of recent girlfriends—we've talked to one and there's no jealous husband involved. Two more, we don't have their names yet. There might well be husbands or partners from previous affairs who've been nursing a grudge for a long time.'

Tidey shook his head. 'If it was a knife or a baseball bat, maybe—but two heavies with guns, hardly an act of passion.'

'We're tiptoeing through every number in his BlackBerry.'

'How bad were his business problems?'

'Apart from running the bank, he had three outside directorships and a company based around his property portfolio—he was in a consortium with some lawyers, doctors, a couple of bankers.'

'Busy man.'

'When the game was in full flow the banks were borrowing billions to lend to the right sort of people—no one could lose. Then—' she flicked an index finger at the chessboard and the king made a clattering noise as he toppled over, scattering pawns—'pop goes the bubble.'

'He must have had something left. This place is worth a fortune.'

'This house—he got a mortgage of four million, then he shopped around and got two more mortgages against the same property, for the same amount. Total—twelve million.'

'Didn't anyone check?'

'A banker, a lawyer, a pillar of society—start asking questions and he might take his business elsewhere.'

'The smart fellas, a friend of mine calls them,' Tidey said.

'That was small change. He had tens of millions—something like a hundred and forty million—invested in property deals. All borrowed—and borrowed against bank shares that aren't worth a cent. It'll never be paid back. Then there's the fraud—Sweetman and his buddies, switching billions from bank to bank, to keep the auditors in the dark, writing up transfers as deposits, to boost share price. That's before you come to the tax dodges—the guy could have written an encyclopedia of scams.'

'He wasn't looking at a slap on the wrist, then.'

'Oh, I don't know about that.'

Tidey smiled. 'He had something to sell? Maybe someone to sell?'

'That was the plan. As soon as Sweetman knew the game was up he called the Revenue and the Financial Regulator. At the time he was murdered he was working on a deal.'

'So, the murder could have been to shut him up?'

'Possible, but improbable. These people, if

121

they're faced with a threat they bribe someone or they hire a lawyer to make a deal.'

'People who had everything—they lost it, their reputations in flitters, maybe even expecting a call from the Fraud Squad. Could be someone went off the deep end.'

'I can see these people smashing Sweetman's fancy chessboard over his head—what I can't see is any of them linking up with a mate and finding a hoodie and an automatic pistol.'

Tidey crossed the room and stood looking up at the large painting over the fireplace. Unlike the other paintings in the room, it was contemporary, an almost photographic reproduction of a modern racing scene under a faultless blue sky. Emmet Sweetman stood beside a light brown horse, holding the reins, the pride of the winning owner glowing in his face as he smiled out into his living room. Behind him, a couple of dozen revellers cheered, most of them waving champagne glasses.

'Butter wouldn't melt,' Cheney said.

Tidey stared at the faces in the painting, every one of them proud, confident, no shadow of doubt in their world. They must have felt like they could get away with anything.

25

Christ sake, missus, leave the fucking kid alone.

Turlough McGuigan tried to focus, to block out the kid's howls, the sound of the mother's hand smacking the back of the kid's matchstick legs. He was walking slowly through the Doonbeg shopping centre. He seldom used the place, although it was within easy reach of his home. The ceiling was low, the tiled floor dirty and cracked, the atmosphere oppressive.

The housing estate surrounding the shopping centre was just as tatty. A monster estate—vast, ugly and unloved. The shopping centre was a sprawling two-storey building that looked from the outside like something designed by a specialist in fortified artillery emplacements. It was an embassy installed by outside forces, representing the country of commerce, built with an undisguised hostility towards an alien environment. The people of the housing estate needed the services the centre provided, the country of commerce needed the profit that came with trade. In more salubrious neighbourhoods, shopping centres might pose as cathedrals of consumerism, offering to upgrade the shopper's self-image. Here, there was no attempt to pretend this was anything other than an exchange of goods and money.

The shopping centre was always busy, always noisy, and there always seemed to be some stressed woman with pursed lips beating her kid with passionless anger.

Focus, Turlough McGuigan told himself.

'You ever hear the expression, "Hesitate, too late"?'

The thug leader had smiled when he said it, back in the coffee shop. He knew about that. He knew about everything.

After a robbery a couple of years back, Turlough McGuigan's Protectica bosses organised a series of morale-boosting seminars. The robbery was a stupid one, a small thing—two wiseguys knocked over a carrier, kicked him in the face and did a runner with a couple of bags, not more than fifteen grand. The guy who ran the seminar was named Finbarr something, full of one-liners. *It's not your fault, but it is your responsibility . . . If you fail to prepare, you're preparing to fail . . . Never let good enough be enough . . . The more you sweat in training the less you bleed in war . . . Excuses are for losers.*

And that one, *Hesitate, too late*.

'If it looks like enemy action, behave accordingly—don't wait for written confirmation. Hesitate, too late.'

In the Doonbeg coffee shop, the thug leader told Turlough McGuigan, 'My information says if I walk up to your guys when they come out of the bank they'll flatten me. Before I get to explain the situation they'll start punching alarm buttons and I'm face down, spitting blood.' He leaned closer. 'What we need is someone who makes them hesitate. Someone they'll listen to as he lays out the facts, so they behave sensibly. That's you.'

Turlough and the thug leader had watched two uniformed Protectica guys—Mick Shine and Paudie McFadden—get out of the van and go into the shopping centre. Now, minutes later, McGuigan watched the two come out of the Doonbeg branch of Bank of Ireland. Both men were helmeted, toughened Perspex face shields tight down over their eyes, armoured vests over their dark green uniforms. Mick was the primary carrier, two black-and-chrome bags of cash in his left hand, two in his right. Behind Mick and two steps to one side, Paudie was the mace—carrying a bag in his left hand, his right hand casually poised close to the extendable baton at the side of his belt.

124

Davey Minogue was podman today, locked into the back of the Protectica van.

Turlough McGuigan had to resist looking back over his shoulder, to where he'd left the thug leader standing casually near the exit. He drew a deep breath and took the mobile out of his pocket.

Mick Shine saw him first, recognised him, inclined his head in a questioning motion. Paudie McFadden slowed at the sight of their depot manager. McGuigan stood in their path and tried to get his face to relax.

'We're being watched. Stay calm, do nothing.'

Apart from a sudden tension in their stance, the two didn't react. 'It's very serious,' McGuigan said, 'but I think we can handle it. Fella gave me this, told me to show you.' McGuigan held up the phone and thumbed a button. 'That's Davey's house.'

'What the fuck?' Mick Shine said.

'Stay calm—I think we'll get out of this OK as long as we stay calm.'

'How did—'

McGuigan thumbed the button and a picture of another house appeared on the screen and Mick Shine shut up. McGuigan thumbed the button again and held the phone towards Paudie McFadden. 'Your house, right?' Then he showed them both the photo of Deirdre, with the thug in the Superman T-shirt holding her breast. 'That's my wife—they've got her right now.'

'Jesus Christ,' McFadden said.

'Stay calm.'

McFadden swore.

Mick Shine said, 'Are you in on this?'

'Don't be fucking stupid.'

125

'What do we do?' McFadden said.

'Are they in my house?' Mick Shine said.

'I don't know, I think so. They've got my wife. They know where we all live, they—'

'Jesus, Jesus.' Behind the Perspex shield, anger and fear contorted Mick Shine's face.

'If we don't stay calm, do as we're told—these fuckers are not kidding.'

'What do they want us to do?' McFadden said.

McGuigan was looking at Mick Shine. 'Mick? You OK?'

None of the shoppers paid any attention to the three men talking quietly. McGuigan could hear the howling kid, taking another whack from his mother.

Mick Shine said, 'Whatever—we do whatever they want.'

McGuigan nodded. 'I don't see how we can do anything else. Play it cool, we get out of this OK, our families too. Just—I'll walk ahead, you follow me outside. OK?'

They stood there silently for maybe ten seconds, then Turlough McGuigan said again, 'OK?'

'Let's go, then,' Mick Shine said.

On the way towards the exit they passed the stressed-out mother, her son silent now, clutching her skirt, an ice cream in his other hand.

26

'That house, two up from this one—big sunroom stuck onto the side of it—guess how much it cost, three years ago?'

'Haven't a clue,' Bob Tidey said.

'Six million—six and a bit.'

Bob Tidey and Rose Cheney were outside the Sweetman home, looking back at it from beside their car. From here, the house had the look of an old-fashioned country hotel. Pillars flanking the entrance, rose bushes off to the left, cast-iron and dark wood benches underneath both the bay windows. And a wide, colourful welcome mat across which Sweetman's killers had stepped.

'Know how much it's worth now?'

'A lot less than six million.'

'Less than three—two million, eight hundred thousand. That's what they're asking, and they won't get it.'

'Tough.'

'Were you ever tempted to get into that game?'

'On my salary?' Tidey said.

'One fella I worked with had three houses—big ones, too—set out in flats. A fair few guards got into that game. In the good old days, all you needed to qualify for a big loan was a pulse.'

'Holly—my ex—and I—a house was somewhere to live, not something to invest in.'

'I thought we were missing out—the newspapers were forever saying you had to be a fool not to get in on the action. My husband was the cautious one. I still feel a bit like I missed a big party.'

'A big orgy,' Tidey said. 'Where everyone got the clap.' He tossed the crime scene photos on the back seat. 'You've got files for me to look at?'

Cheney smiled. 'Back at the station—by the ton.'

*   *   *

127

When Turlough McGuigan and the security guys were almost at the exit, Vincent Naylor turned and faced out onto the shopping centre car park, looking towards where Noel and Kevin were waiting in the black Lexus. He put his hand on top of his head for a moment. Then he stood with both hands in his pockets, one hand gripping the small pistol.

Noel already had the Lexus engine running. Now, the car motored slowly across the fifty feet that separated it from the parked Protectica van.

Vincent turned back and watched Turlough McGuigan lead the two security men out into the sunlight and across the pavement towards the van.

'You'll see a black Lexus coming up slowly,' Vincent had told him. 'The boot will be unlatched. It stops, you swing the lid up, you tell the guys what to do.'

Now, Vincent watched as the Lexus eased to a stop. There was an awkward moment as the two Protectica guards paused. Their training and instinct told them to knock on the van's sliding hatch and to sling the money inside when podman Davey Minogue opened up. Instead, their faces grim, they followed Turlough McGuigan's instructions and dropped the bags of money into the boot of the Lexus. McGuigan slammed the boot shut.

* * *

'Here, you'll need this.' Turlough McGuigan held out the mobile to Mick Shine. Behind the Protectica van, the black Lexus was moving slowly away.

128

'You know we're not allowed private mobiles on the job.'

'Fucking take it. It's been disabled, you can't call anyone. Show Davey the picture of his house. You get back in the van, you tell Davey not to fuck about and you move on to the next collection.'

'The next—'

'Next stop, Harding Avenue, Ulster Bank—I'll meet you there.'

Mick Shine looked at Paudie McFadden, then back at Turlough McGuigan. 'This—'

'They're not finished yet.'

McFadden said, 'Jesus, these—'

Turlough McGuigan's voice quivered. 'We don't have *time* for this. Right now Davey's worrying why there's no package coming through the hole. You wait too long, he gets worried and trips the flare—how are you going to live with what happens to your family?'

A minute later, Turlough McGuigan was sliding into the red Megane, the thug leader at the wheel. At the exit from the car park a woman in a ten-year-old Fiesta cut in front of them and the thug leader called her a cunt. When he got going he made good time and before long he was tucked in behind the Protectica van, ten minutes away from the next collection. Turlough McGuigan looked across and the thug leader was smiling.

'Won't be long now, Turlough—chin up.'

27

Inside the Protectica van, Mick Shine was driving and Paudie McFadden was riding shotgun. Davey Minogue, the podman, was perched on the jump seat at an angle to the lockers that lined the back of the van. He was small for a security man, but fit and bulky, with a bald head and a neat goatee beard. His head was thrust forward between his co-workers and his voice was an urgent hiss. 'Remember your training—'

Mick Shine said, 'Sit the fuck down, Davey.'

'All the hallmarks—it's a scam, it's a bluff.'

'Look at the pictures,' Paudie McFadden said.

Davey snorted derisively. 'They found out where we live, they took pictures of our houses—that's all.'

'Turlough's wife. You think that's a bluff?'

'Who do you think gave them our addresses? The fucker's in on it—that picture's a set-up.'

'We don't know that,' Mick Shine said.

'They have to have someone on the inside. He's here with them, for Jesus sake, giving us orders—what more do you want?' Davey Minogue leaned forward, his face next to Paudie McFadden.

'Sit down, Davey.'

'Pull the flare.'

'You're mad.'

'Pull the flare!'

'Sit fucking down, and shut fucking up!'

Davey Minogue stared at the flare on the dashboard. It was a small unmarked rectangle of black plastic, with a slight ridge along the near side. Press on that ridge and release it and the cover springs open, to reveal a red button inset in the dashboard. Press the button and alarms go off back at the Protectica depot and at Garda HQ, and within seconds the closest Emergency Response Unit receives the alarm, along with the latest GPS information on the van. Within minutes they're slipping the safety catches off their Uzis.

'Lads—'

'Davey, you're wrong—sit down.'

Davey Minogue moved back to the jump seat and belted himself in. Both his co-workers were tense, frightened, and that was to be expected. Davey knew they lacked his composure. They were shocked, in danger of panicking. Give them time and they'd see what he saw—this was a classic inside job. Trouble was, by the time they wised up this whole thing might be over.

Maybe he should have just reached over their shoulders—press, flick, one touch to the red button.

He had an image of Mick Shine jerking the steering wheel, the van swerving—God only knew how that might end.

More ways than one to skin a cat.

The back of the van had rows of numbered lockers, floor to ceiling. A single key opened any locker. If more than one locker at a time was opened an alarm would be triggered back at the depot.

Davey Minogue slid a hand down to his belt and felt the thin steel chain clipped there. His fingers followed the chain to the breast pocket of his uniform, where the key rested.

Maura Coady left the Spar and walked slowly back up Kilcaragh Avenue towards her house. She was carrying a plastic bag with a litre of milk, a small sliced pan and the *Irish Independent*. She averted her gaze from the white van as she passed it, and when she got to her house she looked at everything except the green car parked outside. Once inside, she made tea and toast and promised herself she would stay away from the front window until at least lunchtime.

When she finished her toast she sat for a moment, then she took her cup of tea into the front room and stood behind the net curtain, watching the green car.

28

Davey Minogue wiped a drop of sweat from under his left eye.

Wait too long and it might be over before the cops could get here. There was no telling how many pickups the gang intended to take. The next stop for the Protectica van was on Harding Avenue, on the outskirts of Raheny, and that was no more than five minutes away. Soon as they took the money from the Ulster Bank the gang might pack it in and vanish.

Davey Minogue felt himself waver. Maybe the sensible thing was to watch everything, take it all in, so he could give the cops a complete picture. Blowing the whistle was tempting, but it was dangerous, too. Was it necessary?

When this was over, the cops would pull apart Turlough McGuigan's life. They'd examine his bank account and the bank accounts of everyone he was close to. They'd look up his chimney, poke through his wardrobe and shake out his stamp collection. They'd examine the records of his mobile and his home phone, search his garden shed and his attic, they'd look under his bed—hell, they'd look under anything roomier than his foreskin. If there was anything to find—and Davey Minogue knew there would be—they'd find it.

So—leave it to the cops to pick things up afterwards?

But that wasn't what you did if you had initiative. If you paid attention to your training, you didn't wait for someone else to do the job, you did it yourself. Besides, when this was over, any Protectica employee who sat idly by would be an object of suspicion. Davey Minogue knew there was a way to set himself apart.

His thumb eased the small silvery locker key from his pocket. He enclosed it in his fist, down by his side.

'Davey.'

Hands on the steering wheel, Mick Shine was staring straight ahead at the traffic. There was no internal rear-view mirror, so Shine couldn't have seen anything. Again, he said, 'Davey.'

'What?'

'I know you, Davey.'

Silence.

Then, again, 'I know you.'

Davey Minogue said, 'What does that mean?'

'This is not a game, Davey.'

'Fuck off—what're you getting at?'

Paudie McFadden glanced around at Davey, then turned back to face the road ahead.

'I'll do you,' Mick Shine said. His hands were tight on the steering wheel, his voice steady, his gaze fixed on the road.

Davey Minogue said nothing. He stared at the back of Mick Shine's bullet head.

'And I don't mean that I'll leave you with bad bruises, that's not what I mean.' Shine's voice was calm, clear. 'And I don't mean if you pull a stroke and something goes wrong and someone belonging to me gets hurt. Maybe that's what you think I mean, but that's not what I mean. If you go Rambo on me, you take a chance with my people, my family—no matter how small a chance you think it is—I'll kill you stone fucking dead. Even if it all works out and they give you a medal, I'll put you in the fucking ground, OK?'

They were approaching the right turn for Harding Avenue, and Mick Shine changed lanes.

'Do you hear what I'm saying, Davey?'

There was a traffic light before the turn, and it changed now to red. The van coasted to a stop, third vehicle from the lights. Mick Shine turned in his seat and stared back.

'Do you hear what I'm saying, Davey?'

Head to head, Mick Shine was four or five inches taller than Davey Minogue, and maybe a stone heavier. But Davey looked after himself. As a smaller guy in a tough business, he'd had to work at it, and he knew his heavy shoulders and strong hands could take a bigger man in a fair fight.

But he could see in Mick Shine's eyes something that no amount of training and preparation could

134

match. Fear, held in check by cold anger. In a fight, it was the ingredient that outweighed everything else. If Davey Minogue used the key to alert headquarters he had no doubt that Mick Shine wouldn't wait to see how things turned out.

'I'm just sitting here,' Davey Minogue said.

Mick Shine nodded. The lights had changed and someone behind the van was thumping a car horn. Mick Shine sat and stared at Davey Minogue until he was ready, then he turned back to the wheel, eased the van forward and around the corner, towards the branch of the Ulster Bank on Harding Avenue.

Davey Minogue leaned forward, towards his colleagues in the front of the van. 'Mick—I'm not, that's not me, there's no way I'd put anyone's family at risk, you know that.'

Mick Shine said, 'It's done now, Davey—we're doing what we have to do.'

'All I'm saying—I *know* this is a scam, I know we're being—'

Up ahead, Mick Shine could see the black Lexus, parked this side of the bank.

'It's done now, Davey.'

'I think you're wrong, Mick, but I'll go along—'

The van slowed as it passed the Lexus, and Shine pulled up level with the bank. He switched off the engine and turned round. 'One thing—no offence, Davey, on this stop, and as long as this thing lasts, Paudie's the podman. And you're mace. You come with me—no way you're staying in this van on your own. OK?'

Davey Minogue said, 'That makes sense. I swear, Mick, all I—'

'Let's go, then.

29

The Ulster Bank branch on Harding Avenue was in the middle of a short strip of eight business premises. To the left of the bank, a Londis, a pub, a florist's and a bookie shop. To the right, a Chinese and a video shop and—gone out of business—a boutique that specialised in handmade wedding hats. Noel Naylor was at the wheel of the Lexus, Kevin Broe beside him.

Vincent Naylor's Megane was parked beside the Londis. As he thumbed his mobile, he watched Turlough McGuigan standing twenty-five yards away, outside the Ulster Bank. When Liam answered Vincent said, 'Just checking in.'

'No problems here, everything's ace.'

'OK, then, call you later.'

'How much longer?'

'Depends on traffic, and that's been OK.'

'No rush.'

'Talk to you.'

The two Protectica guys were coming out of the bank, Turlough McGuigan had the boot open, the money was going in.

*   *   *

The boot slammed shut and Turlough McGuigan was turning away when Davey Minogue said, 'Hey, gobshite—a word.'

McGuigan turned. 'What?'

'Don't think you'll get away with this.'

Mick Shine said, 'Fuck this, Davey.'

'Don't worry, Mick, I said I'll go along, but I want this piece of shit to know he isn't fooling anyone.'

'Jesus, Davey—they've got people at our houses—'

'They've got *pictures* of our houses, that's all they've got.'

'They've got my wife,' Turlough McGuigan said.

'Bullshit.'

McGuigan turned to Mick Shine. 'Jesus, man, you don't—'

'I don't know what I believe, but that doesn't matter. I'm taking no chances with my family, or with anyone else's.'

The driver of the Lexus was getting out from behind the wheel. He made a gesture at Turlough McGuigan.

'Just sorting something—' McGuigan turned to Mick Shine. 'Mick, please—'

Shine made eye contact. 'I don't know how long I can hold this together. Is this the last pickup they're taking, or are there more?'

'They didn't say.'

Even behind the Perspex shield, the disgust was clear on Davey Minogue's face. 'It's unprofessional, it's humiliating—'

Mick Shine said, 'We can't stand here—let's go.'

As they turned towards the Protectica van, the driver of the Lexus got back behind the wheel.

*   *   *

When Turlough McGuigan returned to the Megane, Vincent Naylor was holding his pistol in his lap.

'What the fuck was that about?'

137

'The guys—'

'Standing in the street, in civilian clothes, yapping with two security men—you think you can do that and no one gets nosy? You think if a cop car comes by they won't get curious?'

The Lexus was already on the way to the next pickup. The Protectica van was moving out.

'I had no choice. There's a problem, one of the guys thinks—maybe they all do—that I'm involved. They look at the pictures, all they see is a picture of their house.'

'Would this help?' Vincent took his mobile from a pocket in his shorts. 'Say I call my mate at your house—say I tell him to punch your wife in the face a couple of times.'

McGuigan pointed a finger. 'You—'

'A minute later, he sends me another picture.' Vincent held up the phone, looked at an imaginary photo. 'And it's a picture of the blood dribbling down your wife's chin, from her broken nose. Do you think that might help convince your people?'

McGuigan said, 'All I'm saying is if we keep going, one bank to the next, something's going to snap. My guys—'

Vincent hit him, a backhand blow on the face, with the hand holding the mobile. McGuigan made a yelping sound.

Vincent said, 'Probably you haven't been in too many fights, the kinda guy you are. That's what a little slap feels like. Your wife gets a punch in the face, two or three maybe—'

'All I'm saying is this isn't going to work. These guys—the longer it goes on—'

'Two more banks—'

'Jesus, no, this won't—'

'Two more banks. Perrystown, then Coolock—'

Vincent slid the gun into a pocket of his shorts and started the engine. He jerked the wheel and the car moved out, cutting off a Hyundai. Already the Protectica van was out of sight. He put his foot down.

Turlough McGuigan was having trouble keeping the quiver out of his voice. 'Look—I want this to work—I want your people gone from my house, but—'

'How much you reckon we've got, the two banks so far?'

McGuigan shook his head. 'The pickup varies, every time. It could—I don't know—I'd say forty grand, forty-five, from each, minimum.'

'Not enough.'

'On top of that—the Ulster Bank—it's got the takings from the bookie shop, the pub, that's another thirty grand—that's at least a hundred and twenty so far. We do the pickup at Perrystown—a couple of supermarkets there, and I think there's three pubs—Perrystown's probably at least another eighty, ninety.'

'And Coolock?'

'I swear, I know these guys, I know they're arguing among themselves—the chances, right now, someone could be pulling the flare and there'll be police all over the place.' He was leaning forward, both hands on the dashboard, his head turned towards Vincent, his eyes pleading. 'It makes sense.'

Vincent eased off on the speed. He could see the Protectica van, a couple of hundred yards ahead.

'All that, the stuff you said, you add it up, what're we looking at?

139

'After Perrystown, minimum—maybe two hundred thousand.'

Vincent was silent for the best part of a minute. The depot manager was right. It made sense. A shame, really, to miss out on the last pickup—but you had to balance things out. It was always going to be dicey, deciding how many pickups they should go after. This way, he was playing it safe, and there was a price for that. Two hundred grand—a fifth each for Liam and Kevin, three-fifths for Vincent and Noel to share. A good morning's work.

Vincent said, 'After Perrystown, we call it a day.'

30

Detective Garda Rose Cheney pointed to a corner desk. 'You can use that for the moment—we'll sort you out later. Down the corridor, second room on the left—you'll find stationery. That's also where we make coffee. I take mine black.'

The incident room for the Sweetman murder was crammed into what had been the Castlepoint Garda Station's Detectives' Room. The station's detectives were sharing workspace with their uniformed colleagues. When Bob Tidey returned to the incident room with two coffees, Cheney was locking a filing cabinet. She pointed at a thick folder she'd left on his desk. 'Statements and questionnaires.' She dropped a key on top of the folder. 'That's for the bottom drawer in that desk—keep them there until you hand them back to me. You'll find sub-folders—Sweetman's business partners, people he conned, people he was ratting out to the Revenue. Relatives, friends, employees. Notes from interviews with them and their spouses and their lovers and their secretaries and their gardeners.'

'A wide trawl.'

'Not so wide, when you get into it. The Dublin money crowd is fairly inbred. Those that didn't go to the same schools go to the same dinner parties. Or they're members of each other's clubs, they sit on each other's executive boards. Their boats are moored at the same marinas, their racehorses are trained at the same stables.'

'Not since the bubble burst.'

'You might think so, but these people knew what was coming, long before the rest of us. A lot of the important stuff was shifted into their wives' names.'

'If Sweetman did that, his wife might have had a motive to—'

'Nah—it's true love. All the financial carry-on, all the affairs, none of it mattered. She was a true believer.'

Tidey sat behind the desk, pointed to the files. 'Where to start.'

'You could get lucky—the first folder you open, you spot a connection between Sweetman and the Snead kid.'

'Yeah, I find that happens all the time.' Tidey rolled up his sleeves.

As Cheney left the room, Tidey reached for the Sweetman file and took out the first folder, marked *Sweetman: business associates.* He shuffled through the folders until he found *Sweetman: personal life.* Along with a covering note, there

141

were three statements—a lengthy one from Sweetman's wife, and the other two from Sweetman's girlfriends. When he'd read the statements Tidey made his way to the rear exit of the station, went outside and lit a cigarette. He took out his mobile and scrolled down through the contacts list until he found the former colleague he was looking for, a sergeant now working at Clontarf Garda Station.

'Harry—Bob Tidey. You remember a gouger named Gerry FitzGerald?—I had him in for a chat, and I know he was one of your regulars.'

'Our old friend Zippo—last I heard he did a short bit for possession. Should be well out by now. Hold on a minute.'

Tidey and Synnott had once been partners on a murder investigation that ran into the sand. Harry later made inspector, then took a hit back down to sergeant after a spot of bother. When Harry came back to the phone he said, 'I'm afraid you won't be talking to Zippo any time soon. Mr FitzGerald was found in his flat, two months ago. A needle in his arm. One last big blast of the hard stuff, and his heart couldn't take it.'

'That's a pity.'

'Dead at thirty-two.'

'Thanks anyway.'

Tidey took a couple of minutes to work the cigarette down a bit, then he ground it under a heel and headed back to the files.

*   *   *

When Vincent Naylor pulled up across the road from the Perrystown branch of Bank of Ireland, the Protectica crew had already gone inside.

'Time to say goodbye,' Vincent said.

'Here?'

'Last pickup.'

'What about my family?' Turlough McGuigan said.

'You stay with the van—keep those people calm—move on to do your next pickup—it's gonna take maybe fifteen minutes. We'll be long gone, and after that you do what you like.'

McGuigan seemed almost reluctant to leave the Megane. 'Nice knowing you—now fuck off,' Vincent said.

As McGuigan got out of the car, Vincent was already thumbing a text message to Noel, in the Lexus parked just ahead of the Protectica van.

Last pickup.

Noel's replying text—*Right*—arrived just as the two security men emerged from the bank. Turlough McGuigan was waiting for them. He said a few words and it took less than ten seconds to dump the money in the boot of the Lexus. Turlough was getting into the Protectica van when the smaller of the two security men began to move towards Vincent. The bigger guy grabbed at the smaller guy's arm but the smaller guy shook loose and strode out onto the road.

Vincent Naylor took his pistol from the pocket of his shorts and held it between his bare knees.

*   *   *

Standing in the middle of the road, the Protectica guy pushed his helmet up from his face and stared at Vincent Naylor. Just stood there, hands on his

143

hips, like he was burning Vincent's image onto his soul.

Vincent pressed a button and the Megane window slid down. 'Piss off,' he said.

The guy leaned forward. 'I'll remember you, shithead. When you're doing time in the basement of the Joy, I'll come visit.' He poked a finger towards Vincent. 'I've got a couple of mates work in the Joy. Maybe I'll see if I can arrange a little reception party for you.'

'Get the fuck out of here,' Vincent said. Ahead, the Lexus was already steaming off, Noel and Liam on their way, the boot full of Protectica bags.

'Davey!'

Across the road, the other security man was standing at the edge of the pavement, his helmet off, his face red.

'I warned you, Davey!'

Vincent raised his hand and pointed the gun at the mouthy security man. The idiot flinched, took a step back, then paused. He stuck his chin out, like the whole thing was about showing he wasn't scared.

Vincent ignored the fool as he took the Megane away from the kerb, picking up speed as he left the Protectica van behind.

Because of the change of plan, it meant at least a fifteen-minute drive to a change of cars. That was a long way, given that the security guys would almost certainly set up an immediate alarm.

Vincent was already putting a call through to Liam Delaney.

'Yeah?'

'All over—and there's no time to spare, the alarm is already going up.'

144

'Shit.'

'Out of there, right now.'

'Done.'

He made a call to Noel, in the Lexus.

'There's no time cushion—the alarm's already gone off. The Lexus's hot.'

'Gotcha.'

'Where are you?'

'Almost there—we're making good time.'

'Remember—no chances. If it's you or the money, fuck the money.'

'It's cool.'

31

Hard left and they turned off Tonlegee Road, the black Lexus moving at a decent clip, missing the sides of the narrow lane by a few inches. Noel Naylor was some driver, Kevin Broe had to give him that. He was as boring as a Black & Decker, but Noel could handle a wheel. The Lexus hardly slowed until they took the curving turn at the end and he brought the car to a sudden stop in a wide cul-de-sac. Walls on three sides, and the back of a two-storey building on the right. The building, a disused paint factory, fronted onto Mulville Avenue. Noel flipped the wheel and reversed so the boot was close to the back door of the building.

Here, in the dead-end lane off Tonlegee, was where Kevin Broe had planned to kill Noel Naylor. That was before he had a rethink.

It was Noel who'd found the old paint factory, a handy place to store the money until the dust settled. It was away from traffic, it hadn't been vandalised and it wasn't overlooked. Noel and Kevin had broken in and replaced the lock on the back door, so they could come and go at will.

As soon as Kevin Broe had heard that part of the plan he saw this as a golden moment—just Kevin and Noel alone with a rake of money. Kevin's original idea was to take Noel as soon as they arrived, tap him with a bullet from Broe's .38 Colt. After he thought it through, he decided it wasn't a good move. Do Noel now and he'd have to move the money immediately, find somewhere else to store it, travelling in the hot Lexus. And the rest of his life, watching his back for Vincent Naylor coming after him. Why not wait a day, come back alone and shift the money in a hired van? Take it straight up to Larne and across to Stranraer on the ferry—and the world was waiting.

The best thing about doing it that way was not having to cool Noel Naylor.

Kevin Broe had known the Naylor brothers all his life. He lived four houses away on the same road in Finglas, and he always reckoned Vincent was overrated. Liam Delaney lived on the same estate. They'd never been more than casual friends, brought together by acquaintanceship, opportunity and a shared attitude to other people's money.

One thing Kevin envied was Vincent's reputation, puffed up though it was. Everyone knew Vincent blew away a guy's kneecap when the guy mouthed off once too often. What everyone didn't know, though Kevin Broe did, was that Vincent once scratched a guy, just walked up and did it, left the guy leaking blood from the hole in

146

his head. It was something Kevin couldn't claim, and he often wondered what it would feel like. He knew that some day, given his line of work, it might happen, and he knew if the day came he'd have the balls for it. But, Noel Naylor—that would be a rough way to start.

Maybe because Vincent's mother left for London when Vincent was a kid, and his father spent most of his life in a bottle, and Noel had to play Daddy—maybe that was why Vincent treated his big brother like he was a neighbourhood saint. Waste Noel and you could scarper to Timbuktu and you'd still hear Vincent grunting away behind you, looking for payback.

Much better to play it smart. Come back tomorrow, maybe a day later—shift and run. There was a chance he'd be stopped by the cops, or the van would be searched at Larne, but the odds were in his favour. And the reward—a big chunk of change, the kind of money worth taking risks for. The idea of splitting that kind of money with the Naylors and a lightweight fucker like Liam Delaney, that was just plain stupid.

'That's that,' Noel Naylor said. The Protectica bags made a neat pile in a corner on the ground floor of the paint factory. Noel and Kevin each took an end of a scruffy tarp and pulled it across and up onto the bags. Noel tugged at the tarp until it looked like it was casually thrown there, fitting in with the rest of the dead factory's dirt and debris. No point locking the money away somewhere—the only people who might come across it would be kids looking for something to burn or break. They find something locked they're definitely going to smash it open. No reason to look under a tarp thrown carelessly in a corner.

Noel locked the back door of the paint factory and they got back into the Lexus.

*   *   *

Vincent Naylor drove to a quiet back lane behind a string of shops in Whitehall—nothing there but a couple of monster wheelie bins. He opened the boot and changed out of his T-shirt and shorts and into jeans and a plaid shirt. He tossed petrol from one Coke bottle onto the car seats and emptied the second Coke bottle into the boot. He had a dozen matches held together by a thick elastic band. When the inside of the car was in flames he struck another bunch of matches and when he tossed them towards the inside of the boot he was already walking away from the Megane. Vincent was a couple of streets away when the flames reached the petrol tank, but he heard the *whump*.

He was a minute or so away from where the second getaway car was parked.

He glanced at his watch and lengthened his stride.

32

When he turned and saw the cops behind him, Noel Naylor knew it was all over. Two of them, coming out of the back of a white van, bulked up with armour and black helmets. The van swung round, away from the kerb, to block the street. He turned back—already the street ahead was blocked

148

by another white van, two more cops crouched behind cars. Each of the fuckers was holding a rifle or an Uzi or some shit like that. Noel tried to hold back the feeling of dread washing through him—it was all over but there were still different ways this could play out. At best, he'd spend a long time in a smelly cell, but there was a lot worse could happen.

He crouched, took the gun from his pocket and dropped it, kicked it away down the gutter. Not a big help—but he was still wearing the latex gloves and he'd left no prints on the gun. Just might count for something, depending on the mouthpiece he got.

He pulled off the gloves, dropped them and rose, hands above his head. Give them no excuse. To his right Kevin was shouting obscenities, crouched, head weaving this way and that, as though there might be a way out if he could just find it.

'Put your hands up,' Noel yelled, 'don't give them an excuse, let them see your hands over your head.'

They'd left the Lexus on the other side of the rail line, in East Wall, in flames. They'd come round through the arch and down the lane, then turned into Kilcaragh Avenue and walked right past one of the white vans. That was the one behind them, at the end of the street—walked right past it and didn't notice a thing. Soon as he opened the driver's door of the VW Bora he could tell they were fucked—the shades with the guns popping out of the van up ahead.

All over.

Something went wrong, someone grassed, but right now what mattered was staying alive.

'Don't shoot! We're not armed!' His arms stretched to full length above his head. Noel

149

turned to Kevin Broe, his voice low now. 'Put that fucking thing away, get your hands up, you'll get us both killed.'

Noel wondered if somewhere not too far away Vincent was in the same fix. Whoever set them up, if they knew where one getaway car was parked they had to know where the other one was.

Jesus, stay cool, brother.

Oh shit—

Kevin Broe had his head lowered, not in submission, but it was like he was psyching himself up for something, his chest heaving from his deep breaths.

'Kevin, don't be stupid!'

On the far side of the street, a couple of houses down, an old guy was standing, having lowered a black wheelie bin down off his doorstep—frozen by the scene in front of him. Kevin came up straight and stepped out from behind the car, moving fast now, his intentions clear—if he got in through the old guy's open front door, through the house and the backyard and into the next street—

Noel began to shout something and he was interrupted by the *crack-crack-crack* of Kevin's gun, held out at shoulder height, pointing in the general direction of the cops at the far end of the street, firing as he ran.

The police had a limited field of fire. A careless bullet might clip a colleague at the other end of the street. So they fired just three shots at the running figure. The first hit Kevin Broe in the chest, the second in the face, the third caught Noel Naylor in the throat and he went down making gurgling noises.

Phil Heneghan was still standing behind his

150

wheelie bin, his face pale, eyes big. He finally realised the approaching policemen were shouting at him, telling him to get the fuck away. He backed into his hallway. Across the road, that old lady—Maura the nun, he always thought of her, though she'd told his wife Jacinta her name was Maura Coady and Jacinta always called her Miss Coady. Maura the nun was a couple of feet from her open front door, her face frozen, and she was stepping tentatively off the pavement and out onto the road.

*   *   *

Maura Coady bent down beside the body of the man in the middle of the road. There was no doubt he was dead. There was a patch of blood on his chest and one side of his face was missing.

She was aware of urgent shouting.

She straightened up. The other shot man was a few yards away, his chest falling and rising, his legs moving.

'Missus—get away from there!'

She hurried over to the second man. His throat was bloody, the dark red all down his chest. He looked up at her, his mouth making noises. She knelt.

From somewhere behind her, 'Missus!'

One arm cradling the wounded man's head, her lips were close to his ear. 'Oh my God, I am heartily sorry for all my sins—'

He groaned, his eyes moved erratically, fear leaping out of them.

'You'll be all right, you—'

A hand grabbed Maura's arm and hauled her upright, pulling her away, the grip strong and

151

hurting her. The wounded man's eyes were blinking, his lips open.

'Go back in your house, missus.' The man was wearing heavy armour, the word *Garda* printed on his chest. He pushed her, she resisted. 'That man, he needs an Act of Contrition—'

'Go back in your house, we'll look after him.'

At her front door he let go of her arm and she stood staring at him. 'Please,' she said. She raised a hand in appeal, a smear of blood across the backs of her fingers.

Behind the policeman she could see others wearing armour, pointing guns at the bodies of the two men. One of them was reaching down and picking up a handgun from beside the man who was dead. Another was talking urgently into a microphone strapped under his chin.

'Are you OK, Miss Coady?'

Phil Heneghan was standing beside her, his old, lined face chalk white. 'You should go inside, Miss Coady.'

She held a hand to her face, felt her flesh cold. 'I called the police, about the car—they came.' Her mouth was dry, her voice hoarse. 'And—' She gestured weakly towards the man lying on the ground a few yards away. 'Oh God, it's my fault, I called the police, it's my fault—'

There was the sound of a mobile, playing a few bars of jaunty music. Nobody moved for a few moments, then the policeman stopped speaking into the microphone, leaned down and found the mobile in a pocket of the jeans of the man with the throat wound. He tapped a button, held the phone to his ear and said, 'Yeah?'

33

Dumping his second getaway car, Vincent Naylor had a ten-minute walk to the MacClenaghan building on the edge of the Edwardstown estate. Job done. Stride long, arms swinging, the tension of the last few hours had been replaced by an exhilaration he could feel right out to the tips of his fingers.

Nothing left but to collect the money from the old paint factory, move it to the safe house and divvy it up later. He was approaching the MacClenaghan building, looking up towards his fourth-floor squat, when he took out his phone and rang Noel.

'Yeah?'

'Noel?'

Not Noel's voice. What—

Vincent stopped walking, stood there with the phone to his ear.

Fuck, no.

The voice broke the silence. 'He's busy at the moment. I'm a Garda. To whom am I speaking?'

Vincent held the phone up over his head and threw it as hard as he could against the pavement. The phone bounced and landed several feet away. He picked it up and smashed it down again, then stamped on it over and over until bits broke off. A harsh noise escaped him as he walked away, then he turned and came back and took the SIM card from the wrecked mobile. It was a disposable, used just for the Protectica job—nothing the bastards could get out of it now. He stamped again on the

153

broken phone and he walked until he found a drain where he dropped the SIM card in.

It took Vincent a few minutes to get to the fourth floor of the MacClenaghan. He filled a glass with water and stood on the tiny balcony, thinking it through.

If Noel was caught with the money he was fucked, plain and simple. There was no guessing how long they'd put him away for, but it would take a big chunk out of the middle of his life. And Noel, Jesus—coming back from that, that would take time.

What people didn't understand about Noel—he was strong, but he was fragile, too. When Vincent was about twelve, their da left him alone in the house and pissed off to wherever he went that time, Kilkenny or somewhere, with a woman. Vincent wanted to find him and smash his face. Noel—who was eighteen then—said Vincent ought to stop mouthing off that way. Noel talked about how Da was shredded when their mother buggered off, his whole life just went *whoosh*, Noel said, lost everything he'd come to take for granted. Da was still a young man, looking after a ten-year-old and a four-year-old and no notion of what to do with two anxious kids. And when he fucked up over and over—with schools and food and clothes and keeping Vincent from being frightened—the bottle was a good place to get relief.

At the time of the Kilkenny thing, Noel had his own place and he took Vincent in. Then, three years later, Da came back from Kilkenny or wherever the fuck and Noel stopped Vincent from waxing him. 'He's our father—we're his blood.' He had Vincent by the shoulders, not shaking him, just staying in his face. 'He's all the family we have.' And there were tears in Noel's eyes when he said it—not shaky tears—not weak tears. Noel had character—tears that said things weren't what they should be but they were what they were and it was OK to regret the way things had gone, but it wasn't OK to give in to it. Noel said that even if Da was a pathetic cunt, he had the right to be treated properly when he came home.

There was more to Noel than people thought.

'Three things matter in life. First, you do the best you can with the skills God gave you. Second, pick a goal and go for it. And, most important of all—nothing matters more than family.'

Two years after that, Noel was heartbroken when Da did a fade again. Good riddance, as far as Vincent was concerned. Of the two brothers, Noel was the better man, Vincent knew that in his heart. Noel had a code, something to measure his life against. Vincent didn't think about things like that. It rarely bothered him, but he knew that was no way to live. 'You need something bigger than yourself,' Noel said, 'or you're all you are, and that's not enough.'

No need to think the worst. A lot depended on when Noel and Kevin were picked up. If they were lifted with the money in the Lexus—that was the worst-case scenario. Anything else—they could say they were just doing a favour for someone, they thought they were torching the car for the insurance. Not an easy argument to win. But it was a possible runner.

Now, Vincent tried to blank his mind, but it was like trying to hold a door shut against a hurricane. Could be the cops just picked Noel up afterwards, when he was clear of the job, some uniformed shithead recognised him in the street and gave him a pull for old times' sake.

Best thing Vincent could do for the moment was keep his cool. If Noel got clear he'd be in touch soon enough. If not, Vincent would get him an army of lawyers and they'd fight this every fucking step of the way.

34

It was late in the evening when Bob Tidey arrived on Kilcaragh Avenue, near the Fairview Park end of North Strand. A long section of the roadway had been cordoned off, and inside the cordon two white forensic tents had been erected. Small groups of people gathered at each end of the street, with uniforms allowing access only to residents. Tidey had to explain himself to a Garda, who insisted he speak to the officer in charge, who turned out to be a snotty detective inspector with whom he'd shared an office at Cavendish Avenue up to two years back.

'Hi, Polly.'

Detective Inspector Martin Pollard was as frosty as ever. Many of those who had worked with Polly—Tidey being just one—insisted on using the nickname, knowing the Detective Inspector detested it. Precise and pernickety, Pollard was one of those people who, without ever doing anything downright blameworthy, somehow managed to piss people off.

'You have business here?'

156

'The old lady who lives in that fourth house down, she's a friend. Gave me the tip on the car—that's what got the ERU lads involved. I should speak to her.'

Pollard pursed his lips for a moment, then said, 'I'll expect a note on anything she may say—we've taken statements up and down the street, but if she has anything useful—'

Pollard handed Tidey a card.

'Sure, no problem.' Tidey pointed towards the white forensic tents, about twenty yards apart. 'Both of them?'

Pollard nodded. 'The pathologist has almost finished the preliminary. One was dead before he hit the ground, the other was gone soon after.'

'You've got an ID?'

'Small-timers. One of them started shooting. There's no accounting for stupidity.'

Back at Castlepoint station, Tidey had spent the afternoon and evening reading the Sweetman files. He was taking a coffee break, half inclined to quit until the next morning, when he heard two uniforms talking about an ERU shooting at North Strand. After a quick call to a friend in Garda HQ, he locked away the Sweetman files and hurried to his car.

When Maura Coady opened her front door the lines in her face seemed to have deepened since last he saw her. She did the one thing he couldn't have imagined. She circled his waist with her arms and rested her head against his shoulder. His embrace absorbed the shaking in her slender frame. After a while he eased her back into the hallway and closed the door. 'You're OK, Maura, it's just the shock.'

'I'm sorry.' Her voice was a thin whisper.

'Have you seen a doctor?'

'The police brought someone—I think he was— he gave me something, said it would calm me.'

He sat her down in the front room and when he reached for the light switch she said, 'No, please.' He made tea and sat across from her. It was still a bright summer evening outside but the street was narrow and little daylight reached into the front room. She sipped the tea and for a long while neither of them spoke. Then Tidey said, 'I'm sorry you got caught up in all this.'

She looked up at him. 'He was frightened, the second man. The first man was dead, died immediately. The other man was alive, his throat was all bloody, he was making noises. I started saying—I didn't think—it's as natural as making the sign of the cross. I started saying the Act of Contrition. And—the poor man—it was just a moment, but I could see the fear. He knew, when he heard me—'

'It was a comfort, I'm sure it was.'

'He was afraid and I made it worse.'

'Most people wouldn't even think of going out onto the street, with something like that happening.'

'I was in here, just looking out at the street— sometimes I do that. I saw them, they were the men who left the car there, I was going to ring you. One of them opened the driver's door, he looked up and I could see the panic, one of them put his hands up, the other one—'

She sat silently, as if seeing the events again.

'Have you eaten?'

'I couldn't.'

158

'A time like this, you have to look after yourself. I can make you something.'

'If I hadn't said anything. Those two young men. Lying out there in the street.'

'The technical people are nearly done, the bodies will be removed soon, everything will be back to normal.'

'If I hadn't called you—'

'You did the right thing. They had guns, they were putting other people's lives at risk.'

'What did they do?'

'I don't know—a robbery, I'm not sure where. I'll find out, if you like.'

'It doesn't matter.'

He leaned forward. 'Maura, the shock, a thing like this—it'd drain anyone. You ought to lie down, try to get some sleep.'

'I couldn't. I keep thinking—'

'No need to worry—there'll be a Garda on duty all night, it's routine when something like this happens. You're safe here.'

'It's not that—' She closed her eyes.

'I'll stay here. It'll be OK.'

She looked at him for a long time, her eyes older and more tired than he'd ever seen them. 'Would you?'

'I promise.'

*   *   *

Vincent Naylor's eyes were shut tight. He was lying on his side on the laminated wooden floor of his squat, wearing just boxer shorts. The volume on his iPod was beyond comfortable and the relentless pounding of Fear Factory filled his head, dissolving all thought. He'd been lying like this for a long while, buried deep inside the pulsing sound, hiding from grief and time, his body rocking with the beat.

Before that, when Liam Delaney called, Vincent was taking a Marks & Spencer ready-made Indian meal out of the microwave.

'Vincent—Jesus, man—'

Vincent's first thought was to switch off the phone, lose it somewhere. *Strict radio silence.* Liam had no business calling anyone involved in the job. Him calling might mean he'd been snagged and he was obliging the shades in the hope of a good word.

'I just heard—'

'What you calling me for?'

'Shit, Vincent, I just heard.' There was silence, then Liam's voice was rushed, getting high-pitched, louder. 'Vincent, it's on the television, for fuck's sake—North Strand, it has to be them—haven't you heard?'

In the hours since then, Vincent had needed noise, something to hold stuff at bay so he didn't have to think about anything. He'd picked up on Fear Factory from Noel, and it did the job tonight. For a while. Then, above the insistent bass and the relentless drums and the slashing guitar, something—some combination of the overwhelming presence and the irreversible absence of his brother—attached itself to his mind and exploded. As Vincent Naylor rocked and threshed on the floor, the noise of the band and the pain of his grief were locked into his head, surrounded by the silence of the room. And beyond that the silence of the flat and the six soundless floors of the abandoned apartment block.

35

The crime scene tents had gone, taken down after the bodies had been removed last night. The blue-and-white tape had been taken away and the street was its unexceptional self. Detective Sergeant Bob Tidey had slept for a while in the fireside chair in the front room, woke with a crick in his neck and couldn't get back to sleep. He got a glass of water from the kitchen and sat by the window for a while, looking out at the dark street. When his watch said it was almost 4 a.m. he went back to the kitchen and when he couldn't find any coffee he made two mugs of tea, went to the front door and gestured to the Garda dawdling around the pavement on overnight duty. Grateful for having his boredom eased, the Garda stood at the door, drinking tea, chatting, both their voices kept low. After a while, the Garda took a twenty from Tidey and headed down to the all-night Spar on the corner. He came back with half a dozen newspapers and a packet of Rothmans. Tidey opened the cigarettes and the two lit up at the doorstep and the uniform went back to his pointless duty, the cigarette cupped in his hand.

Both the *Irish Times* and the *Irish Independent* carried the story of the double shooting low down on the front page. The two dead men were 'known to the police'. The Garda ombudsman had already launched an inquiry into the circumstances. The stories were light on facts and the newspapers bulked things up with comments from politicians. A statement from the leader of the opposition praised the Gardai and condemned the government for its softness on crime. Most of the tabloids rehashed the bare details in clichés about shoot-outs and streets of death. The *Irish Daily Record* carried the shooting on page 4 and half of page 5, complete with grinning photos of the two dead men. It also had a fair amount of detail, gleaned from locals, about the shooting. One story said that one of the gunmen was surrendering and he called out to the other one.

'Something about not giving them an excuse, that's what I heard,' Phil Heneghan, aged 79, a resident of Kilcaragh Avenue told the *Irish Daily Record*. 'I was putting out my wheelie bin when it happened, I was standing a few yards away.' A statement from Garda HQ said the Emergency Response Unit had fired only after being fired on.

It wasn't a duty Tidey could imagine for himself—carrying a gun, facing panicking criminals, making instant decisions about whether to shoot. Move too quickly, you maybe kill someone trying to surrender. Hesitate and you or a colleague or a civilian gets shot. The *Record* story might be on to something—someone moved too soon. Or it was just media shit-stirring. Either way, Tidey felt regret for the two gobshites in the morgue, and for whatever policeman put them there.

This would be another day for immersing himself in the investigation file on the Sweetman murder. The bad night's sleep meant he'd need a lot of coffee as the day went on. So far, the file was mostly interviews with people who said they didn't know much about anything. Detective Chief Superintendent Hogg's people had been thorough but unproductive. And there was nothing at all suggesting any possible link to the Oliver Snead murder.

If Maura Coady was still edgy tonight he'd have to find someone with rank who'd put a uniform outside the house for a couple of nights, just for comfort. These days, every minute of overtime had to be approved in triplicate, but the force owed her for this.

He could hear Maura moving upstairs. She'd be OK, he decided. The nuns were tough old birds— had to be, to stay sane while living that kind of narrow life. When Tidey first met Maura Coady several years back she'd walked into Cavendish Avenue Garda Station looking to talk to someone dealing with the Teresa O'Brien murder. Tidey was involved in the case, a prostitute found in a builder's skip in a lane off Capel Street, beaten to death with a brick. At that time, Maura was living in a house with three other nuns from the Sisters of the Merciful Heart. The convent in which she'd lived for decades had been sold at the height of the property bubble and the sisters dispersed to rented houses. Since then, through death and further property sales, the sisters had been reduced to a handful, and Maura opted to live alone.

'I know who did it.'

'Sorry?'

'Teresa O'Brien—I know who killed her. It was Mossy Doyle.'

'And you are?'

'Maura Coady—I was a teacher, a nun, and

163

Teresa used to be a pupil of mine. She came to me a few months back, she needed somewhere to stay and I fixed her up.'

'We'd better talk.' Tidey waved a hand towards the door leading into the interview rooms and twenty minutes later he had a very concise statement. She'd been having a cup of tea with Teresa in a cafe in Talbot Street when Mossy Doyle arrived and began roaring at them. Doyle was a less than successful pimp, who felt he still had some claim on Teresa. 'I'll swing for you, bitch, I'll beat every breath of life out of you.'

Maura Coady repeated the words to Bob Tidey that day in Cavendish Avenue station, and she said them again on oath, in the Central Criminal Court, with Doyle a few yards away, staring daggers at her. Maura's initial statement led to a search of Doyle's home and the recovery of a pair of shoes stained with what turned out to be Teresa's blood. The result of the trial was never in doubt. Giving the evidence that put him away, Maura hadn't so much as glanced in Doyle's direction, her voice steady and certain.

The nuns were tough old birds, all right.

36

When he came out of it, sometime during the night, his brain bruised by the hours of pounding music, Vincent Naylor moved slowly. Lying on his back, body limp, he raised his hand to his chest, took hold of the iPod lead and pulled out the earphones. Eyes closed, he threw them and the

164

iPod across the room. The silence assaulted his ears and he lay there a long time, dazed, allowing his senses to gradually awaken. He was aware of a massive dread at the centre of everything. After a while he identified a scent.

Petrol—

He wondered what that might mean.

He felt a dull wave lapping at his consciousness and recognised it as sleep. He let it take him.

*   *   *

When he heard footsteps coming down the stairs, Bob Tidey glanced at his watch. Just gone five fifteen. Maura Coady was wearing a dark check dressing gown. 'Morning, Sergeant Tidey. I hope you got some sleep.'

Tidey stood up. 'I think it's probably OK to call me Bob, now that we've spent the night together.' He immediately regretted the quip, but she smiled.

'There was a time when you'd have gone straight to hell for a remark like that.'

'Sorry. You slept OK?'

'I'm fine, thank you. It was just the shock—I'm fine now.' She crossed to the window and looked out for a moment. 'It's like nothing happened out there—two lives.'

'It's in the papers. The reporters will probably come knocking, looking for witnesses.'

'They've already been. A young man, wanted to know what I saw.'

'What did you say?'

'I looked him right in the eye and I lied. Said I wasn't home when it happened.'

'Best thing to do.'

'I don't see the point of yapping about it, for the entertainment of others.' She moved towards the kitchen. 'Would you like some tea?'

'I've just made a pot.'

'That's great.'

He realised they were both speaking in low tones. No one to disturb, but it was instinctive, this time of the morning.

Sitting in the living room, sipping from her mug, Maura Coady said, 'I'm sure you've got more important things to do today'.

'I'll head off soon. You're sure you're feeling OK?'

She smiled. 'Contemplative—it's what nuns do.'

Tidey put his mug down. 'Do you have someone—do you have contact with the other nuns, the convent, whatever?—I'm not sure how that works these days.'

'You know how it was with those veterans from the First World War? Every year there'd be an anniversary and someone did a headcount, until there was just a handful left and it got to be like a death-watch. We're not reduced to that yet, but the structure's threadbare. Pretty soon. Anyway, no, I have very little contact.'

'That's your choice, yes?'

'I had friends in the Order, they died. And, these days, the way things went, there isn't much reason for reunions and celebrations.'

Tidey nodded.

Maura said, 'I know what you're thinking.'

'What am I thinking?'

'You're thinking what everyone thinks when they talk with a nun or a priest, especially one who's been around as long as I have. How much did she know? That's what you're thinking. Did she cover things up, or maybe she was one of the ones who beat the kids, or worse?'

'That's not what I was thinking.'

'It's what everyone thinks.'

'You forget—I'm a member of an outfit that's had its own troubles. After the Donegal scandal, people assumed we were all stitching people up. Every policeman was bullying witnesses or blackmailing touts and jailing the innocent.'

'And some of you did.'

He nodded. 'Some of us did. But not all of us. Not even most of us. And not all the priests were raping children, not all the nuns were beating them black and blue. In this job, if you're going to be any use to anyone, you learn early on that you need an open mind.'

'Innocent until proven guilty?'

'Something like that.'

She sat there, like she was working something out in her head. Then she said, 'I'm guilty.'

*   *   *

The sound of boots on the stairs, coming up from the third floor. Vincent Naylor finished making a cup of instant coffee. He reached for another mug, ladled a spoonful of coffee, poured again, and by the time the security man came into the flat Vincent had his morning cuppa ready.

'Bit chilly,' the security man said.

Vincent handed him the mug, sat down near the window, looked out towards the Edwardstown estate. When he'd woken there was no confusion in his mind, he knew Noel was dead, he knew he

167

was waking to a whole new world. He hadn't had anything to drink last night, but this morning he felt hung-over.

'Biscuit?'

The security man held out an opened packet of custard creams, taken from a pocket of his anorak. Vincent took a couple, bit off half a biscuit and it tasted as good as anything he'd ever eaten. He remembered that he'd thrown last night's Marks & Spencer meal into the waste bin.

The security man was in his fifties, tubby, unshaven. Part of his minimum-wage job required him to look in on the MacClenaghan building each morning, the rest of his day was spent visiting similar withered development projects on the Northside of the city. The first time he arrived, he'd asked for a backhander and Vincent offered him a fiver and a cup of coffee.

'Fiver a night?'

'A week.'

The security man had nodded. He looked at Vincent now, his head tilted to one side, one eyebrow raised.

'You OK? You look a bit fucked, if you don't mind me saying.'

'Yeah,' Vincent said. 'Didn't get much sleep.'

The security man said, 'Bit of a smell of petrol.'

Vincent pointed at the jerrycan, standing in a corner. He'd kicked it over during his bad time, threshing about. He'd cleaned up, but the smell lingered.

'Had to get that yesterday—need to fill my car, first thing,' he said. 'Must have spilled some.'

The security man sat in silence until he finished his coffee, then he said, 'I'll be off, then.'

'Right.'

'Hang onto the biscuits,' the security man said.

Vincent's nod acknowledged the generosity. 'Mind how you go.'

37

Maura Coady came back from the kitchen with a glass of water. She sat down across from Bob Tidey and took a sip. Her voice was still close to a whisper. 'You've seen the Ryan Report?'

'I read the newspapers when it came out,' Tidey said. 'I decided I already knew more than I wanted to know about all that.'

'I'm in there, Volume Two—there's a chapter on the Sisters of the Merciful Heart. It's not much, just one short chapter in five whole volumes—it's between the chapter on the orphanage at Goldenbridge and the chapter on St Michael's at Cappoquin. Compared with some of the evidence, we were far from the worst. But we're there—and I'm there. Three witnesses gave evidence against me.'

'What did they say?'

'Some of what they said, I remember those things happening. Some of it—it was like they were talking about someone else. A lawyer came to see me, put the allegations to me. I told him what I remembered, and I said I knew they were telling the truth. Even if I didn't remember all the details, I know it all happened, I know, I—'

'You don't have to talk about this.'

She shook her head. 'When you do something

169

terrible, after a while—the daily routine, the people around you, the work, the worries—after a while all that takes over. So many layers of time settling on the memories—and the big things, even the awful things, they end up buried under all the other stuff. Sometimes it feels like it happened to someone else.'

She stared out the window, at the street beyond the net curtain. 'It was a different country, when I took the veil. The way people thought, it was normal that a young woman should go off behind a wall. Cover herself from head to toe in black, never once do anything that wasn't ordained by someone else. Never touch a man, or let herself long for a child.'

'Maura—'

'Looking at it now, I'm on the last lap, an old woman from a different age—and I can see how strange it must seem. Unnatural, even. But it was normal back then, when the Church was so powerful. It was more than normal, it was something that made everyone proud—to have a priest or a nun in the family. It was a blessing.'

'It was a simpler world back then.'

'Not really. Different things mattered, but the world was always complicated. There were a lot of unwanted babies. Sometimes they were taken from mothers who weren't married, sometimes a parent died and families broke up. Sometimes parents couldn't look after their children—there were a whole lot of babies with no one to look after them.'

'And you got the job, whether you wanted it or not.'

'Oh, we wanted it. It suited everyone. The bishops got to run the schools and the hospitals—

the politicians liked not having to worry about the bothersome kids.'

Tidey leaned forward, forearms resting on his knees, his head close to Maura Coady. He waited while she swallowed some more water. 'What age were you?'

'When I went into the convent—seventeen. I had a calling, a vocation. I was earning my place in heaven. When I was twenty-three I was in charge of more than thirty very loud, very troubled kids. Feed them, teach them, mother them. Nourish their bodies and protect their souls. I filled their heads with prayer and when they got awkward I hit them with a leather strap. There were Department of Education guidelines that told me when I was allowed to do that.'

She took another sip of water. She held the glass with both hands. 'One girl—I don't remember her name, but I can see her face even now. She did something wrong, something petty, and instead of saying sorry she shrugged. That was all. She looked me in the eye when she did it. Stubborn girl, rebellious—out there in front of all the others. So, I hit her. Open hand across the cheek. A big step. It wasn't just about impudence any more, I had to show her—and the rest of them—who was in charge.' There was a silence. Her eyes were seeing something not in the room. 'It should have worked. She should have shown fear, she should have lowered her eyes. Instead, she just looked straight at me, like she hadn't felt a thing, and she called me *rabbit face*. So, I hit her again. And again she pretended it was nothing and again I hit her. I don't remember how many times I hit her before she cried.'

171

Maura sounded strained, as though the words themselves were heavy.

'When I was a child, the priests told us how to recognise the dividing line between a venial sin and the mortal sin that put your soul in danger. *Did you take pleasure in it?*—that was the measure of things back then. Your instincts could lead you astray, but you were in real trouble if you took pleasure in it. I think it's that kind of thinking that let some of the priests do the things they did. They told themselves it was something they couldn't help, a curse of the flesh. They were struggling with the Devil, and as long as they could convince themselves they weren't taking pleasure in it—'

'There was no pleasure to take from what you did.'

'Oh, there was.' Maura shook her head. 'I remember the feeling of achievement when that girl cried. There'd been a challenge to the natural order of things, and I faced it down. It was a great feeling. Looking back, I think maybe I felt shame even then—but maybe that's me remembering things the way I want to remember them. The girl's a middle-aged woman now—and if she's still alive I know she still remembers what happened that day and I know she still hates me, and she's right.'

'Did she give evidence?'

'No—and I don't know why. Maybe she's buried it inside. Maybe she left the country. Maybe she's dead. Maybe she was one of the ones who never said anything to anyone about it, the quiet, defeated ones.' She took a long breath. 'She wasn't the last. When you find yourself with power, you use it to solve problems—and you never know where that's going to lead. It wasn't just the physical hurt—there were the ones who vanished into themselves. The ones who couldn't fight back, the ones who—I've heard some of them talk, on the radio these past couple of years, people crying, all these decades later, people who lived thwarted lives, people so hurt they let whole parts of themselves wither and die. That's the worst part of what we did.'

'You were young, in an impossible situation—we all do what we think is right at the time.'

'Beating a child into submission—and there were worse things than that. Things I can't think about. Day after day, year after year, until it became so routine we didn't even notice. Most of them took it as normal, and those that didn't—we broke them. It wasn't just the violence, it was the humiliation. Back then it was called chastisement. We chastised them. We were guiding them through the valley of temptation—from birth to death—keeping them pure for the life eternal. We made them afraid of us, and we didn't mind that a lot of them hated us. We were saving their souls.'

After a few moments of silence, Tidey said, 'You've done your penance, Maura. We can't go back and do things again, the way we know they should have been done.'

'There were times when I was feeling bad. Locked into that life—I know now I wasn't OK with that and I wonder. Any chance of another life slipped away—maybe there was disappointment, unhappiness, frustration, things I didn't recognise in myself back then. Maybe that kind of unhappiness is where the cruelty comes from. Or maybe there were times when I just enjoyed having the control.'

'What about—you said—what the priests did?'

Maura stared at the table. 'The first time—there was a priest used to visit the school, a very nice man, very jolly. One of the girls—I thought she was lying. Leave it with me, I told her. And I did nothing. She never said anything more. It was—you couldn't be sure. There were times he'd spend a lot of time with a child, all smiles and joking, and the child wouldn't seem all that happy about it. Children can be like that, they—'

'You never said anything to him?'

'Once, I tried. I asked him if he was perhaps spending too much time—I put it delicately, like he might be overloading his schedule.'

'And?'

'It was awful. He smiled at me, just looked me in the eye and smiled at me. Said nothing. I stood there and he smiled and smiled and I stood there and I knew. It was like he was challenging me—did I dare confront him straight on, and question the natural order of things? Of course I didn't. After a moment I turned and left and that was that.'

'He was the first, you said?'

Her voice was bare, raw. 'I never saw it happen, that's what I tell myself. So I couldn't be certain it did. And the truth is I didn't want to know. There were signs—looking back it's clear as day—but I was afraid, so—'

Tidey let the silence draw out, then he said, 'It was a long time ago.'

Maura gave him her empty smile. 'Tell that to the kids.'

'I know. But it's a fact—decades have passed, you gave evidence, you admitted what you did, what you failed to do. Isn't that what you're

174

supposed to believe? It's a long time since I was a believer, but I remember the prayers. *Forgive us our trespasses, as we forgive those who trespass against us.*'

She nodded. 'Sometimes I tell myself things like that.'

38

When Bob Tidey left Maura Coady's house it was after seven o'clock. The sun was out but it hadn't yet had time to take the chill out of the air. He'd gone several yards when a voice said, 'You live there?'

He turned and saw a small young man with a grey suit and over-gelled black hair. The man poked his chin up at Tidey. 'You see the shooting?'

'Who are you?'

The young guy flashed a card from his breast pocket. 'Anthony Prendergast, *Daily Record*.'

'Nice suit, Anthony.' Tidey turned and walked towards the North Strand Road.

'You're a Garda, right?'

'A bit baggy about the knees.'

Walking a little faster to catch up, the reporter couldn't resist glancing down at his legs, checking that his suit was hanging right. 'That old lady in there, is she a witness?'

'Fierce ambitious, you are, Anthony—to be asking so many questions this early in the morning.'

The reporter held out a small white rectangle. 'My card.'

'Thank you, Anthony, I'll treasure it.'

A few yards on, Tidey looked back and saw Anthony writing something in a notebook.

*   *   *

Vincent Naylor walked away from the MacClenaghan building, across the open ground towards a back road skirting the M50. Once he got there he'd have no bother picking up a taxi. Behind him, the dawn was creeping up the sky.

Noel dead, Liam keeping radio silence. Vincent was walking away from a world of debris, a possible future forming in his mind.

Pick a goal and go for it.

After the security man buggered off, Vincent knew he needed to get out of there, get started on what he had to do. There was always the chance that the security man would put a couple of things together, ring the cops just to be on the safe side.

Can't go to Noel's place.

Michelle.

No. She shouldn't get caught up in this.

And safer to stay away from Liam Delaney.

The smart thing to do would be to turn up at a Garda station, let them see how upset he was about Noel, tell them he'd been off on a bender, knew nothing about the robbery until he heard Noel was dead. Let them try to prove otherwise. To go missing was as good as a confession in their eyes. But fuck doing the smart thing.

First, do the right thing by Noel. Then— whatever. You can't live without a code, without something bigger than yourself.

Do the best you can with the skills God gave you.

Pick a goal and go for it.
Nothing matters more than family.

Vincent spent an hour opening windows and doors, smashing holes in the flimsy walls in the MacClenaghan building, giving the fire easy access from flat to flat, heaping furniture and clothes and curtains and bits of carpet where they would do most good. Now, walking away across the open space, he glanced back, saw the flames on the fourth floor, his own squat already destroyed, the fire taking hold on the fifth and sixth floors.

Tall against the lightening sky, the MacClenaghan building was burning like a torch. Vincent faced front, his stride lengthening, feeling the strength back in his body after the exhausting hours of grief.

It's a start.

Part 3

The Calm

39

Or sumpthin'.

Detective Sergeant Bob Tidey decided he'd finally identified the Homer Simpson of the team investigating the Emmet Sweetman murder. His name was Eddery, the exhibits officer, a large, square-jawed Garda with an ill-matched crew cut and long sideburns. He was holding up a key on a black leather Armani key ring.

'I checked with his missus and his secretary— they identified everything on his regular key ring— this key—it was in the top drawer of his office desk.'

'And?' Tidey said.

'Just a key. A front door, a house, an apartment. Maybe a gym locker, a garden shed or sumpthin'.'

'Did you get anyone to check it out?'

'How? Sure, it's just a key—I can't check it against every lock in the country.'

It had started with a question Tidey asked of Detective Rose Cheney. 'Where did he screw his girlfriends?'

'Hotel room?'

'Not according to Orla McGettigan's statement.'

The team had concluded, after interviewing two close male friends of Sweetman's, that he'd at least three affairs going over the past couple of years. Orla McGettigan was the only woman who'd been identified. She was a director of a marketing firm in the IFSC.

'She says she met him at a product launch, something her firm was working on.' Tidey looked down at his notebook. 'According to her statement, *We went to his place.*'

Cheney said, 'We didn't make a big deal about that one—McGettigan has no husband or partner, so it wasn't like there might be someone with a reason to go gunning for Sweetman.'

'*His place*, is what she said. Not his home, presumably. Where? Did he have an apartment in town?'

'No—not according to his wife and his accountants.'

'If he's got another place, it's definitely worth a look.'

Cheney took the job of checking again with Sweetman's wife, secretary and friends, to find out if they knew of any flat he might have occasionally borrowed or rented if he had to stay over in town. Bob Tidey went to see Orla McGettigan.

'How often do I have to tell you people?—I'm not an expert on Emmet Sweetman. There's a limit to my knowledge of the man.'

'This won't take a minute.'

She was small, mid-thirties, neat-featured and impeccably dressed for the office. When Tidey arrived at her workplace McGettigan insisted that they move to a coffee shop round the corner. 'No offence, but a visit from you people isn't something I want to flaunt.' Her voice was level, calm and she spoke like she spent a lot of her day giving orders.

In the coffee shop they immediately brought her regular latte to the table. Tidey didn't order anything.

'I know what happens to people who get involved in this kind of thing. Someone gets charged and it ends up in court. And no matter how peripheral

182

you are to the case, if there's a sex angle it gets trotted out for the amusement of all and sundry.'

'That's true,' Tidey said. 'But there's just one thing I need to clear up, and it might be important.'

She made a show of suppressing her irritation, then she leaned back in her chair and nodded.

'In your statement,' Tidey said, 'you said the evening you met Emmet Sweetman you went back to his place. Where was that?'

'He drove, I paid little attention.'

'Northside, Southside?'

'North.'

'Any rough idea where?'

'I know we crossed the river, I'm pretty sure he took the Malahide Road, but—' She smiled. 'I'm not terribly familiar with the geography over there.'

'What kind of place did he take you?'

'An apartment.'

'Did you use the same apartment throughout the affair?'

'What the tabloids, if this ever comes out, will no doubt call a love nest.'

'If you like.'

'We went back there once, maybe twice. Mostly we used my place, sometimes we used the Shelbourne Hotel.'

'Was the apartment—did it seem well used, was he at home there?'

'It was pretty basic. He had some clothes, some bits and pieces. He seemed comfortable with the place.'

'Were there—'

'I think I've done my civic duty now, Sergeant.

183

I'm a single woman, I've done nothing wrong. I'm not in any way important to this case, but I know the odds are I'll get dragged into it—it's funny how the juicy bits always turn out to be relevant.' She was on her feet. 'All my work, and my talents, and my achievements will be brushed aside. And to anyone I know or anyone I come to know, for the rest of my life I'll be defined as the murdered man's bit on the side.'

'You're right, and it's not fair. It's called collateral damage. A crooked banker got taken out by men with guns—which puts him at the centre of a media explosion. And everyone around him gets to take a piece of the blast.'

'Will you find whoever murdered him?'

'We'll continue to do everything possible.'

'In other words, I'm involved enough in this thing to have my life destroyed, but not enough to be told anything more than what's in the standard press release?'

'Sorry.'

'I hope you get whoever did it.' For the first time, there was a softness in her tone. 'Emmet might well have been a crooked banker—but he was a nice man.'

Back at Castlepoint Garda Station, Bob Tidey sought out a folder that held a list of Sweetman's business interests. There was a maze of property holdings—some buildings Tidey reckoned Sweetman owned, others were a group thing, deals within deals. It took Tidey over an hour on the phone with a friendly business journalist before he could translate the jargon. Sweetman had property interests in three Irish cities, plus London, Manchester, Prague and Berlin. His holdings gave

184

him access to six apartment blocks in Dublin—two of them on the Northside.

Tidey found the exhibits officer and asked about Emmet Sweetman's effects. 'Any unidentified keys?'

Which was when Eddery produced the key on the black leather Armani key ring. 'Just a key. A front door, a house, an apartment. Maybe a gym locker, a garden shed or sumpthin'.'

40

Bob Tidey was late arriving and the pub was already filling up. There was barely an inch left of Trixie Dixon's pint. Tidey joined him at the bar and gestured to a barman, but Trixie cut across him. 'I'll get it—you're well entitled to a thank-you drink.'

'Jameson and ice, so. Is this as good as the bribes get?'

'Afraid so, Mr Tidey. And Christy sends his thanks, too.'

'It was a fair result. As long as he doesn't come out of prison and turn into John Dillinger.'

Trixie's smile was weak. Bob Tidey figured there was a reason he'd been asked for a meeting, apart from the thank-you. It didn't take Trixie long to get to the point. When the drinks arrived he said, 'I don't want to impose, Mr Tidey, but, there's something—can I talk to you in confidence?'

Tidey said, 'You know I won't mess you around.'

'It's Christy.'

'You surprise me. What's he done now?'

185

'Nothing, it's just—'

Trixie took an envelope from inside his jacket. He turned so his body blocked the envelope from the rest of the pub and passed it to Tidey.

'Jesus, Trixie, the bribes are certainly improving. Where the hell did this come from?'

'It's for Christy.'

Tidey ran a thumb through the fifties. 'How much?'

'Five grand. Fella came to see me at the GAA hall—all he said was, "That's for Christy", and he gave me the envelope and pissed off.'

'One of Roly Blount's people?'

'I didn't recognise him, but it had to be.'

'I see your problem.'

Keeping his mouth shut, taking the rap for the gun, Christy had shown he could be trusted. The gift wasn't just a thank-you, it was a welcome aboard.

Trixie said, 'The last thing he needs when he comes out is to be at the beck and call of those fuckers. Kids get into a situation like that, they can end up killing someone or getting killed.'

'Go see Roly, be polite. You're grateful but worried, you'd rather Christy kept to himself. It's Frank Tucker who pulls Roly's strings and Tucker's a businessman, he doesn't need to press-gang anyone. Christ knows, there's enough young gobshites queuing to sign up.'

Trixie said, 'They'd see that as Christy giving him the brush-off. You can't tell how those bastards will react—if they think you're turning bolshie they can take it as an insult, or a threat.' Trixie took a sip of his pint. 'I was hoping you might have some ideas.'

Tidey shook his head. 'I'd have a word with

186

Frank Tucker, if you like. But, to be honest, I think that would make things worse. Might start them wondering if Christy's got friends he shouldn't have.'

Trixie said, 'Jesus, it used to be you could go stroking and make a bad living at it, and if you got a decent job and you liked it you got out of the game. Now, it's like the fucking army. You fall in with these people, you have to bow and scrape and salute the little cunts. And if you step over some line—maybe a line you don't even know is there—you get a bullet in the head.'

Tidey rattled the ice in his Jameson. 'All I can say is, let it lie for the moment. Christy won't be out until the end of next year—anything might happen in the meantime. When it's near his release, if things are still the same, maybe the smart thing to do is get him out of the country for a while.'

There was a hoarseness in Trixie's voice that had nothing to do with his damaged lungs. 'He was just doing a favour. Roly Blount needed to stash a gun, for someone in the neighbourhood to pick up. Do me a favour, he says. And Christy thought these guys are cool, like something from *The Sopranos*. And now—some choice—be a toady for those fuckers, or leave your own country, just to be on the safe side.'

They finished their drinks in silence. Outside, Tidey's voice was gentle. 'It may not come to that, Trixie. The way things go with these types, by the time Christy gets out Roly could be dead—problem solved. If not, keep in touch—we'll see what we can do.'

'Thanks.' Trixie patted his jacket pocket. 'At least, if he has to do a flit, the five grand will come in handy.'

41

Liam Delaney spent the morning chasing himself around the inside of his head, trying to decide what was for the best. He was crap at that—that's what Vincent was good at, thinking things through.

Pick up the money at the paint factory?
Assume the whole job has gone sour, cut and run?
Wait to hear from Vincent?

The original plan was to meet up with Noel Naylor this afternoon and move the money. They needed somewhere to count it, split it—somewhere the coming and going wouldn't attract attention. Noel had rented a house at Rathfillan Terrace, in Santry. Since any one or more of them might have been picked up after the job, all four had keys to the Santry house.

Trouble was, go for the money as planned and maybe Noel or Kevin had written down the address of the house in Santry, maybe the cops found it when they searched their homes. Or maybe someone saw something, made a call and the shades had already found the money and they were waiting with guns drawn. They might not be the brightest, strutting around like they're CSI Dublin, but even deadheads can catch a lucky break.

Shortly after three o'clock Liam parked on Tonlegee Road. He walked around to Mulville Avenue and scoped the front of the paint factory. Nothing stirring. He made his way back to

Tonlegee. As he got into his car he admitted to himself that the cops mightn't all be as dim as he liked to think. He started the engine and half a minute later he was turning down the lane that led to the old paint factory.

He parked and pulled on a pair of latex gloves.

When he got inside he found the Protectica money bags untouched beneath the tarp. It took him four journeys to get them into the boot of the car.

When he turned the key in the ignition it occurred to him that the noise might be the cue for a sudden burst of police activity, but nothing happened.

There was a garage in the rented house on Rathfillan Terrace and he drove inside and closed the door before he began unloading the bags. After about a minute he said, 'Fuck it,' dropped the bags where they were and spent the next five minutes checking rooms. When he realised he was down on one knee, looking under a bed, he told himself not to be a total spanner and went back to unloading the bags.

He spent over an hour getting the money sorted. He used a Stanley knife and a high-leverage cable cutter to get into the Protectica bags. Then he pocketed some money—not enough that he couldn't explain if he was pulled in—and sorted the rest into large beige envelopes. He put the envelopes into six plastic Tesco bags. Noel had prepared a hiding place under some stripped-back insulation in the attic. There wasn't enough room there, so Liam brought the leftover money to the bathroom and stuffed it behind a bath panel.

From the upstairs front window everything

outside seemed normal. Two men who'd been working on a car engine across the road when he'd arrived were still at it. One of them was scratching his head now, and staring into the engine like it was an impossible crossword. Next door, a woman was using a hooked garden weeder to scrape dirt from between paving stones. It looked normal enough, the whole street. He peeled off the latex gloves and used the side of one hand to lever the front door shut behind him. On the way to his car he listened to the scraping of the woman's weeder, half expecting it to suddenly stop. As he slid behind the wheel he kept an eye on the two amateur mechanics across the road.

Liam Delaney was halfway down Oscar Traynor Road before he admitted to himself that he was free and clear. Whooping, he thumped the steering wheel. What had happened to Noel and Kevin was shit, but those are the breaks. He was suddenly convinced that the bummer had bottomed out and the only way was up.

When he got home there was a small padded envelope lying in the hallway below the letter box. It was addressed to Liam in block capitals. When he tore it open he found a mobile phone inside. He stared at it for a moment, then checked the inside of the envelope. Nothing.

He switched on the phone and when it asked for a PIN he tried four zeros, the likely factory default, and it worked. He tapped into the call list—nothing. No texts in the inbox, no sent messages. He tried the address book and there was just one number. He highlighted the number and tapped *Call*.

When the call went through, Vincent Naylor

190

said, 'It's me.'

42

Bob Tidey said, 'Sorry about that—bit of a waste of time.'

Rose Cheney said, 'Had to be done.'

Tidey dangled Emmet Sweetman's key from its leather Armani key ring. He was beginning to think that maybe Garda Homer Simpson was right—it was just a key. 'Maybe it *is* the key to a gym locker, a spare one, an old one, whatever.'

Tidey and Cheney had spent the afternoon at an apartment block five minutes off the Malahide Road, trying the key in apartment doors. It was slow, boring work. They pressed buttons on the front-door intercom until they found someone in, explained who they were and that they needed to find a particular flat. After that, it meant going from apartment to apartment—ringing bells and asking permission to try the key in the lock. If there was no one home they tried it anyway. Over and over, hope waning as lock after lock rejected the key.

There was a second apartment block, close to the Swords Road. 'You want to do this again tomorrow?' Tidey asked.

'The first apartment tomorrow—first apartment, ground floor,' Cheney said, 'I know we're gonna get lucky.'

Tidey grinned. 'Sure,' he said. 'I've found it usually works like that.'

Anthony Prendergast was hunched at his work-station, deadline coming up fast and a final paragraph to write. You need to finish on a punchy last par, something that'll stay with the skulls when they put down the newspaper. He did a Control/Home and the cursor shot up to the top of the story.

> When you go up against a city's deadliest bad men you need more than a quick mind and a sense of justice. You need armour covering your vital organs. You need a state-of-the-art automatic weapon in your hands.
> John is not this man's name, but it's the name we'll use to protect him. It's the least we can do, given that every working day he puts his life on the line to protect us.

Tight, clear, immediate. A killer opening.

The thing a lot of hacks don't understand is that sometimes all you have to do is ask. The way Anthony saw it, journalists are so used to being told to piss off by people with real inside information, they assume the worst and get lazy and don't even try.

'A ten-par follow-up on the North Strand shootings,' his news editor had told him. 'Something on the ERU lads.'

Dead easy. No way those hard nuts would talk, but he could tap his Garda contacts for anecdotes, get a formal briefing on the unit, string together a few of the ERU's Greatest Hits, with a short par

192

on the Abbeylara controversy. Because he wasn't lazy, first thing this morning Anthony made a formal request for an interview with the Garda who fired the fatal shots. Then he worked the phones for an hour and was preparing to go down two floors and check the ERU file in the newspaper's library when he got a call.

'The answer to your request is no—the member of the Emergency Response Unit involved in the shooting is on leave and we don't allow individuals to talk to the media.'

'Thanks, I—'

'My name is Sergeant David Dowd. I was in charge of that detail and I'll talk to you—unofficially and off the record—if you can meet me in twenty minutes.'

At the *Daily Record*, the suits had taken their regular penny-pinching to new levels. A round of wage cuts was followed by a memo advising staff that usage of soap, towels, stationery and toilet paper was at unsustainably high levels. For years now, all taxi expenses had to be pre-approved by one of a small circle of executives. Anthony Prendergast decided that going through the hoops would leave him no time to make it to Rathmines to meet Sergeant Dowd. He decided to break a sacred rule of journalism and pay for his own taxi ride.

They met in a cafe in Rathmines. Dowd was in civvies, on mandatory rest after yesterday's shooting, and mightily pissed off. He had a copy of the *Daily Record*, open to Anthony's article. They were sitting at a table near the door and Anthony was about to ask what the Garda wanted to drink, but Dowd wasn't interested in the social niceties.

'This shit here—*A resident of Kilcaragh Avenue said that one of the robbers appeared to be surrendering when he was shot.* That's bollocks.'

Anthony said, 'It's a quote—there was an old man, his name is in there—'

'Yeah, Heneghan. This says that one of those fuckers tried to surrender but we shot him.'

'It doesn't say that, it's just what the old guy said he saw—it's not like *I* was saying that's what happened.'

'That's what people will read into it. Don't you people care about what actually happened? Does it always have to have an anti-police angle?'

'Look, no way am I anti-police. That's—' Then, he spotted the opening. 'All I can do is talk to people who were there—and you know what it's like, trying to get a first-hand account from official sources. So, I had to depend on this old guy, and I know he was sincere, he was just—'

Dowd's chin was up. 'The man who fired those shots is one of the most dedicated policemen on the force. He's no gun nut, he's not trigger-happy—he fired those shots because—'

'I never said—'

'—he had to. And he went home last night in a state because of how it worked out. And when his leave is up he'll report right back and be prepared to do exactly the same again. Because he believes in what he does.'

Two women at the next table were staring at Dowd.

He lowered his voice. 'It doesn't help, when a decent policeman is treated like a fucking Wild West gunslinger.'

Anthony Prendergast leaned across the table and

194

said, 'Tell me about it—about what happened, about what it's like. Tell me about the reality of what you have to do.'

Dowd sat there for a moment, then he said, 'Off the record?'

'Completely on your terms.'

'I didn't get permission to talk to you and if I'd asked I'd have been told to piss off.' Dowd said he didn't want to do this in public. He stood up and Anthony followed him out. It took them five minutes to walk to a quiet street lined with old houses. Dowd led the way into a neat semi with a bay window. He went into the kitchen for a minute, spoke to his wife, then took Anthony into the front room.

In the hour that followed, Dowd several times displayed annoyance and anger, but mostly he was matter-of-fact.

'I've never killed anyone, I very much never want to ever kill anyone. I know what bullets do to people and the thought of it makes me sick. I'd prefer if there were no armed police at all, but what do we do when some little fucker shows up waving a weapon?'

'I know that makes—'

'The man who shot those two people, he feels the same. I'm not speaking for every policeman, or even everyone in the unit. But there's no one setting out to get a notch on their gun—and in particular not the man who had to do what he did.'

Anthony Prendergast said, 'Tell me exactly what happened yesterday.'

Back at his desk, Anthony found that the story wrote itself.

'We had the situation under control. It wasn't possible to evacuate the whole neighbourhood but we had the street blocked at both ends.

'One of the suspects had put down his gun, the other one was holding on to his. They had to know they hadn't an earthly. But sometimes people, when they're trapped, can get crazy.

'The second suspect started shooting. He ran for it—Kevin Broe, his name was. It was a street with occupied houses, at least one civilian standing in the open within yards of the gunman. We had members at both ends of the street, so we had to watch out for crossfire.

'We had no option but to return fire, and one member—just one—fired three aimed shots at the man who was shooting. Two of them hit their target. The gunman ran across in front of his companion and the third bullet hit the other suspect, Noel Naylor, in the throat. It's regrettable, but it couldn't be helped.'

'Won't you get into trouble?' Anthony asked Dowd. 'It's off the record, but they'll know it had to be one of a very few people.'

'Let them prove it. Long as you keep your mouth shut.'

'I swear.'

Reading the story back, Anthony felt a glow. A story like that, an exclusive with a member of the Emergency Response Unit—there wasn't a reporter or editor in town who wouldn't read that and note the byline.

Sitting in the living room of his modest house, with his wife in the kitchen making coffee and sandwiches, it's easy to recognise that this is no storm trooper, this is no itchy-fingered heavy—this is a decent citizen doing a difficult and dangerous public service.

All he needed now was an end paragraph that would finish the job in style.

He glanced again at the opening. Sometimes the old tricks are best—you make the end par echo the opening par, gives the piece a feeling of coming full circle. He thought about it for a moment, then he typed quickly.

There are people we depend on to protect us from the bad guys. They're our armour against the vicious hoodlums who desecrate our country. And when these policemen do what we need them to do, and when controversy inevitably arises, it's our turn to be their armour.

To protect them.

Without question.

A killer finish.

He typed *Ends* at the bottom, clicked the mouse a couple of times and the story was on its way to the news editor's basket.

Ten minutes later the news editor wandered over to Anthony's workstation, holding a hard copy of the piece. 'Love the ending,' he said. 'Sheer poetry.' He sounded sincere, but Anthony could tell he was taking the piss. 'By the way, you'll see I tightened up the opening and cut the last line. We never, ever, *ever* report what anyone does or says *without question*. When we accept anything without question, that's not journalism, it's stenography.'

He turned away, then turned back. 'Nice work. Now, go out there again and get me something better.'

43

Liam Delaney parked on a parallel street and walked to the rented house on Rathfillan Terrace. He was carrying a briefcase. Vincent Naylor hadn't been terribly clear about what kind of piece he needed—all he said was *bring stuff*—so Liam had brought him some choices.

'Take your pick,' he said, the briefcase open on the floor of the little kitchen, three guns showing on the table—two automatics and a revolver.

'Whichever,' Vincent said. 'Which one's the best?'

'It depends on what you want to do with it. Say you're walking in somewhere, you want everyone to shit themselves, so no one feels like playing hero—I'd take the Taurus.' He picked up the revolver, passed it to Vincent. 'Forty-four calibre—it's got Clint Eastwood all over it.'

'Heavy, though.'

'The Chiefs Special—that one's light. Seven rounds, nine mil. Some American cops use them. Reliable. But, if it was me, I'd use the Bernardelli. It's a combat pistol, nine mil, sixteen rounds. It'll do just about any job.'

He passed the gun to Vincent, who hefted it, then held it level with his eye and took aim at an imaginary target. 'Feels OK.' He nodded. 'I don't need the Eastwood, too showy. The cop gun—no, I'll need more than seven bullets. I'll take this one.'

Liam put the Taurus and the Chiefs Special back in the briefcase. He took out two magazines for the Bernardelli. 'Enough there, unless you're planning to invade a country.'

'Thanks—how much did this cost you?'

'Forget it.'

Vincent nodded his thanks.

'You really need to do this?' Liam asked.

Vincent didn't say anything.

'It's not my style, Vincent—otherwise, you know, I'd—'

Vincent said, 'It's me has got to do it.'

Vincent was filling the kettle when Liam said, 'You any idea who ratted us out?'

Vincent spooned Maxwell House into a couple of mugs. He did it slowly, as though part of him was off somewhere else. Liam began to wonder if Vincent had heard the question. Standing at the kitchen counter, looking out into the back garden, Vincent said, 'I know who's top of the list.'

*   *   *

Bob Tidey rang the bell for Apartment 1, ground floor, in the Swords apartment block, and there was someone home. 'Of course, Garda, no bother.' He was a small, neat septuagenarian and he was delighted to cooperate with the police. The key didn't fit his lock.

Ninety minutes later, on the third floor,

Apartment 327, there was no one home, and after Cheney slid the key into the lock there was a click and they were in.

Cheney said, '*Yes.*'

'Gotcha.' Tidey immediately pulled the door shut.

Fifteen minutes later, a uniform arrived from Swords Garda Station. By then, Tidey had borrowed a kitchen chair from the nice old man in Apartment 1 and had installed it outside 327.

'Got something to read?' Tidey asked. The uniform smiled, took an iPod Nano from his breast pocket and settled down on the kitchen chair.

It took two hours to get a search warrant.

*　　　*　　　*

Outside Vincent Naylor's hotel-room door, two or three young women were laughing as they passed down the corridor. One of them said, 'Oh my God,' over and over until their voices faded in the distance. Vincent was sitting at a dressing table, a sheet of Westbury Hotel stationery in front of him. His handwriting had always been neat, but he took special care writing his list. It had four names.

He sat there for a long while, staring at the sheet of paper, picturing faces—enjoying the anticipation.

*　　　*　　　*

'Socks,' Bob Tidey said. 'Dark blue, three pairs. And three pairs of dark blue Ralph Lauren boxer shorts.' It was the first sign of personal possessions in Emmet Sweetman's very bare love nest. The

200

apartment was small. Two bedrooms and a living room and a tiny kitchen. It was bare and characterless. No food in the kitchen cabinets or the fridge, no washing-up liquid, no newspapers or magazines in the living room, no clothes thrown casually anywhere. A duvet pulled more or less straight on the bed suggested a minimal attempt at tidying.

A randomly used apartment known to few others would be an ideal place to stash any business material that required an extra layer of security. Tidey had hoped for a briefcase, a file, some papers—anything that might connect with Sweetman's murder. It was too much to expect, and he wouldn't say it to Cheney, but his hope was for something like a threatening letter—the kind of thing that murderers are sometimes thick enough to do.

Cheney opened a closet and found four suits of varying colours. 'Nice,' she said. She checked the labels. 'Same as his closet at home—all Ralph Lauren. If this guy was as loyal to his wife as he was to Ralph, maybe he wouldn't be pushing up daisies.'

'You tending towards the wronged husband theory?' Tidey said.

'Nah—I'm just partial to a bit of gossip.'

Tidey reached into the back of a drawer—nothing there. He pulled back the lining paper and checked underneath. He did the same with the other three drawers—all of them empty. He felt under the bottom of each drawer to check if there was anything taped there. Nothing.

'At last,' Rose Cheney said, 'a sign of life.' She had a shallow drawer open in the bedside table and she was holding up an opened box of condoms. 'The passion kit.' She threw the condoms on the bed, then a sleep mask, a blue bottle of massage oil and some wispy scarves. 'A bit skimpy, for a passion kit.'

'Enough to get a lad through a midlife crisis.'

'You speak from experience?'

When Tidey didn't answer, Cheney said, 'Oops. Sore point? Sorry.'

Tidey smiled. 'No problem. I'm the one brought it up. But, yeah, sore point.'

Cheney put the passion kit back in the drawer and Tidey tilted the mattress while she checked underneath. Nothing.

Cheney went into the other bedroom, Tidey went into the bathroom. A bottle of shower gel was half empty, the Head & Shoulders shampoo lying on its side, the cap open. There was a towel on the floor, in a corner, another hanging untidily from a rail. Tidey touched them both. Dry.

He joined Cheney in the second bedroom. She was opening and closing drawers. 'Empty, empty, empty.' The only sign that anyone had used the bedroom recently was a jacket casually thrown on the bed.

'You checked the pockets?'

'I like to keep the most promising for last.'

She checked a tall, narrow closet. Completely empty. Then she turned to the jacket. 'Bet there'll be a thick envelope full of documents in the inside pocket,' Cheney said.

Tidey shook his head. 'A diary in the side pocket.'

When Cheney lifted the jacket there was a mobile phone lying underneath.

*   *   *

It took forty-five minutes to get the mobile phone to Crime and Security, and another two hours for them to secure the call records from the mobile carrier and email a preliminary report to Castlepoint Garda Station. Sitting in the incident room, Bob Tidey gave a low whistle. 'Some more gossip for you.'

Rose Cheney said, 'Make my day.'

The phone was a pay-as-you-go, the report said. It had been activated eight months ago and had never been used to call Sweetman's home or office. Sweetman appeared to have it solely for his off-the-books social activities. Apart from Orla McGettigan, the phone log showed just four other numbers, all mobiles. Crime and Security had connected the numbers to three named women, two of whom were married. The third woman was an analyst in the loans department of Sweetman's bank.

'Could be the analyst was part of his frauds,' Cheney said. 'Hogg wants the numbers—he'll have people knocking on doors first thing in the morning.'

Tidey said, 'I want to deal with that last number myself.'

Cheney glanced at the report. 'Cornelius Wintour—sounds like a bookkeeper who still uses ledgers and quills.'

'Not quite.'

'It would help on the gossip front if he's young and pretty and Sweetman liked to vary his diet.'

Tidey smiled. 'It's a long time since Connie Wintour was young, and he's never been pretty.

203

He's a solicitor, exclusively criminal cases. According to the Crime and Security report, Sweetman made or received calls from Connie several times a week, including two calls he exchanged with Connie on the day he was murdered.' Tidey stood up, took out his cigarettes.

Cheney said, 'When you're facing criminal charges you spend a lot of time talking to lawyers.'

'Sweetman had a firm of solicitors fronting for him. The kind of clients Connie usually handles—they don't use banking scams and property deals to steal money, they use balaclavas and guns. Connie could be the link between the murders.' Tidey put an unlit cigarette between his lips. 'Now, if I don't go outside and light this thing I'm going to start kicking lumps out of the wall. Do me a favour?'

'As long as it doesn't involve your midlife crisis.'

'Get onto the DPP's office. We had a suspect in the Oliver Snead killing, a junkie named Gerry FitzGerald—Zippo to his friends. He's dead now. Get them to look up Zippo's file, see if Connie Wintour ever represented him. If he did, we just might have a connection between the two killings.'

Tidey made himself a coffee. He took it to the back exit of the Garda station and lit his cigarette. He took out his mobile and rang Holly's number. When the voicemail invited him to leave a message he clicked off.

When he finished the cigarette, Tidey lit a second Rothmans. He was halfway through it when Rose Cheney came out the back exit. 'Two things—the DPP's office say Connie Wintour never represented this Gerry FitzGerald guy.' She started moving past Tidey, towards the car park. 'And, two, Hogg just called. There's been another

204

killing—possibly related. A couple of minutes' drive from here.' Tidey flicked away his cigarette and followed her.

At the wheel of her Hyundai, Cheney said, 'He's already at the scene, with the uniforms—the call was red-flagged to Hogg. He says the victim's some kind of property developer, his name came up in the Emmet Sweetman inquiry—the two of them had a business connection. And now, someone's blown his head off.'

Nosing out onto the street, Cheney cut off a blue van, turned left and leaned on the pedal.

Part 4

The Storm

44

Vincent Naylor picked up the newspaper from the floor. There was a tiny piece at the bottom of an inside page about the funeral plans for the 'North Strand shoot-out robbers'. The lazy bastards don't care what they write—there was no shoot-out, Noel was unarmed when the cops shot him. The piece said Noel Naylor was being cremated at Glasnevin and Kevin Broe was being buried in Balgriffin. It said that police had contacted Naylor's father, who was home from Scotland to organise the funeral. They were still hoping to make contact with the dead man's brother.

Yeah, right.

Vincent had been sitting by the window for a couple of hours. Nothing to see outside except the back of another building. He'd read the piece half a dozen times. Every now and then he put the newspaper down on the floor, and in a while he picked it up and looked at it again. Before this happened, Noel had never had his name in the papers. Now—

One paper had some shit about 'the Naylor Gang', and how it had 'terrorised large areas of Northside Dublin'. Another had a photograph of Noel, a bit blurry—must have been taken on someone's phone. Some cheap fuck, some so-called friend, must have sold it to a nosy reporter. It showed Noel with a big grin on his face, his mouth open, his hair messy, maybe at a party. Vincent had read shit about himself, about how he had just recently been released from jail after being sentenced for 'a vicious and unprovoked assault on an innocent young man'. And one piece of crap described Noel as 'a notorious thug and a leading figure in Dublin's drug-drenched gangland'.

Noel didn't fuck with drugs. Didn't take them, didn't sell them. Noel always said you get into that game and you're playing chicken with a bunch of psychos. Noel wasn't a leading figure in anything. Noel robbed.

They even brought Da into it. Some thick fuck of a cop was quoted about how the old man had been done for violent behaviour in Aberdeen—sounded like he'd clocked a barman at closing time. Now he's in the papers as the head of a 'criminal family'. Almost made Vincent feel sorry for the prick.

Vincent let the paper fall to the floor again. It was down there with several newspapers, collected over the past couple of days. The first reports of the shooting and the robbery, the piece from the *Daily Record* about the bastard from the ERU, explaining why it was OK to shoot Noel and Kevin. Strangest thing of all was reading the tiny piece that mentioned the plans for Noel's funeral. It was unreal. All that decency, all the fun and the clever stuff—the little things that made him special—all melted to nothing. It was over, Noel was all he'd ever be, and that wasn't enough. He deserved a whole life. Not this broken-off part of a life.

Vincent stared out the window, focused on some spot in mid-air between here and the back of the building across the way.

After a long while, he looked at his watch. Almost time to get ready.

One of the three uniforms was pale and blinking a lot. He shook his head when he saw Rose Cheney and said, 'I don't think you should get too close.' The corpse was about twenty yards away, in a seated position, leaning back against a wall. What was left of him.

Cheney waved a thumb at Bob Tidey and asked the uniform, 'Do you think he might manage to keep his lunch down?'

'I just meant, I didn't mean—'

'Not to worry,' Cheney said, 'no one's going any closer to that poor sod than they need to.'

Two of the uniforms were guarding the entrance and exit to the underground garage. The third, the nervous one, was standing as close to the body as he dared. Detective Superintendent Hogg finished talking to three people from Technical, each clothed head to foot in white forensics suits, each carrying a couple of small cases. He joined Tidey and Cheney. 'Justin Kennedy's the victim's name, according to the apartment manager.'

Tidey raised an eyebrow. 'He identified *that*?'

For once, the claim that someone blew someone's head off wasn't an exaggeration. Most of the victim's head was splattered up the wall above the rest of the body. 'It's his car, Kennedy's car, that he's sitting beside—the manager says that's how he usually dresses. A property guy, puts deals together, well known in the business—his name popped up as an associate of Emmet Sweetman. He shared an apartment upstairs with his girlfriend.'

The body was dressed in an expensive light grey

business suit, the look somewhat spoiled by the volume of blood that covered the shoulders.

Bob Tidey said, 'Anyone hear anything, see anything?'

'We need to do a canvass, but I doubt it. The fella that found the body—a young man, lives on the third floor—came down to collect his car, saw the blood, called the apartment manager.'

Tidey and Cheney walked closer. The double-barrelled shotgun was lying about six feet in front of the body. The door of the car, an Alfa Romeo, was slightly open.

'It's like he got out of the car,' Tidey said, 'turned round, maybe he got pushed or whatever, ended up sitting like that, you think? Maybe the shooter made the poor bastard sit down for a chat before he blew him away?'

Hogg said, 'I've put in for some more uniforms— we need to start the canvass, and this area needs to be fingertipped.'

Bob Tidey told Hogg about Sweetman's spare mobile, about the calls to Connie Wintour. 'A crooked banker and a dodgy lawyer—the dodgy lawyer has a lot of clients who know their way around a gun. He could be the connection between the Sweetman and Snead murders.'

Hogg said, 'All you've got's a record of a call from Sweetman's mobile to the dodgy lawyer. You need to firm that up. Go talk to Wintour, see if he admits knowing Sweetman, if he talked to him the day of the murder.'

'You need us here?'

'Go see Wintour.'

'Sure, but he'll hide behind his rights as a lawyer.'

Hogg snorted. 'This is a murder inquiry. Mr

Wintour is an officer of the court and he should be honoured to help us with our inquiries—err on the side of recklessness.'

45

Lifting the teacup to her lips, Maura Coady sighed when the doorbell rang. She put the cup down. When she opened the door, her neighbours Phil and Jacinta were standing with a smaller, much younger man.

'Everything OK, Miss Coady?'

'Fine, Phil—everything's fine.'

Jacinta said, 'This young man here, his name is Anthony, he's from the newspapers.'

The younger man nodded and held out a hand. 'Ms Coady, pleased to meet you. Phil here tells me—'

Phil was leaning forward. 'Anthony wrote about the shooting, described it just as it happened.'

Maura said, 'I'm afraid I really can't—'

'Don't worry, Ms Coady, I know how distressing this must have been, and I'll only take a moment of your time. I was wondering—'

Maura backed away. 'I really can't talk right now, I've got something on the stove.'

'I can wait, it's no bother—'

'You'll have to excuse me—' Maura was closing the door.

'Ms Coady—'

She closed the door, surprised to find herself at ease with her rudeness. She'd managed to push the shooting to the back of her mind and she wanted to keep it that way. If she'd had a list of things she didn't want to do, talking to a newspaper reporter would be near the top.

As she sat by the table, lifting the teacup, she noticed her hand trembling.

Outside, Phil and Jacinta Heneghan were explaining to Anthony Prendergast that Maura Coady was a *real* lady. 'Old school, they call it—old values,' Phil said.

'She's special, Miss Coady,' Jacinta said. 'You know she's a nun, don't you?'

'Is that right?' Anthony Prendergast said.

*　　　*　　　*

Either you win or you lose. And this afternoon, in this bookie shop, Shay Harrison was a winner. Shay never saw the point of place betting. There's a horse you like, you put your money on the nose, it either makes it first past the post or it's an also-ran. The notion of betting that a horse will be placed second or third—that might be all right if the horse is up against an Arkle or a Red Rum. Mostly, a gambler has to have the balls to make a choice, no hedging his bets.

Shay collected his winnings on Iolanthe Bear, in the two thirty at Leicester. To put your wad on the nose for a long shot, with a strong favourite in the field, you have to be mad. Except when it turns out like this. Shay Harrison wasn't a guesser, he was a thinker. He thought about the owner, the trainer, the jockey, the course, the weather, the form—and when it was all done whirling around inside his head and he looked at the runners and riders it was like there was a glow coming off just one of them,

and that's when he knew. Didn't always work out—
didn't *often* work out—but when it did . . .

Iolanthe Bear, twenty to bloody one, skating
home in front of the evens favourite. Part of Shay
wished he'd dared put more on it, but a tenner at
twenty to one wasn't to be sneezed at. The thing
that made Shay special, the way he saw it, was that
he knew when to put his winnings in his pocket and
head home. You lose on a long shot, it's OK to
hang around, to try to make up for it by taking the
short odds on a couple of favourites. That way,
maybe you end up losing not too much. But if you
bingo a long shot you have to watch out you don't
lose the run of yourself, hanging on, feeding the
machine until it's like the long shot never came in.
Which is when you feel like the fool you are.

Shay knew at least half of the dozen punters in
the betting shop. He'd talk about this some other
time, probably over a pint, but on the day, no—it
was bad form to boast or to whinge. You stay cool.
The thing to do was to take winning or losing as
the same thing—a result. In the long run, with
luck, they even out. This past year, for Shay, the
results had been bloody brilliant. Shay nodded to a
neighbour, Jimmy Higgins, turned for the door and
a man said to him, quietly, 'All that stuff about
wood choppers, about feeding you into a
machine—that was all bullshit.'

Shay looked round and the man was standing
there, hoodie up, and a hand rising with a gun, and
Shay wanted to say I didn't, I swear, I didn't say a
fucking—

He jerked his head down and to one side, but the
man adjusted his aim and fired the bullet into his
temple and Shay Harrison, Protectica employee

215

and lucky gambler, felt nothing when his face hit the floor of the bookie shop.

*   *   *

When Maura Coady answered the doorbell she found the reporter chap standing there, a big smile on his face. 'Ms Coady, I wonder—' He held a small camera to his face and it clicked and he smiled again. 'It won't take a minute, just a couple of words—'

'No, please, I've nothing—'

'It's about the—'

Maura closed the door, turned and stood trembling in her hallway. She suddenly wanted the walls to be closer, the hallway smaller, everything that mattered within reach and the rest of the world gone away.

46

Connie Wintour's office was on the second floor of an old building within walking distance of the Criminal Courts of Justice. The hall and stairs were narrow, the decor was mid-twentieth-century shabby. Inside, the office was one part chrome to two parts beech. Wintour's secretary glanced away from her Mac long enough to recognise Bob Tidey, then returned to her work. 'I'm afraid Mr Wintour is unavailable.' Her voice distant, without inflection.

Bob Tidey said, 'But he's here?'

'He's not available.'

'Is he with a client?'

'He's not available.'

Tidey said, 'Not to worry, Linda, he's always glad to see me.' She was still getting to her feet when Tidey opened the pebbled-glass door that led to the inner office.

In another chrome-and-wood room, the walls behind him lined with legal volumes, Connie Wintour was sitting back, feet up on a desk big enough to use as a landing pad for a small helicopter. The desk was almost bare—just a mobile, a large notepad, a pen and a worn leather desk diary, arranged symmetrically on either side of a fashionably retro white Bakelite desk phone. Connie's eyes were closed, his expression one of intense concentration. He was wearing a large set of wireless earphones. One hand rested on the desk, two fingers gently keeping time, patiently coaxing inaudible music from his invisible orchestra.

'You'll have to leave. Mr Wintour doesn't—'

Tidey said, 'Shh, Linda, don't spoil the concert.'

Wintour's fingers made a series of short, emphatic taps, as though bringing a musical passage to a peak.

Tidey took a couple of steps to the right, towards the bank of filing cabinets along one wall. He pulled a drawer all the way out, then slammed it shut. Wintour's eyes opened, he took in the scene, stared for several moments. Then he closed his eyes again. One hand made a lazy *bye-bye* motion.

Tidey jerked the drawer open and slammed it again. And again. Wearily, Wintour slid off the earphones and shook his head. 'Childish as ever, Sergeant Tidey.'

217

'Just a word or two, Connie.'

Wintour lowered his feet from the desk and said to Rose, 'Cornelius Wintour, my dear. And you are?'

'Detective Garda Rose Cheney.'

'Delighted,' Connie said. He turned to Tidey. 'And who are you stitching up today, Sergeant?'

It was one of Connie Wintour's selling points as a lawyer—he never tired of passionately accusing Garda witnesses of framing his clients. He had a lengthy list of regulars who used his services primarily because they got a kick out of watching him throw insults and allegations at Gardai on the witness stand. The fact that such clients more often than not went to jail didn't lessen the kick they got from Connie's cross-examinations.

Tidey said, 'Why did Emmet Sweetman call you on the day he was murdered?'

Wintour raised one eyebrow. 'You're a bit old, Sergeant, for using the Garda College book of trick questions.'

'The question was very simple, Connie. Why did Emmet Sweetman call you on the day he was murdered?'

'You ask *why* he called me—but the purpose of the question is to establish *whether* he called me. Am I right?'

'As it happens—no.'

Wintour smiled. 'I can confirm, then, Sergeant, that I've never spoken to Mr Sweetman in my life.'

Tidey nodded. 'You say no—our inquiries say yes.'

Rose Cheney leaned across the desk and lifted Connie's mobile. 'And this looks like a relevant piece of evidence in sorting out who's telling the truth.'

Wintour was on his feet. 'Don't be fucking absurd. Fishing expeditions aren't—Put that phone back or I'll have an injunction with your name on it before you get to the bottom of the stairs.'

'No need to rush, Connie,' Tidey said. He took a grey evidence envelope from a jacket pocket and held it out. Cheney slid the phone into the envelope. Tidey licked the envelope, then he signed and dated it. He passed the envelope to Cheney, who also signed it, then put it in her handbag. 'You get hold of your favourite judge, Connie, and we present our evidence and let him sort it out.'

'You've no right to conduct a search without a warrant.'

'No search, Connie—the mobile was in plain sight, and it's relevant to a murder inquiry. Since there's a conflict about whether or not you got a call from a murder victim on the day of his death, we're just safeguarding a vital piece of evidence.'

Cheney said, 'Now, if you'll call that judge, we can arrange a hearing and get this over with.'

*   *   *

Vincent Naylor watched Michelle Flood arrive in the second-floor lobby of the Westbury Hotel. The lobby was wide and long, with a couple of dozen coffee tables scattered around, along with couches and deep chairs. It was busy, a lot of people here for afternoon tea. In the centre of the lobby there was a guy playing the piano.

Vincent sat in a wingback chair near the entrance to the bar, sipping coffee and watching Michelle

219

approach. *I'll be close to the bar*, he'd told her. She was wearing black slacks and a lacy black top over a white blouse. Nothing showy, but classy all the same. She walked right past him, stopped, looked around, this way and that.

The piano player was working on a pimped-up version of a Sinatra number. Vincent stood up. Michelle looked right past him, into the small bar. Vincent stared at her from about six feet away, until he made eye contact. Her face became a mix of surprise, confusion and relief. She walked towards him, kissed him on the cheek and murmured, 'Jesus, what's happened to you?'

*   *   *

A waiter brought more coffee and a second cup. 'I can't get used to it,' Michelle said. 'The difference.'

Vincent Naylor's hair was barely there. His dark curls were gone. What was left was cropped so tight it might have been sprayed on. He was wearing a black suit, a blue shirt and a dark grey tie. His shoes were black leather, highly polished. He looked like a creep from a television show about wannabe entrepreneurs. Only his nails, bitten short, betrayed him.

'No one would look for me here.'

'When I didn't hear from you, when I heard about Noel—you must—' Her voice was soft. 'I know how much he meant to you.'

Vincent shook his head. He looked down at the table and said nothing for a while. Then, leaning forward, his face close to Michelle's, he said, 'I'm in trouble. I have to leave the country.'

'For how long?'

'Have the police been to see you?

'Why would they?'

'I was worried there might be some comeback on—someone might connect you to me.'

'What's happening, Vincent?'

He held her gaze. 'This thing with Noel—I can't stay in Dublin.'

'How can I help?'

'There are ways—people I know, I can get whatever papers I need, transport. But I have things I need to do.'

'Then what?'

He touched a finger to the side of his mouth, the nail scraping at the skin. 'I didn't want to leave without seeing you.'

'Have you decided where you're going?'

'England, to start—then, maybe—'

'It has to be a city. No way do I end up in the sticks.'

After a moment, Vincent said, 'You mean it?'

'God help me.'

*　　　*　　　*

He brought her up to his room and after a while she said, 'Let's go now, tonight.'

'I haven't got the stuff I need.'

Vincent was lying back, hands behind his head. Michelle laid her cheek against his chest, breathing in his scent. 'How long will that take?' she said.

'Couple of days, maybe.'

'Then—we go?'

'There are other things I need to do.'

'Such as?'

It was a while before he replied.

When she came back from the bathroom, Michelle's eyes were rough. The tissue in her hand was crushed and wet.

'Vincent, please, this isn't you.'

He looked into her clear blue eyes and he'd never seen anything so pure, so beautiful, so full of everything he never thought he would have. And he nodded slowly and he said, 'This is me.'

*   *   *

He told her about the supermarket. He'd been buying a toothbrush, paste, food, bits and pieces, after he left the MacCleneghan building.

'Middle of the aisle, couple of old geezers—husband and wife, whatever—and the old guy's standing a couple of feet out from the shelves, holding up a packet of something, squinting at it like it's got the Third Secret of Fatima written on the back. And she's got her trolley parked sideways—fucking *sideways*, across the aisle—and I lost it.'

He could have walked around them, squeezed past, but Vincent's mouth twisted and he dropped the basket he was carrying, turned the old guy round, knocking the packet of something out of his hand, pushing his arms up and out, like the stupid fucker was walking a tightrope. And Vincent said, 'Like *that*—stand like *that*. OK? *OK*, you stupid piece of *shit*?'

The fear in the old man was so strong Vincent could smell it. 'What?' he said, not daring to lower

222

his outstretched arms. 'Why?'

'Cos, you and your stupid missus—if you hold your fucking arms out you can block the *whole* fucking aisle, right?'

The old bitch said something high-pitched, but Vincent gave her trolley a shove and walked on towards the checkout, leaving his basket on the floor. He heard the noise from behind as the trolley crashed into shelves, things falling, things breaking and he didn't look back.

It was an idiotic thing to do.

As it happened, Vincent walked clear, no problem. But there could have been a couple of security thugs and they might have taken Vincent, then called the police, and that would have been that.

He couldn't help himself. When he calmed down later he knew the anger was dangerous, but what could he do about that? A couple of nothings like those two, the walking dead, hanging on, taking up space, while Noel was lying cold in a coroner's drawer. What a fucking waste.

It was a thought that inflamed him half a dozen times a day—fat stupids walking down the street, big-mouth idiots on the television screen in the room at the Westbury. Wherever he looked, alive and fouling up the world, while—

It wasn't right.

'They're making ashes of him,' he said to Michelle. 'And I'll be in another country.'

*　　　*　　　*

Before she left the Westbury, Vincent gave Michelle a thick envelope full of money.

223

'How long?' she said.

'I can't say for sure. When you're settled, buy a new phone, text me. Soon as I get to London—'

'Please, Vincent.'

'I can't, not yet. Things, the way—'

One hand gently brushed his thin layer of hair. Close to her ear, Vincent's voice was low, insistent. 'If I don't do this, it's like I'm saying what happened to Noel doesn't matter.'

When they kissed she held him long and tight.

47

Inside Castlepoint Garda Station, Detective Chief Superintendent Malachy Hogg approached the corner desk where Bob Tidey was working. 'Just got word—the hearing's at lunchtime, the judge'll see us in his office, five past one. You ready?'

Tidey indicated the computer screen in front of him. 'Ten minutes, I'll have it done.' Several yards away, Rose Cheney held up a single folded sheet. 'That's it, keep it simple—best thing,' Hogg said. He took her statement.

As promised, Connie Wintour had found a judge to give him an interim injunction, putting a stay on the seizure of his mobile phone. This afternoon, the judge would read evidential statements and hear submissions on whether the injunction should be confirmed or discontinued.

When Hogg went back to his office, Bob Tidey sat staring into space for a couple of minutes. Then he took his personal laptop from a drawer and went down the corridor, found an empty office and sat behind a desk. It took him a couple of minutes to start up the laptop and connect a card reader, then he took from his inside jacket pocket the sealed envelope holding Connie Wintour's phone and tore it open. Within another two minutes, he'd downloaded Connie's contact list and call information. He found another evidence envelope, put the phone in, sealed it and signed it.

Back in the detectives' office, he put the envelope in front of Rose Cheney and handed her a pen. 'The envelope got torn, I had to replace it.'

Cheney stared at him.

Tidey said, 'Accidentally—taking it out of my pocket, it got torn.'

Cheney said, 'I won't lie.'

'That's OK—just sign it. No harm done.'

Cheney signed the envelope. 'Anyone asks, I'll tell them exactly what happened—you told me the envelope got torn, I signed again.'

Bob Tidey nodded. 'No one will ask.'

*   *   *

Detective Chief Superintendent Hogg came into the detectives' office, crooked a finger and said, 'You two.' Cheney stood up, and Tidey put away the file he'd been reading. In Hogg's office, the Detective Chief Superintendent held up a thin file. 'From Technical—the death of one Justin Kennedy, last seen with most of his head missing. It was suicide. His prints confirm his identity, his fingermarks are all over the shotgun. The weapon belonged to his brother, who's now living in Turkey.'

Cheney said, 'He shot himself and then threw the

225

shotgun halfway across the car park?'

'Seven feet away, the shotgun was. And he didn't throw it. He sat down, tucked the muzzle under his chin, the stock resting on the floor, and squeezed the trigger. The recoil sent the shotgun flying, and it landed where it did. Beyond doubt, according to Technical. There's impact marks on the floor, traces on the stock, and all the angles are right.'

Tidey said, 'Where does that leave us?'

'Kennedy was involved in a couple of deals with Emmet Sweetman—and that was a nightmare even before Sweetman was murdered. They seemed to have pulled a couple of strokes, the two of them. Now, the Revenue had their hooks into him and several of his associates were taking him to court. Criminal charges were a possibility. His marriage ended a year ago. His girlfriend says he's been missing for days at a time. All the signs are he just decided it was time to rest his chin on a shotgun.'

'Sounds reasonable.'

'We'll head off for the courts in twenty minutes.'

Back at Bob Tidey's desk, Rose Cheney said, 'There's no way you can use anything you found in Wintour's phone, you know that? This hearing—the best we get is we confirm Emmet Sweetman called Connie Wintour on the day of his murder.'

'Anything else I might find out from the phone—it can't be used in court, but it might point us in the right direction.'

'I hope you—'

Bob Tidey wasn't listening.

Across the room, Detective Garda Eddery was leaning back behind his desk, reading the back page of a tabloid. Facing Tidey, the top of the front page carried photos of a footballer and a blonde

226

woman. Most of the bottom half of the page was taken up by a large headline and a photograph.

Tidey whispered, 'Ah, Jesus.'

He crossed the room and said, 'Sorry, I need that, just for a second,' and took the newspaper from Eddery. A minute later, Tidey gave the newspaper back to Eddery, then tapped at his phone and when Maura Coady answered he said, 'I'm sorry, Maura, I've no idea how this happened.'

She hung up.

*   *   *

Vincent Naylor sat on a bench in Stephen's Green, reading the newspapers. People strolled along the pathways, stood near the water and fed the ducks, or just watched them. On the grass, kids played, couples lay close. Somewhere, a brass band was playing. Vincent finished the broadsheets, skimming page after page. Not a word. It was like the papers had moved on to other business.

He put the *Mirror* aside and turned to the *Daily Record*, glanced at the front page—

Jesus fuck.

He read quickly through the opening paragraphs, his breathing heavy. There were just three paragraphs of the story on the front page, the rest of the story carried over to an inside page. Vincent stared at the headline. ABUSE NUN IS SHOOT-OUT HERO. To the right of the headline, there was a photo of the bitch—a bucktoothed old biddy. And a name—Maura Coady.

'Jesus fucking Christ!'

It was only when he saw the man with the laptop bag dangling from his shoulder, stopping, staring

227

at him, that Vincent realised he must have sworn aloud. The guy was tall and thin. What was left of his hair had been allowed to grow long and was brushed across his head. He looked like a worn-out mop. The mop's face was a picture of disdain. Vincent stood up from the park bench, dropped his newspapers, put a hand to the worn-out mop's face and pushed and kept pushing. The guy back-pedalled, making indignant noises, until he ran out of footpath and went backwards into the water, landing on his arse, ducks scattering.

The gobshite was screaming as Vincent walked away. Standing up in the water, ranting after Vincent and flailing around in search of his laptop. When Vincent got to the exit from Stephen's Green he looked back. A young guy in jeans and a T-shirt was making a hopeless effort at pretending he wasn't following Vincent. The guy had a mobile to his ear.

He tried to run but Vincent caught him within a few yards and pushed his face into the ground, hard. Then he took the guy's mobile and smashed it.

Ten minutes later, he checked out of the Westbury.

48

The injunction hearing was to be held in Judge Daddley's office, and he was in no hurry. Detective Superintendent Hogg, Bob Tidey, Rose Cheney and a lawyer from the Chief State Solicitor's office stood a few yards to the left of the door to the judge's office. Connie Wintour and his lawyer stood to the right. The conversations were muted, with little eye contact between the two sides.

'Bugger's probably having a sandwich,' Hogg said.

'What's he like?' Cheney asked.

'Not much nonsense about him, fairly new to the job. We live in hope.'

Bob Tidey was mentally rehearsing his evidence, in case he was grilled. Whether it's on the witness stand or in a judge's office, the trick is to be clear about what you want to say, say it and give as little as possible beyond that. Above all, don't get into a pissing contest with the other side's lawyer— lawyers live in the urinal, they know all the angles.

Tidey had his evidence stripped down to basics. Police work turned up a previously undiscovered phone belonging to murder victim Emmet Sweetman. It had been used sparingly, for numbers Sweetman didn't want recorded on his regular phone—namely his girlfriends. And calls to Connie Wintour. The police wished to confirm that Wintour had spoken with the deceased on the day he died, and when the lawyer denied receiving such a call it became necessary to obtain access to his phone, to establish the truth.

When the judge's clerk beckoned them into the office they found the judge sitting at his desk, swallowing what was left of a cup of coffee, then wiping his lips with a napkin. He lacked the bloated look that barristers and judges inevitably acquired as their careers advanced. Off to the left, a young woman sat behind a stenographer's machine mounted on a collapsible table.

'This won't take long,' Daddley said. He tapped

229

the file on the desk and said, 'Anyone leave anything important out of their statements?'

To say yes was to invite a reprimand for wasting the court's time. No one said anything.

'Having examined the submissions, I think I understand the facts and the issues.' He looked up, from one lawyer to the other. 'Unless anyone has a burning desire to clarify anything that passeth my understanding?'

The lawyers for each side took maybe three seconds to decide if they wished to piss off the judge by suggesting he mightn't have a full grasp of the issues.

'In that case—which is Detective Sergeant Tidey?'

Bob Tidey raised a finger.

'Nice try, Sergeant, and I can't blame you. I wouldn't mind knowing myself why an officer of the court would deny receiving a call, when there seems to be evidence that such a call was made to his phone. Perhaps there's a simple explanation.'

He looked towards Connie Wintour, who kept his mouth shut and his expression blank.

'However, the facts are plain. The police are entitled to ask anyone whether they got a phone call. The person being questioned—any person, but in this case a lawyer—is entitled to privacy. The explanation might be that someone else answered the phone, even that it was a wrong number. It doesn't matter. Suppose you were allowed to check Mr Wintour's phone to see what calls he received that day—suppose the late Mr Sweetman's number shows up—Mr Wintour might merely say he answered a wrong number. If his phone contained conclusive evidence of anything illegal, the circumstances might be different. Beyond that—' He opened the file, tapped the top page, Bob Tidey's statement of evidence. 'If the courts approve a police officer seizing a lawyer's phone on the basis of a need to confirm he got a call, where would it end? There's the issue of personal privacy, and there's also the issue of professional confidentiality, not to mention client confidentiality. In short, I'm far from convinced that the evidential value of the seizure trumps the intrusion into the rights of the applicant.'

Before leaving the judge's office, Bob Tidey handed over the envelope containing Connie Wintour's phone. Wintour's lawyer passed it to his client and Connie favoured Tidey with an unctuous smile.

'Bollocks to that,' Detective Superintendent Hogg said, leading the way out through the main doors. Standing on the steps of the Criminal Courts building, he faced Bob Tidey and Rose Cheney. 'Off the record—give me the scenario, tell me how you see this. I take it you used the opportunity to have a sneaky look at what's on Wintour's phone?'

Tidey said, 'I wish I had, sir, but it never occurred to me.'

'How do you see this?'

'What I'm thinking, sir—Sweetman and Connie, what if they had a stroke going, a property deal? What if Connie was fronting for someone else? When things started unravelling, all sorts of people got into bed with each other. Then, when Sweetman started making deals with the Revenue, making statements, he became a danger to someone.'

Rose Cheney said, 'In Sweetman's world, the worst thing you expect is a lawsuit. Connie knows a lot of people who do things another way.'

Hogg nodded. 'It's worth a whirl. See if you can follow it anywhere.'

After Hogg left for Castlepoint station, Tidey and Cheney walked down to Ryan's pub. When they'd been served two soups, Cheney said, 'Show me what you found on Wintour's phone.'

'It's on my laptop.'

'You can't do this officially. You run those numbers through the usual channels it will leave a trail.'

'So?'

'I've got a contact. Used to work together, long time ago.' She took out her mobile and began tapping.

49

Maura Coady said, 'At first, to be honest, I thought it might have been you. Apart from a couple of the sisters, I've never talked to anyone else about any of that.'

'Maura, I—'

'I know, I realised—I just had to ask myself, why would you?'

'For the record, I didn't, I wouldn't.'

'I know that reporter spoke to Phil, across the road, and Phil and Jacinta know I was in the convent. They're good people, but Phil loves chatter. And, on the day of the shooting, I think I told Phil it was me who called the police—that it was my fault, what happened.'

'Maura—'

'But I've never spoken to them about the other stuff.'

Tidey said, 'The way the newspapers work—I guess once the reporter found out you were a nun, and that you'd called the police, he decided he had a story. "Hero nun catches armed robbers." These days, the way things have gone, whenever a bishop or a priest or a nun pops up in a story—the reports are public records, and they've got everything on computer—Ferns, Ryan, Murphy, volumes of them.'

Maura's smile was grim. 'No end to the scandals.'

'Even where the reports use pseudonyms, these guys have sources they can tap.'

Maura was sitting across the kitchen table from Tidey, her forearms resting in front of her. 'I spent half an hour cleaning the eggs from my front door this afternoon. Someone—some person who believed they were avenging the victims of the clergy—they threw two or three eggs at the door. First thing this morning, that newspaper was stuffed through the letter box—with obscenities written on it, in thick red marker. Later, twice, there was loud banging on the door and when I went out there was no one there.'

'Kids—'

'The kids are at school. That will start tonight or tomorrow, when someone tells them about the witch living on their street. Today, those were adults.'

'It won't last.'

'It will last—once the witch is identified, there'll be no going back from it. I'll always be the

233

neighbourhood child abuser.'

'I'll have a word with the local station.'

'Thanks—but I'm sure those policemen have more important things to do with their time.' She shook her head. 'This is no more than a nuisance. Believe me, I can put up with it—it'll calm down, maybe I'll move somewhere else, it isn't important.'

'All the same—'

'Really—thanks for coming, thanks for comforting me, but in the grand scale of things—'

'You did the right thing, Maura. You stepped in when thugs with guns put people's lives at risk. And you shouldn't pay a price for that. I promise, I'll do whatever I can to make this OK.'

Maura's smile was lighter this time. 'A few hours ago, after I saw that newspaper headline, I cursed you.'

Tidey smiled. 'Oh ye of little faith.'

* * *

Vincent Naylor was tempted to order something stronger, but it was best to stick with coffee. When the man he was waiting for came into the bar of the Four Seasons Hotel Vincent stood up and they shook hands. The man said he'd have a Ballygowan and Vincent told the waiter.

Vincent assumed that by now the coppers in charge of the Protectica robbery had circulated his photo. The Westbury had suited the look he was counting on for camouflage, the young business nerd, but it was best to leave after the trouble in Stephen's Green—too risky, hanging around the same area. He felt a little less at ease in the Four

Seasons—the suits were more expensive, the bellies bigger and the faces redder. But it was even less likely that a passing cop, with Vincent's photo in his head, would make the connection between an armed robber and a suit in a Ballsbridge hotel.

After the Ballygowan was served, they talked about people they knew in common, avoiding specifics. The man sympathised about Noel and Vincent just nodded. After a while, Vincent indicated a folded copy of the *Irish Independent* on the table, and the man said, yeah. Vincent said the passport photos were with the money. He asked how long and the man said it wasn't a big job. 'It's just a matter of stripping in the details.'

'Terrific.'

The man took a set of car keys from a pocket and left them on the table. 'Blue Renault, third level of the Ilac—the bay number is 332.' He put a card on the table, with the reg number. Vincent nodded.

When the man stood up, they shook hands again, then the man left with the folded copy of the *Irish Independent* under his arm.

In his room, Vincent sat at a table. His neat list now had scribbling down at the bottom. He tore the paper in two, took a sheet of Four Seasons stationery and wrote the names again.

No matter how much you frighten a guy, there's always a chance he can't keep his mouth shut. Maybe it was the nun—the paper said the nosy bitch had called the police about the getaway car, but Vincent doubted that was all the police had to go on. Shay Harrison had to have blabbed.

It wasn't about settling scores before he left the country. Vincent saw it like there was an old-style weighing scales in his head, with Noel on one side,

235

and a lot of stuff on the other. It was about getting the balance right. It was something he'd tried to explain to Michelle, but no one else could understand it. Vincent wouldn't be all right with Noel until that balance felt right.

The restaurant in the Four Seasons wasn't his kind of place. He decided to order room service and get an early night. Big day tomorrow.

*   *   *

Bob Tidey's text to his ex-wife said *Hi* and Holly's reply said *Out and about*, so that was that for the evening. He went to an Italian restaurant close to Grafton Street and they brought him something with a cream sauce—he was sure he'd ordered something with a tomato sauce, but not sure enough to bother making an issue of it. He was sipping coffee when he got a call from Rose Cheney's home number.

'My contact came through—I just got an email.'

'Anything useful?'

'He kept it to the calls made or received by Wintour on the day of the murder and on the two days either side of it.'

'Fair enough.'

'Both times that Wintour got a call from Sweetman, he called another number within minutes. Belongs to someone called Stephen Hill. Ring any bells?'

'Nothing.'

'Me neither—maybe something will pop up when we run the name.'

In no hurry to go home to his apartment, Tidey went to a pub, which was a mistake. The taste of the cream sauce lingered and he didn't enjoy his whiskey. He was in a taxi ten minutes from home when his phone buzzed. The text from Holly said *Home*. Tidey gave the driver the change of destination.

50

'First of all,' Detective Chief Superintendent Malachy Hogg said, 'congratulations to all of you on the work you've done on this case—it's no more than I expected, but it's been a pleasure to work with such a professional squad.' The members of the Sweetman murder inquiry team were gathered in the conference room at Castlepoint Garda Station.

It's *been*?

Bob Tidey glanced across the room at Rose Cheney. She arched an eyebrow. Until now, there was no hint that this was anything other than a routine morning conference.

'The good news is that we've come to a conclusion on the case. Last night, at HQ, along with Assistant Commissioner Colin O'Keefe and several senior officers, we reviewed the files and put together some final details—had a look at the entire picture. We met again this morning and some more pieces fell into place.'

Bob Tidey felt the relief that comes with knowing a case isn't going to end in an open file. Only a fraction of the country's gun killings resulted in a trial—too many ended in files that were as thick as they were inconclusive. He also felt puzzled.

237

Usually, a case moves towards a conclusion when there's a strong lead. It gets the resources necessary to confirm the team is on the right track, the evidence is tested until it's persuasive—no surprises. He'd never seen a case jump upstairs, to be assessed at brass level, without going through the staging points.

'The breakthrough—it came in a statement by one Marisa Cosgrave,' Hogg said. 'She was the girlfriend of the late Justin Kennedy—businessman, lawyer, property speculator, suicide victim. Mr Kennedy, as some of you will be aware, was involved in a number of questionable property schemes with Emmet Sweetman. According to Ms Cosgrave, in recent times this led to some enmity between Sweetman and Kennedy. There were threats—each threatened the other—and we have confirmation from the Revenue that a week before his murder Sweetman made a preliminary statement naming a number of people, including Kennedy, as participants in a tax fraud. He was due to make a further, detailed, statement outlining the specifics of the fraud—his murder prevented that.'

'Kennedy killed Sweetman, then killed himself?' Rose Cheney couldn't keep the scepticism out of her voice.

'Obviously it's not possible to link an individual shotgun to a specific shooting—lead pellets can't be matched to a weapon. But it was the same type of ammunition that killed Sweetman and that Kennedy used to kill himself—RC twenty-gauge, thirty-two-gram semi-magnum. We've consulted Kennedy's diary and that of Ms Cosgrave and there's nothing to account for his movements on

238

the night of the murder.'

'Nothing to say he was in the vicinity of Sweetman's house, then?' Tidey said.

'Nothing to place Kennedy anywhere in particular on the evening of the murder—it's the other evidence that suggests he was at Sweetman's house.'

'Such as?'

'Ms Cosgrave's statement includes the detail that Mr Kennedy made a specific threat—in her presence—in a phone call to Sweetman. This, she quotes him as saying, was Sweetman's last warning. That was two days before Sweetman was shotgunned.'

One of the team, a sergeant called Bowman, spoke from the end of the table. 'There were two killers—if Kennedy had a shotgun, who used the handgun?'

Bob Tidey said, 'Specifically, a handgun used to murder Oliver Snead? We're not saying Kennedy linked up with some gangland tosser to kill Sweetman?'

Hogg said, 'We have no idea who the second shooter was—someone Kennedy roped in as backup—obviously we'll continue inquiries into that aspect of the case. I'm inclined to conclude that the gun was floating on the market. The point was made at one of our conferences—someone sold a gun to someone who sold it to someone else. Guns have an unfortunate habit of migrating between criminal elements.'

Tidey made eye contact with Hogg. 'Some gangland thug killed Oliver Snead, the gun sort of floated around, then someone in a business suit bought it and used it on Emmet Sweetman?'

239

'We don't yet know the precise provenance of the weapon, but when you put it all together, the bigger picture is convincing. Prior association between Sweetman and Kennedy, motive, opportunity, threats, shotgun, same type of ammunition, no alibi. Kennedy kills himself out of remorse, or fear that he's about to be found out. You have doubts, Bob?'

'I've never seen a case go upstairs before the evidence has been assessed by the inquiry team.'

'As you know, this case has been a matter of concern at all levels—so it was natural that the conclusion of the case would be overseen at a higher echelon.'

Bowman said, 'The conclusion? This second killer—that's still open?'

Hogg nodded. 'Of course—that aspect will be pursued vigorously. Obviously, now that we've identified Kennedy, and we know what the murder's about, the inquiry will be scaled back somewhat. But every effort will be made to identify and arrest the second shooter.'

'Scaled back to—what?'

'Garda Eddery was exhibits officer from the beginning, and therefore has a comprehensive grasp of the case—he'll stay on with me. And since Assistant Commissioner O'Keefe will continue to play a hands-on role in the inquiry, he will be supplying two of his own people to help out. We'll have a full complement of uniformed support.'

Rose Cheney said, 'The rest of us bugger off?'

'Thanks to all, for your conscientious efforts—I've arranged for three days' leave before you return to your units. Now, if you'll excuse me, I've an appointment at HQ within the hour. I'd like you all to note that my door is always open, should any of you feel you have anything to add to specific aspects of the case. And again, thank you and congratulations.'

Bob Tidey leaned back in his chair, the front legs raised a few inches. 'What happened to following the evidence?'

Hogg kept his voice level. 'As of now, you're on leave, Bob—lots of time for idle chatter. I have work to do.'

Tidey's gaze followed the Detective Chief Superintendent as he gathered his papers and moved towards the door, Eddery in his wake. Hogg never looked back.

'So, another one bites the dust?' Rose Cheney was standing to Tidey's left.

'You buying this?'

'I'm heading home—my eldest's birthday is the day after tomorrow. Then, I'm back to Macken Road, to pick up where I left off. And you're back to Cavendish Avenue. As far as the brass are concerned, ours not to reason why.'

Tidey shook his head. 'I always thought reasoning why was part of the job description.'

51

It took a few minutes before it dawned on Albert Bannerman that something was wrong. Vincent had used his mobile from outside the house, said he was leaving town. 'I need your help—I can't stay here.' When Albert opened the front door Vincent said, 'Thanks, man, you're a star—I won't stay long.'

Albert had a towel around his neck. He was wearing dark red pyjamas. He gestured towards Vincent's suit. 'The Mormon gear, it works—come in.'

Vincent had a black leather bag dangling from his shoulder. Standing in the hallway, he said, 'You know about Noel?' There was an ache in his voice. Poor fucker. Noel Naylor was something else, but Vincent was all right, he knew how things worked. And the hurt was in his eyes, in the line of his mouth, in the way his shoulders sagged.

'It passes, mate.' Holding Vincent's hand, shaking it, the other hand patting his shoulder. 'I know it won't help now, but time—it's true, it makes the pain bearable, believe me.'

Vincent nodding, a distance in his eyes.

'Can't stay here, Albert—apart from the cops, this city won't be the same, not now.'

In the living room, Lorraine stood up from an armchair. She was wearing a dressing gown with an elaborate floral pattern. Her unease was clear when she saw Vincent. Her lips parted, like she was about to say something, then she thought better of it. Vincent said, 'He was a good man, Noel was,' and Lorraine said, 'He was great company—we had a lot of fun together,' and Vincent nodded.

Vincent Naylor in a suit—Vincent being polite to Lorraine, Vincent coming for favours when the cops were out beating the bushes for him, Vincent saying there was nothing in Dublin for him now that Noel was gone, Vincent running his hand back over his almost bald head. Something in Albert Bannerman's gut was screaming this isn't right and when Vincent reached into the shoulder bag, pulling out a big fucking piece and pointing it at Albert—it was almost a relief. Over by the window, Lorraine released a short, high-pitched scream.

Albert's mouth twisted in anger and contempt. 'You piece of shit—you come into my house, I offer you my sympathy. And you bring a fucking *gun*?'

'Face down on the floor.'

'Vincent—'

'Face *down*.'

Lorraine screamed 'Albert!' and Vincent pointed the gun at her and she twisted her face away from the weapon, cowered, screamed again.

'Tell her to shut the fuck up.'

Another scream from Lorraine.

Albert shouted, 'Shut the fuck *up*.'

Vincent gestured with the gun. As Albert knelt, the towel fell from around his neck. He lay face down on the floor.

'Hands behind you,' Vincent said.

'This is—Jesus, Vincent, this doesn't make sense.'

Vincent leaned down, stuck the muzzle of the Bernardelli into the back of Albert's neck and said, 'Hands behind you, *now*.'

Albert did as he was told and Vincent took a plastic tie from a pocket, looped it around Albert's hands and pulled it tight. He straightened up, told Lorraine to hold her hands out in front, and when she did he bound them with another plastic tie. Lorraine closed her eyes and began a scream. Vincent hit her across the face with the gun and she ended up lying across a vast purple armchair, half conscious, whimpering.

243

'Fuck you,' Albert said. 'Leave her out of this.'

'She's what this is about,' Vincent said.

*   *   *

When Vincent returned from checking the rest of the house, Albert was on his feet in the kitchen, hands tied behind him. His back was to the door leading out to the garden, his hands awkwardly trying to turn the knob.

'Come in here, Albert. Lie down.'

Albert came back slowly, muscles tensed in his thick neck. He knelt, then leaned forward, easing himself face down. 'You know I didn't have a choice,' he said. 'A fella comes for me with a knife, what the fuck would you do?'

'This isn't about that, Albert. This isn't about you.'

'Vincent, this is crazy.'

Vincent stood a couple of feet from Albert's upturned face, inclined his head, leaned down and said, 'You think I can walk away from here, from this city—you think I can piss off to wherever? Make a new life—you think I can do that knowing this bitch is walking around Dublin on her hind legs?'

Lorraine whimpered.

'Ah, Vincent, Jesus, man, she's a ride, that's all, these things happen, people lose out—Noel, he lost out—it happens, it's happened to me, to you, to everyone. It's just the way things are.'

Vincent went down on one knee, his face closer to Albert, his voice low. 'You think I'm going to wake up every day, go about my business, do all the normal stuff, and put my head on a pillow at

244

night—and every single moment I know that cow is strolling around? Noel in ashes, and that cow waltzing around like he never existed? You think I could live with that?'

Albert said nothing. His neck twisted at an angle, he looked up at Vincent, his breathing heavy.

'What you gonna do?'

Vincent straightened up. 'No option.'

'Why me?'

'You think—no matter where I end up—you think I can leave you looking for me?'

'Vincent, I swear—'

'Albert—' Lorraine's voice was a high-pitched moan.

'Shut *up*.'

Vincent shook his head. Albert tucked his legs under him and levered himself into a half-sitting position. 'We can work this out, Vincent—there's no need.'

'Albert—'

'There's no need, Vincent, I swear to you—look, there's things we can—you and me—wherever you're heading off to, I can help you—'

'I'm sorry, Albert.' Vincent stood up straight. He looked Albert in the eye. 'If you were in my place, you know it's what makes sense.'

Albert stretched his neck, thrust his big, bald head towards Vincent and said, 'I'll do her.'

'Oh, Jesus, Albert, Jesus—' Lorraine struggled to her feet, moving awkwardly, her hands tied in front of her. She was a couple of yards from the living-room door when Vincent hit her on the side of the head with the Bernardelli. She made no noise, stunned, just collapsed face down onto the floor.

'It'll work,' Albert said. 'I'll do her. There's a gun

taped to the back of the bookcase in the front room.'

Standing over Lorraine, Vincent turned, looked at Albert.

'Get it for me,' Albert said. 'Leave one bullet, that's all. You've got me covered. Think about it, Vincent—I do it, it's on me. We do this together it means I've got no beef with you. You leave, I clean up—she's gone. I'll have a story—everyone knows she's a tramp—she went away somewhere, there's nothing for either of us to worry about.'

Vincent leaned down and put the gun to the back of Lorraine's head and squeezed the trigger. Her head bounced on the floor and a spray of blood flew away and landed on the blue carpet.

'Fuck you!' Albert swivelled his legs and tried to push himself up from the floor. He made it to his knees just as Vincent shot him in the head.

52

From the window of his apartment, Bob Tidey's view was of a short stretch of Glasnevin Road. There was only so much to be got from watching cars shoot past, and the progress of the occasional pedestrian had little to offer. In the background, the radio was babbling. *Morning Ireland* was finishing an interview with a minister for something or other. The minister kept saying there was no alternative. The interviewer moved on to an economist who worked for a bank, who began by saying he agreed with the politician, it was the only game in town. Tidey reached out and stabbed a button on the front of the radio, jumping to Country Mix FM, where Christy Moore was singing 'John O'Dreams'.

Instead of adding his mug, plate, cutlery and glass to the dishwasher, Tidey took them to the sink and washed them by hand. It gave him something to do while he tried to put a shape to the coming day. The plan was to stroll down to the Botanic Gardens and spend an hour among the flowers, then kill another hour with a brisk walk. In the afternoon, he planned to visit a man who lived in Finglas, a shopkeeper with a sideline in fencing stolen goods. With three days' leave, he had an opportunity to touch base with informants, a tedious but useful exercise. The shopkeeper occasionally passed on scraps of information he picked up in the course of his work. He wasn't after payment—it was just an insurance policy, for the day when he might need someone to put in a good word.

He intended calling on a small-time thief in Coolock, an occasional driver for various gangs, with whom he had a similar arrangement.

Sometime during the day, Tidey promised himself, he'd text Holly, see if she was free this evening.

Tidey was five minutes from the Botanic Gardens when he changed his mind about strolling amid the flowers. He walked home, went round the back of the apartment block and got into his car. Halfway down Collins Avenue he found his Bluetooth earpiece and called Clontarf Garda Station.

'You got time for a bit of brain-picking?'

His former colleague, Harry Synnott, said, 'I've

247

got a meeting—no more than an hour—after that, any time you like.' Tidey parked at the station and walked up along the seafront for half an hour, then back. Standing across the road from the station he rang Harry again. 'Come ahead,' Harry said.

Sitting in the office Harry shared with four others, Bob Tidey talked about the sudden end to the Sweetman case. 'Maybe I'm making too much of it.'

'Someone's pulling strings?'

'Not necessarily,' Tidey said. 'It could be they believe this Kennedy fella did the killing. Or it could be they see some other possibilities opening up—roads they don't want to go down—and Kennedy's a plausible story to justify wrapping things up.'

'Either way, Bob—they've drawn a line.' Synnott, who had crossed an occasional line in his time, smiled ruefully. 'Some kinds of lines, you step across them and you're in the twilight zone.'

Tidey said, 'Stephen Hill. You know the name?'

Harry Synnott shook his head. 'Nothing comes to mind. Who is he?'

'Emmet Sweetman, the day he was murdered, twice called a dodgy lawyer. The dodgy lawyer immediately called this Stephen Hill. The only way I can run a check is if I turn up for work—which means risking a head-butting contest with Hogg. I was hoping—' Tidey gestured towards the monitor on Synnott's desk.

Synnott eased his chair towards the desk, pulled his keyboard closer. After a minute he turned the monitor towards Tidey. 'Stephen Hill—two robberies, aggravated assault. Interviewed in the course of two murder investigations, but nothing

248

came of either.'

'That's someone who might turn up on a doorstep with a shotgun.'

'And there's a connection. You asked me the other day about Gerry FitzGerald—Zippo. Says here both he and Stephen Hill were pulled in for questioning on an aggravated assault. The two lads said nothing, walked away from it.'

It took Tidey ten minutes on the phone to the DPP's office to find out that Stephen Hill had four times been represented in court by Connie Wintour.

*　　　*　　　*

When Connie Wintour came out of the lift on the fourth floor of the Criminal Courts of Justice, he saw Bob Tidey and gave him a big smile. 'Ah, Sergeant, we meet again. Are you down here to prosecute a case, or perhaps you've come for a wee chinwag?' He turned left and headed towards the courtrooms.

'When was the last time you spoke to Stephen Hill?'

Wintour didn't react, just kept strolling. 'Stephen—I still have hopes for the lad.'

'I'm sure he comes in handy, if someone needs to send someone else to hospital.'

Wintour stopped and smiled. 'Still fond of the view from your high horse, Sergeant?'

'Injured innocence doesn't suit you, Connie.'

'Did I ever tell you, Sergeant, about the third case I handled, the first that mattered? A bloody daft burglar who spent more time in jail than out. He was caught twenty yards from the broken window of a parish priest's house, carrying a set of golf clubs. And when the prosecuting Garda suggested that eighteen other counts of burglary should be taken into consideration, he just nodded. Open and shut.'

'I'm sure you did a crackerjack job.'

'Better than that—I went through every document, checking every detail. And six of the burglaries he confessed to—they happened when he was in jail.'

'Aren't you the clever lad?'

'Not really. My mistake was when I stood up and triumphantly informed the judge of this unsavoury state of affairs. He deleted the six counts and gave my chap the maximum on the rest. What I didn't know was that the police were clearing their books—adding unsolved crimes to open-and-shut cases. The judge was cooperating, and my client was furious with me because he expected a shorter sentence for taking it on the chin.'

Wintour continued walking, casually swinging his briefcase. 'We live and learn, Sergeant. It's a funny old business, law and order.'

'I've a suggestion, Connie.' Wintour paused. Tidey gave him what he hoped was a confident smile. Connie would be approachable if he believed his personal position was under threat. The first step was to give him a reason to consider opening negotiations.

'I think you know where the Sweetman murder inquiry is heading.'

Connie looked genuinely puzzled. 'And that should concern me—why?'

'What it looks like—Sweetman was about to roll over and start blabbing to the Revenue about a bent property deal. And I think maybe that upset the heavies you and Sweetman were both involved with. I think you talked to Sweetman that day—one last try to get him to shut up. When he wouldn't, you rang someone else.'

Wintour stopped again. 'And that was?'

'Stephen Hill. Trigger man.'

Connie gave him a warm smile. 'You're here to rattle me, Sergeant. Shouldn't you be wearing your Columbo raincoat, so you can pretend you're done with me, then you turn back—*just one more thing, Mr Wintour,* right? Well, I'm afraid, Sergeant, the days when a policeman could rattle me, inside a courtroom or out, are long gone.'

'That might well be, but—'

'The Sweetman inquiry, as you're well aware, Sergeant, is over.' Wintour began walking. 'Before long, the awful truth about the late Mr Kennedy and his ease with a shotgun will doubtless be leaked to an obliging reporter. The hack will in turn announce that he's cracked the Emmet Sweetman mystery.'

'Who told you?'

'A city is made up of many villages, many circles, many layers, and with modern means of communication—' He stopped at the entrance to a courtroom. 'Here we are, today's bear pit.' He turned away and pulled the door open. 'Take care, Sergeant.'

'You did ring Stephen Hill. He's the killer.'

Wintour looked back. 'Stephen—not a bad chap, easily led astray. With time and patience I hope to see him become a useful member of society. Mind how you go, Sergeant.' He let the door swing shut behind him.

251

53

If you're not in, Anthony Prendergast believed, you can't win. For every ten tip-offs a reporter follows, maybe one pays off with a story. The rest—well, you work for a newspaper, so people with a bee in their bonnet assume you can help them swat it. Some are decent people who've truly been screwed, others have surfaced from the bottomless swamp of paranoia and obsession. The trouble with conspiracy theories is that when you reject them you're immediately accused of helping the conspirators suppress the truth. Which is when your name turns up on websites, listed among the agents of Satan.

But if you don't wade through the crap you miss the occasional worthwhile story. Anthony Prendergast knew his talent didn't lie in the quality of his prose. And his contact book wasn't heavy with high-level sources. But he had a young reporter's hunger—he'd wade through the deepest crap, across the widest fields of codswallop, as long as there was a chance of a story at the end of it. This afternoon was an example of casting your bread upon the waters, with little expectation of getting back anything other than soggy bread.

'He sells guns.' The voice on the phone was slightly hoarse.

'A policeman?'

'A sergeant.'

'Do you have any personal knowledge of this?'

'I know what I know.'

'Are you a Garda yourself?'

'I know someone who bought one.'

'A gun?'

'Yeah.'

'From a policeman?'

'That's what I said.'

'Can you give me your name?'

'You can call me Matthew.'

'You know this cop's name?'

'Yeah.'

'What is it?'

'Not on the phone.'

'What station?'

'I have a file.'

Oh dear.

Civilians who keep files on people tend to be secret-agent fantasists. The files are laced with underlined words and exclamation marks, a coded index and key sentences typed in capital letters. Anthony's interest went down a couple of notches.

'Can I see it?'

'Meet me this afternoon.'

Walking down along the south side of the quays, Anthony had already tagged this one as a loser. But, if you're not in you can't win.

As promised, the would-be Deep Throat was sitting in Sorohan's, at a table near the door, a glass of Coke in front of him. A surly-looking guy in his twenties, with a lower-level Civil Service look to him. Anthony introduced himself, relieved he wasn't expected to go through a password ritual.

Anthony pointed at the Coke. 'Get you another?'

'I'm OK.'

Anthony got himself a coffee and sat down next to Matthew.

'Are you in the force yourself?'

'No.'

'The civilian end of things?'

'You want to see the file?'

'Sure.'

'It's in the car.'

It took less than a minute to get to the car, a large Renault, in the car park behind Sorohan's. 'How did you find out about this?'

'I have my ways.'

Anthony said, 'Yeah.'

The would-be informant opened the boot, leaned in and said, 'I bet you thought I was talking through my arse?'

'I wouldn't say that, it's just—'

Matthew took a gun out of the boot and pointed it at Anthony. He gestured towards the boot. 'Get in,' he said.

*   *   *

When they got to the house at Rathfillan Terrace, Vincent Naylor drove the Renault inside the garage, closed the door and opened the boot. He reached down and held the reporter by the front of his shirt, pulled him up and out. There was a yelp as the reporter hit his shin off something, then Vincent was opening the internal door, pushing the reporter inside, through the kitchen, moving fast.

'What's this about?' The reporter's voice was high-pitched, panicky.

When Vincent got him into the living room he pushed him backwards into the armchair facing the door. The pussy was sweating.

'What's this about?'

Vincent stood there, looking down at him, the

reporter's lower lip quivering.

'This is very simple,' Vincent said. 'I'm going to ask you questions, you're going to answer them. You don't answer them, you're no use to me. I put you back in the boot of the car and wait until the middle of the night. Then I drive you to a spot along the Royal Canal and I push the car in.'

'Jesus, come on—what am I supposed to know? I've no idea who you are, I've no—this isn't—'

Vincent leaned down and picked up a folded tabloid from the floor. He made eye contact with the reporter as he smoothed the paper, then he looked down and read from it. ' "Sitting in the living room of his modest house, with his wife in the kitchen making coffee and sandwiches, it's easy to recognise that this is no storm trooper—" ' Vincent looked up from the paper. 'You remember that shit?'

'That—'

'Easy question—you remember that shit?'

'Yes, the robbery story—the ERU guy—'

'That was my brother he shot.'

'That's not—'

'What's his name and where does he live?'

The reporter sat there, his mouth open, his eyes wide, breathing hard. 'Jesus—I can't tell you that—I—look—'

Vincent leaned in so close that when he whispered Anthony could feel his breath on his cheek. 'Is that your final answer?'

54

When he got the reporter upstairs, Vincent made him kneel beside the radiator, then he used plastic ties to bind his hands to the pipes. He used a twisted shirt to fasten the reporter's legs together—kneeling, leaning against the radiator, head down near the floor.

'Awkward, I know, and you'll probably get cramp, lying like that. But if your information checks out I'll be back to untie you. If you're pissing me about, I'll be back to shoot you in the head. One way or the other, this won't take long.'

'Please, this won't—' His neck straining, his head half turned so he could look up at Vincent, the reporter's face was pale and sweaty. There was blood around his mouth, a cut above his right eye. 'He didn't shoot your brother—'

'You had your chance. You knew—and don't say you didn't—that if you gave me the cop's address he's as good as dead. You had a choice—your life or Sergeant Dowd's, remember that? My opinion—you made the sensible choice. Don't spoil it now, bitching and begging.'

'He was just doing his job—'

'One last little thing.' Vincent leaned right down, his face close to the reporter. 'This nun, this bitch, Maura Coady—Kilcaragh Avenue, North Strand, right? In the paper, you didn't mention a house number.'

'I don't remember.'

'Well, that's a pity.' Vincent straightened up. 'You've made the cop die—and now you're going

256

to die anyway.'

'I really don't remember the number, I swear.'

'I believe you.'

Vincent reached for the Bernardelli on the bedside table. 'Sorry it ends like this—'

'Forty-one.'

'Kilcaragh Avenue?'

'Yeah.' Anthony looked away from Vincent, staring straight at the wall.

'You know if I go there and—'

Anthony said something, his voice so low that Vincent had to lean forward.

'Say what?'

'I said it's the truth.'

'North Strand and Rathmines—a bit of a drag. This evening, I do one of them. The cop or the nun? What do you think? Which of them goes to God tonight? Eeny meeny miney mo?'

*   *   *

The birthday boy had already received his presents and cut his cake and it was time to drain some of the hyper energy out of the party guests. Rose Cheney's husband threw a switch and the guests cheered as a bouncy castle shimmied into its upright position. When it was fully inflated Rose yelled, 'Three, two—one!' and stepped back as a dozen screaming kids rushed forward. For a moment she watched them jumping, bouncing, tumbling, then she joined Bob Tidey, who was nursing a can of Heineken on the raised deck at the end of the back garden.

'I'm not sure that's such a good idea, Bob—the investigation is over, at least our part in it. The

257

brass aren't overfond of foot soldiers who play detective.'

'You're buying the Kennedy theory?'

'He had a shotgun—he had the nerve to turn it on himself, so he more than likely would have had the nerve to use it on Sweetman. Put it this way—it's an explanation. You or I might want to put firmer ground under it, but we have our place in the scheme of things.'

'What pisses me off is that Connie Wintour knew—probably before we were told—he knew the investigation was being closed down.'

'Cosy cartels, golden circles—whatever you call them, they're as much a part of this country as the mountains and the bogs. They watch out for each other.'

Tidey finished his Heineken. 'Let it be?'

'There's no percentage in fighting a battle you can't win.'

At the bouncy castle, a kid was crying. Cheney went to help a parent soothe the hurt.

*   *   *

Home—it's like when you're a kid and you build a hidey-hole from where you can look out onto a world in which you don't feel entirely safe. Maybe the hidey-hole period lasted just one summer, maybe only a couple of weeks, but that idea of sanctuary never left Garda Sergeant David Dowd. Even with all the confidence and knowledge he retained from his ERU training, the part of the day he most enjoyed was when work and social obligations were done with, when he closed off the outside and relaxed into his hidey-hole.

He'd changed into T-shirt and shorts, he'd read two Mr Men books to his daughter—chosen at random from her enormous stack. Now, time to go downstairs and chill with his wife. There was a time when that would have meant a couple of beers or whiskeys, but not now. In the years since joining the ERU he hadn't touched a drop. He would stay that way until he moved on to some unit where he would never be called out at short notice to deal with potentially fatal circumstances.

He raised both arms to pull the bedroom curtains closed and pieces of glass hit him in the face. He went down, screaming his wife's name, telling her to drop to the floor—two more shots shattered window glass and he was belly down, moving fast across the floor, out the bedroom door, up onto his feet, running towards his daughter's bedroom. The sound of two, three more shots, glass breaking.

Fuck, fuck, fuck. Not here. Not here.

*　　　*　　　*

The city centre pub was crowded and noisy. It had never bothered Bob Tidey when he drank here back in the days when he was stationed nearby at Store Street. Back then, the crush and the noise was part of the fun, now he found the raised voices and the slight hysteria oppressive. He'd dropped in on his way back from Rose Cheney's home, but after a single whiskey he left. He'd texted Holly and got another *Out and about* reply, so he took a taxi home to Glasnevin.

After a while, sitting in his flat, he found himself having an imaginary conversation about the

259

Sweetman case—the reasons for believing that a business partner did it and then committed suicide, and the holes in that theory. He wondered if having imaginary conversations was a sign of mental deterioration. He switched on the television and clicked his way through a jungle of old sitcoms, showbiz gossip and obscure sports, along with documentaries offering all he needed to know about Nazis, ancient Romans or air crashes. He didn't notice himself nodding off and when he jolted awake he was still sitting in the armchair, his head tilted at an awkward angle. On the television, a man was explaining something about Stonehenge. Tidey's watch said it was just after two o'clock. He made it to the bedroom and slipped back into sleep.

*   *   *

In the dim light from inside the open boot, Vincent Naylor could see that the reporter's tied hands were trembling, his lips quivering as though he'd just surfaced from an arctic sea. For a moment, Vincent thought the creep had gone into shock.

'Please.'

'Shut up.'

Vincent leaned down and pulled the reporter out, dumped him in a heap on the ground. They were out beyond Tallaght, in a wooded area in the foothills of the Dublin mountains. Below, the lights of the western suburbs glowed. It was almost three in the morning, the air was chilly, the whole world quiet.

Vincent took a knife from his pocket, unfolded the blade and cut the bindings on the reporter's

260

hands and legs.

'You gave me everything I needed, right? No reason to worry, then—right?'

The thing at the cop's house had been sweet. Vincent was prepared for a false start, maybe a darkened house, maybe a long wait until the bastard arrived home. Instead, an SUV in the driveway, lights on upstairs and down. Stoking himself up to ring the doorbell and put the muzzle of the gun in the bastard's face, Vincent looked up and there the bastard was at the bedroom window and it took Vincent just a second to get the Bernardelli out of his shoulder bag. *Blam blam blam*—the cop went down like someone took his legs away. And again, *Blam blam blam*, for good measure. The only maybe in Vincent's mind was what if that wasn't him? But who else would be in a bedroom of the guy's house at that time of evening? Had to be.

Vincent took the reporter by the back of his jacket and dragged him—the guy's legs scrambling awkwardly on the uneven ground—until they were in front of the car, in the beam from the headlights.

'Please—'

'A bone to pick.'

'Please—'

'My brother Noel—' Vincent leaned down so his lips were a couple of inches from the reporter's ear—'all his life, he never got his name in the papers.' Vincent straightened up. The little creep cowered, carefully avoiding eye contact. 'First time he got his name in the papers was when he was shot dead by the cops. Shot dead trying to surrender.'

'Please—'

'Never got his name in the papers, his whole life. Then, his name was all over the papers and some of it was fair enough, it just said what happened. Even if it didn't say he'd been surrendering.'

The reporter tilted his chin up towards Vincent. 'I said that, about surrendering—I put that in—there was an old man, he told me—thousands of people read that, they—'

Vincent punched the reporter in the face. Anthony said, 'Ah,' then he said it again, almost a sigh, over and over. There was blood on his mouth, where his lip split when it was crushed against his teeth. Vincent leaned down again. 'A notorious thug, you called him. A drug dealer, you called him. Thousands of people read that too. Why'd you have to tell lies? Why?'

'It's—I talked to the police, they said there were things he was never charged with, and—'

'And those bastards never lie?'

'Please—'

'You expect to get away with that?'

'Please—'

Vincent reared back and his hand with the Bernardelli came swinging, the gun smashing into the side of the reporter's head. Which was a mistake. Vincent shook him, slapped his face, tried to bring him round—no use. The smack in the head probably gave him a concussion. Pity, that. When Vincent put the gun to the reporter's forehead and squeezed the trigger the bastard never saw it coming.

55

Rising up from a deep sleep, Bob Tidey was already reaching for his bleating mobile before he was fully awake.

'Yeah?'

'Detective Sergeant Tidey?'

'Yeah?'

'There's a car waiting, out front. Instructions from Detective Chief Superintendent Hogg.'

It took several moments of silence to make sense of this. At first, Tidey thought he might have slept in and missed an appointment.

'A car? What for?'

'Detective Chief Superintendent wants to see you, directly.'

'What about? I'm on leave.'

'Those are my instructions.'

Tidey muttered, 'Bollocks.' He looked at his watch—quarter past ten. 'Give me a minute.' He ended the call.

He was ready in twenty.

*　　　*　　　*

Vincent Naylor sat down to a late breakfast at the Four Seasons Hotel. Usually, a coffee and a slice of toast was enough, but today he felt like treating himself. He glanced inside the large envelope he'd collected at the car park at the Ilac. All in order.

These were people it was a pleasure to deal with. They could supply anything, and take your dirty money and launder it for a sizeable commission.

The envelope held a driving licence, a real passport with a fake name, a debit card to match, linked to an account with three grand. There were details of the options for his trip via Belfast to Glasgow, and it was up to him to make his own way to London. He had a choice of when to leave—one phone call, twenty-four hours' notice, and they'd slot the final pieces into place. These people knew how to charge, but they did a first-rate job.

The scales inside Vincent's head were more balanced, and that made him feel like he was paying Noel the respect he deserved. He could leave the country right now and he'd feel he'd done the right thing—but he hadn't cleared the entire list. He'd done the Protectica guy, Lorraine and Albert, the reporter and the cop. Almost finished.

The waiter came to take his order. Vincent said he'd have the full Irish, with extra sausages.

*   *   *

Detective Chief Superintendent Malachy Hogg was sitting behind his large oak desk. He didn't rise to greet Bob Tidey. 'Right to the point, Detective Sergeant. After consultation with Assistant Commissioner O'Keefe, I am to inform you that you're suspended from duty, on full pay, as and from this moment, pending a disciplinary inquiry.'

The words were delivered flatly, as though Hogg was reading aloud from a set of instructions. 'You will be informed within forty-eight hours of the particulars of the conduct that led to this suspension. I suggest you notify the Association of Garda Sergeants and Inspectors, with a view to acquiring represen-tation.'

Tidey waited. Hogg remained silent.

'That's it? I've done something unspecified, to someone unknown—and—'

'You know damn well—you received specific instructions regarding a major murder case, and you ignored them and ploughed your own furrow.'

'It never occurred to me you and Connie were close.'

'Don't be stupid. This isn't about Connie Wintour, it's about you. Decisions were made, but you decided you're above all that chain-of-command shit. Well, we don't have lone crusaders in this force.' Hogg's voice was now more brisk. 'Wintour complained about being harassed, as he was entitled to do. And when it trickled down to Assistant Commissioner O'Keefe—when he learned that you'd ignored orders—he had no option.'

'Trickled down to an AC. How high up the political ladder do Connie's protectors go?'

'Off the record, Bob, leaving rank aside—you're way out of line. Senior officers reached a conclusion based on the evidence. You're entitled to your opinion, but we can't have freelance investigators second-guessing official findings.'

'Off the record, leaving rank aside—do you believe the Sweetman murder was just a falling-out between two businessmen?'

'I do.'

'You don't think it's a convenient story—a little drama to distract the skulls?'

'I believe the evidence supports our conclusion.'

'You're ready to stand over that, Chief Superintendent?'

265

Hogg had drained his face of empathy. When you're giving someone a kicking, there's no point wearing fluffy slippers. 'Remember, you got a reprimand from a judge, in open court, over the quality of your evidence in a criminal trial. If you've any notion of making a song and dance about this, that reprimand can be picked up and run as a perjury allegation.' He waited a moment, and when Tidey didn't respond he said, 'Now, fuck off, Bob.'

*   *   *

Twice Bob Tidey called Colin O'Keefe's number, and twice there was no answer. He adjusted his mobile so his number wouldn't appear on the receiving phone. He called again and the Assistant Commissioner answered.

'Colin, you know this murder–suicide shit is dodgy. Hogg is so set on closing the case that he's threatening me with trumped-up perjury charges if I follow an open lead.'

'This is inappropriate.'

'Colin, this stinks.'

'We were colleagues, we were friends. We'll be colleagues again, and I hope we'll be friends again—but right now you're one of the many problems I have to deal with. I wish it was different—but that's the way it is. Now, I'm ringing off.'

The phone went dead.

*   *   *

Almost noon.

266

The car that had brought Bob Tidey to Garda headquarters in the Phoenix Park was nowhere to be seen. He walked a while and picked up a taxi on the North Circular Road. He was sitting in the back, oblivious to his surroundings, when the driver turned and said, 'We're going where?'

Tidey didn't want to go home, to be alone. He didn't want to go anywhere, to be with anyone else. 'O'Connell Bridge.'

At the end of the journey, standing on the bridge, he knew of no reason to go this way rather than that. It was as if all points of reference had been removed. He crossed the bridge and walked up past College Green and found a Starbucks.

This could be sorted out. The suspension didn't have to lead to anything drastic. He was a good detective, valuable to the force, and he wouldn't be shafted as long as he got back into line. It was the sensible thing to do. The notion of forcing the issue, watching his career flame out for the sake of the Sweetman case was too foolish to consider. Outside the force, for the rest of his life, he'd be as adrift as he felt when he got out of the taxi—all points of reference gone.

When his mobile rang he didn't recognise the number that showed.

'Yeah?'

'Martin Pollard.'

'Polly, how's it going?'

'There's something you should know.'

'Yeah? What about?'

'Not on the phone.'

Tidey said, 'You're in luck—suddenly, I find myself with a lot of time on my hands.'

56

Michelle Flood said, 'I miss you,' and Vincent Naylor said, 'I miss you too.' He was lying on the bed in his room at the Four Seasons. 'Won't be long, now.'

'I can't help it.' Her voice was faint. He held the phone closer to his ear. 'Every hour you stay in Dublin, I'm thinking is this the hour they take you?'

'There's a delay, I can't leave yet. The passport's taking longer than I thought.'

'How much longer?'

'You know how these things work. People say they'll have something done—then there's a delay.'

She told him about the apartment, the area. As she spoke, Vincent reached down towards the bottom of the bed and tucked the top of the passport back into the envelope—he knew it was silly, but he didn't want it staring at him while he spoke to Michelle.

'It doesn't have to be permanent,' she said, 'we can move on, it depends—but it's a lovely neighbourhood and I think you'll like it.' He said he was sure he would.

*　　　*　　　*

Bob Tidey was sipping his coffee, in Gaffney's pub in Fairview, when Detective Inspector Martin Pollard arrived. Pollard ordered a vodka and tonic. Balding since his twenties, his hair had now receded over the horizon of his polished head. As ever, he didn't waste time on chit-chat. 'This is all on the quiet, we never talked, right?'

Tidey nodded.

'Someone tried to kill an ERU sergeant, at his home. Several shots through the window of his bedroom—he got away with a few cuts from flying glass.'

'Someone's asking for trouble.'

'Technical fast-tracked the forensics. The same gun has been used to kill a hood named Albert Bannerman—and his girlfriend. And a man named Shay Harrison, who worked for Protectica.'

'Someone's gone berserk.'

'We're trying to keep a lid on the fact that the incidents are connected. We think it was a hood called Vincent Naylor. He's the brother of one of the men shot dead on Kilcaragh Avenue—he hasn't been seen since the Protectica job.'

Tidey shook his head. 'Never heard of him.'

'He used to work for Mickey Kavanagh, did at least one killing for him. He just finished a stretch in the Joy for assault. A couple of years back I spent several weeks trying to tie him into a kneecapping. I know he did it, but the victim was too scared to make a statement.'

'Some fruitcake—three dead and he's shooting at an ERU sergeant?'

Pollard poured a small amount of mixer into his vodka and lowered half of the drink. 'He tried to kill the leader of the ERU team, he's killed a Protectica employee, who may have been the inside man. Which is why I wanted to let you know. That friend of yours, the woman who tipped us off about the car—'

'Maura Coady.'

'We don't know how many people he's mad at, but her name was in the papers—the hero nun who gave police the tip-off.'

'Ah, Jesus. She's in her seventies—she said a prayer over one of the guys when he was dying.'

'If Vincent Naylor's read the papers—' Pollard shrugged.

'She's going to get protection, right?'

Pollard looked uncomfortable. 'That's where it gets complicated. We've got a list of people we've been told have priority. Assuming this Shay Harrison was the inside man, there may be other Protectica people in danger. Other ERU members—any Garda who might have pissed off Vincent Naylor in the past.'

'Maura Coady—without her, there wouldn't have been an ERU operation.'

'It's not that anyone's excluding her, it's just that they had to draw the line somewhere and she happened to be on the other side of it.'

'Budgets, right?'

'I've had a chat with my Super, and he's approved an unmarked car, parked close to her house, for a day or two. The reason I contacted you—maybe you can do something more.'

'Such as?'

'I'm told you're an old buddy of Assistant Commissioner O'Keefe—maybe you can put a word in, get her shifted up the list? I'm told O'Keefe is a reasonable man.' Martin Pollard finished what was left of his vodka.

Tidey stood and hesitated a moment, then he said, 'I better head.'

Pollard said, 'Yes, keep in touch.' As Tidey left, Pollard took his glass to the bar.

Walking towards the city centre, Bob Tidey called a friend at Garda headquarters and found out where Colin O'Keefe was scheduled to be this evening. Given Tidey's suspension, approaching O'Keefe would be tricky, but manageable. The Sweetman case made things awkward, but that could be finessed. Bow the knee, throw in a bit of the old mea culpa. Keep the focus on getting protection for Maura Coady.

Tidey rang Harry Synnott at Clontarf station and asked for another favour. Then he hailed a taxi. When he got home to his flat in Glasnevin a lengthy fax from Synnott had arrived. Tidey made a coffee and sat at the kitchen table, reading excerpts from Vincent Naylor's file. There was a lot of background stuff on Naylor and on the people he'd worked with and for. There were two pages on the killing he did for Mickey Kavanagh, and three pages of background on Mickey and his operations.

Tidey sipped his coffee, his gaze fixed on a mugshot of Vincent Naylor. In pictures taken by their captors, criminals sometimes look subdued, sometimes angry or defiant. Naylor faced the camera with the air of a footballer who's just learned he's been voted Man of the Match.

57

The President, her voice laden with emotion, said that the republic—in this, its hour of need—was calling on its daughters and sons, at home and abroad, to rally to its cause. 'And we make this call, knowing that our people's love for their country is matched only by their spirit, by their creativity, by their ingenuity and by their energy.'

The President spoke from a platform in the courtyard of Dublin Castle. Behind her, seated in three tiers, representatives of the state and of civic society had come to demonstrate their support for the project being launched this evening. Among them were the Garda Commissioner and two of his Assistant Commissioners, including Colin O'Keefe.

'Almost four score and ten years ago, within the precincts of this very Castle, in a solemn two-hour ceremony, the soon-to-be-martyred Michael Collins accepted the transfer of government from Viscount FitzAlan, the British Lord Lieutenant. Shortly afterwards, the flag of another country was solemnly lowered, and with equal solemnity the flag of the reborn nation was raised aloft. Many times in the decades since then, this country has known tough times. Yet the challenges we face today are as great as the gravest test endured by our forebears.'

The President's audience of several hundred was standing on cobblestones in the centre of the courtyard, hemmed in by barriers. Bob Tidey was standing at the back of the crowd. He noted the beefed-up security that had become standard at official events, to discourage public expressions of anger against executive incompetence and corruption. There were, however, no politicians on the platform, apart from the presidential figurehead. Nothing would kill off potential support as quickly as the presence of a nervously grinning government minister.

The new project invited citizens to go online at a tastefully designed website and reveal their entrepreneurial ideas on how to get the country out of the massive hole of debt into which the bankers had driven it. It seemed to be a kind of national suggestion box, with prizes for the best submissions. Tidey pitied the poor sods who had to sort through the crank proposals and the inevitable tide of obscenities.

Three speakers followed the President, each more emotional and flowery than the speaker before. Finally, with a ringing call from the Master of Ceremonies, an RTÉ celebrity, the event ended. Bob Tidey showed his ID and was allowed through the barrier. Colin O'Keefe saw him coming and held up a palm—he smiled and silently mouthed, 'Five.' Tidey lit a cigarette and waited twenty minutes while O'Keefe mingled. The President went indoors after a while, accompanied by her retinue. The crowd's smiles, handshakes and enthusiastically nodding heads suggested that the launch was considered a great success. The sound of excited chatter covered the courtyard like a fluffy blanket.

Eventually, as the crowd began to dwindle, O'Keefe beckoned and Tidey followed him to a corner of the courtyard.

'I'm due inside for dinner, Bob—and, like I said, this is inappropriate, given your suspension.'

'It'll take a minute.'

'I can't speak to you about the suspension, or about the Sweetman case.'

'It's not that.'

O'Keefe leaned closer, his voice lowered, although there was no one within several yards. 'A word to the wise, Bob—these disciplinary things, they're a ritual dance. Once you understand the choreography, there's no need for it to come to anything.'

Tidey said, 'I follow orders—so, it's over, the Sweetman case. Believe me, I'd no intention of challenging anyone's authority. But there's something I need, there's a problem that—'

'You trying to do a deal with me?' O'Keefe seemed offended. 'There's something you need? And in return you'll accept the decision of senior officers on the Sweetman case?'

'Nothing like that. This Vincent Naylor thing— the guy who's on a rampage—'

O'Keefe shook his head. 'We need the lid kept on that—you shouldn't even—'

'There's a woman, a witness—without her there'd have been no ERU on Kilcaragh Avenue that day. With this Naylor thug on the warpath, she needs protection.'

'Send me the details. I'll look into it.'

'Colin—she's vulnerable, she needs cover now.'

'Jesus, Bob—what is this? Have you borrowed Bob Geldof's halo? The Naylor problem, it's not your case, it's none of your business—but you'd like someone fast-tracked onto a security list.' O'Keefe's voice was rising. 'Four shootings in a couple of days, the work of one lunatic. Have you any *idea* of the pressure—the panic, Jesus— keeping the lid on—there are *dozens* of people— including members of the force—people who might or might not be in this nutcase's sights. Scarce resources have to be—'

'There's a real danger to a civilian—'

'That's the judgement of an officer—let's be blunt, Bob—an officer who's recently been reprimanded by a judge in open court and suspended due to a breach of discipline.'

'Colin—'

'I'm expected at dinner.' O'Keefe began moving away.

'Fuck this, Colin—this woman is entitled—'

O'Keefe stopped. 'You're speaking out of turn— again.'

'It keeps coming back to Sweetman, right? You're pissed off with what you have to do, but you'll do it anyway. You know it's wrong—and you know I know it's wrong. And that pisses you off.'

'The Sweetman case is solved.'

'Not solved, closed down.'

Some yards away, one of O'Keefe's minders was staring, poised to intervene. O'Keefe waved him away and stepped closer to Tidey. 'Let me explain something, Bob. You're not Sherlock Holmes, you're not Sam Spade. You don't have a mandate to go down mean streets looking for mysteries to solve. And you're not Batman—you're not here to clean up Gotham City.'

'I know my job.'

'You're a public servant. You're handed a file and told to ask questions of anyone who might have answers. Then you hand the file back and you move on. Then other people decide what happens to the file.'

For a moment, Tidey considered whether it was worth the waste of his breath. Then, keeping his voice under control, he said, 'We didn't finish asking questions. The Sweetman case—for whatever reason, it's being shut down before all lines of inquiry have been exhausted.'

'Your job is to gather the raw material, to pass it up the line. It's for others to decide where it fits into the bigger picture.'

'Whatever happened to following the evidence, wherever it leads?'

'Grow up, Bob. We've got an explanation of the Sweetman case, entirely plausible—but we're supposed to keep the inquiry going endlessly, exploring every crackpot theory until we find an explanation that rings your bell?'

'Blame it on the dead guy. That's a sacred Irish tradition.'

'If we didn't have a perfectly feasible explanation of the crime I'd be happy to continue our inquiries—but what's your alternative explanation?'

'Somebody with something to hide needed to shut down Sweetman, and they hired a couple of heavies.'

'Who? Who did the hiring? Who did they hire, how, when, where—or is this all something you saw in a dream?'

'A man named Stephen Hill—gun for hire. He regularly worked with a criminal we believed was one of the two men who killed Oliver Snead. Suppose Hill was the second man in the Snead murder, and he still had the gun. Suppose he used it on Sweetman.'

'Why?'

'Sweetman was talking to the Revenue, and maybe his pals panicked. Who might they go to? Maybe a shady lawyer who was up to his neck in the property game? And Connie Wintour was Stephen Hill's lawyer. We know he talked with both Hill and Sweetman on the day Sweetman was murdered.'

'And for this you want us trampling all over the landscape, on a fishing expedition, casting suspicion where it doesn't belong?'

'What if you're wrong? What if some frightened businessmen asked Connie to arrange for Sweetman to be shut down?'

'That's why we have people like me—to assess the evidence, to bear in mind the bigger picture. To decide when and if an inquiry is productive. You're throwing around allegations about the very people who have an important role in getting this country up from its knees. Maybe you don't give a shit, but those of us who have to keep the bigger picture in mind, we'd rather not try an experiment in reckless justice, thank you very much.'

'So, we shut up shop?'

'Bob—the kind of people you're talking about—you really think there's going to be solid evidence for any of this? You want us to go finger-pointing at a time when it's never been more important for everyone to pull on the green jersey?'

'That's not—'

'You want to give every malcontent, crank and lefty head-banger a licence to stir shit? And for what? So we can get that warm feeling in our tummy for ten minutes—justice served, every avenue exhaustively explored, even if we know it's going to run into the sand.'

Tidey spoke calmly, his voice low. 'This country, we're great at looking back at things. Something awkward happens, we run away from it. And when the smell won't go away—ten years later, twenty, thirty—we have an inquiry, or a tribunal, and we write a report that no one reads and that's it. We're great at looking back. But when it's happening, when we need to do something—there's always someone to tell us we have to pull on the green jersey and shut the fuck up.'

They stood silently for a moment. Then O'Keefe said, 'This suspension doesn't have to be a big deal, Bob. You'll be OK. You keep your head down, time goes by—it's like it never happened.'

'Maura Coady?'

'Send me the details. We'll do what we can, within the resources at our disposal.'

'Which means she's on her own.'

'We'll do what we can.'

Colin O'Keefe turned abruptly and walked towards the wide doorway through which the President and her retinue had gone.

Only stragglers remained in the courtyard. Bob Tidey felt like he'd lost a lot more than an old friend.

58

Do him?

There were two sides to this.

Sitting at the writing table in his room at the Four Seasons, Vincent Naylor was staring at the wall, seeing the Geek walking towards the HMV exit, watching him turn and look back, the contempt all over his face.

'Scumbag! Skanger!'

It was the insolence of the little freak that mattered, almost as much as the eight months in the Joy. Noel was right. 'He's got it coming.'

Vincent opened his wallet and took out the slip of paper Noel had given him. He unfolded it and looked at the Geek's address for a while. Then he placed the paper on the writing table in front of him and used the edge of his hand to smooth it out.

It was doable, without messing up his plans.

Vincent loved the notion of watching the Geek's face, the Geek recognising Vincent and knowing this wasn't going to be good. Seeing the Bernardelli come out. Vincent could feel the weight of the gun in his hand, though it was still in the leather bag lying on the bed. He could see the Geek's mouth opening, lips moving, no sound coming out. The gun coming up.

Vincent felt the kick of the gun against his hand.

He realised he'd been holding his breath and he let it out slowly. He was sitting upright, his chin raised, the muscles rigid in his face.

That would be cool.

But there was something not right about doing the Geek. It would be like he was giving in to his instincts, maybe even losing control. Lorraine and Albert, the others—that shit was righteous. It connected to Noel, it balanced things out. Doing the Geek would be indulging himself. Vincent was better than that. He broke the little freak's nose, he made him curl up in fear, and he did time for that—and maybe the little freak shouldn't get away with it, but it was important to Vincent to maintain the purity of what he was doing.

This was about Noel. It shouldn't be tainted by anything else.

Live your pointless life, you little freak, and die your meaningless death.

Vincent knew he wasn't just a man with a gun and a grudge. He was a man who carried the sword of justice. And the gift of life.

He tore the slip of paper in half and let the pieces fall to the carpet.

*　　　*　　　*

Two seagulls came in low over the Liffey boardwalk, then wheeled around and set out across the waters towards the south side of the river. Despite the whiskey, Bob Tidey felt icily clear-headed as he approached the boardwalk. He'd dropped into the Porterhouse on impulse, minutes after leaving Dublin Castle, and as the third Jameson went down he knew that staying any longer would mean the night would descend into a maudlin, self-pitying mess. He crossed Capel Street Bridge, stepped onto the boardwalk and immediately felt more at ease. It was one of his favourite places for a stroll in the city centre. If it was a sunny day, maybe sit and have a coffee. It was a simple, agreeable place, if you ignored the junkies—and mostly they ignored everyone else.

The run-up to the millennium, ten years earlier, had seen an eruption of celebratory ideas—expensive and often silly. Up at O'Connell Bridge, the council installed a luminous digital clock, floating just below the surface of the Liffey, counting down the seconds to the millennium. After a while it stopped working, so it was junked. Easy come, easy go. Few felt strongly about erecting the Dublin Spire, in O'Connell Street, but there was a committee with a brief to spend a few million, so they spent it—even though the thing went up three years late for the millennium. Bob Tidey thought the Spire was halfway pleasant to look at sometimes, in the early evening, coming up Henry Street, the sun reflecting from the steel. Mostly, it was just there, neither pleasing nor repulsive. A steel pole reaching up into the sky for no particular reason. It wasn't ugly, oppressive or irritating, like so much left behind by the Celtic Tiger bubble, but it wasn't much else either.

The boardwalk, though, put something useful where nothing had been before—overhanging the river on the north quays. And if the junkies liked to hang out there when the weather was good, that was OK. They were citizens too.

There were two of them now, chatting a few yards from where Bob Tidey stood. The evening was still warm, the sun waning. The Sweetman business was done and dusted. Let it go, get on with the job. Further resistance would quickly lead to tough choices—and Tidey found himself rearing back from even thinking about life without his police job. Almost everything he did revolved around the continuous flow of casework. It engaged him like nothing else. Even the ceaseless recurrence of crime didn't weary him, though he'd long let go of the illusion that he was making the world a better place. It was the effort that mattered. To quietly accept the hopelessness, to fail to struggle, was to live without meaning.

The vibration of his mobile alerted him to an incoming call, a second before the phone rang.

'Tidey? Martin Pollard. Bit of bad news—my Chief Superintendent has found another use for that car I sent to Kilcaragh Avenue.'

'You're kidding.'

'He's short-handed. I argued we need someone watching the witness's house—he said she had to join the queue. Have you had a chance to talk to O'Keefe yet?'

'If I send him the details he'll do what he can.'

'That means a week of consideration—with probably bugger all coming out of it.'

'This isn't right.'

'Let's not assume the worst—chances are it won't come to that. Naylor may be out of the country already.'

Tidey was about to say something about betting Maura Coady's life on that, but instead he said, 'Thanks for calling—I'll, I don't know—'

'If there's any change, I'll be in touch.'

Halfway through the conversation, staring down into the dark waters, Tidey suddenly knew, as though seeing in his head a sketched map of the world around him, how things were and what he had to do. He had to do it and he didn't dare. It had to work and it couldn't possibly. The consequences if he failed were dreadful, the consequences if he succeeded were hardly less so.

Now, it was like there was something expanding inside his chest, his mind rippling, thoughts spinning past each other, nothing connecting. He recognised the signs of something he hadn't experienced in a couple of decades—a panic attack. He held onto the boardwalk rail, both hands clenching so hard that it felt like he might crush the wood to splinters.

*   *   *

Liam Delaney was right—the Bernardelli was a good piece. Vincent Naylor thought maybe in future he should make sure he had a gun he felt comfortable with, instead of making do with whatever piece of hardware was handy. Mind you, the Bernardelli was too bulky to carry on his belt or in a pocket, and with the black leather bag hanging from his shoulder Vincent Naylor felt like a fag—but it was the only way to do it. He had the top of the bag unzipped now, coming out of the Four Seasons. No way of knowing when he'd need to get the gun out, and he didn't want to have to fiddle with a zip. He walked out onto the main road and turned towards the city centre.

He waited until he was some distance from the hotel before he hailed a taxi.

'Northside,' he said, 'out towards Fairview. I'll give you a shout when to stop.'

'Weather's holding up,' the taxi driver said.

'Looking good,' Vincent said.

As Bob Tidey lit a cigarette he noticed and tried to
still the shaking in his hands. He took a deep drag,
exhaled slowly, then began to walk up along the
boardwalk towards O'Connell Bridge. He had
no idea how long he'd been standing on the
boardwalk. The panic attack had gone, the
dreadful alternatives still massive in his mind.

What he'd decided to do was simple enough, but
at any stage something might go wrong. In which
case he'd adapt, or he'd try to come up with
something else. Or let it all fall apart.

There were no guarantees, and doing nothing
wasn't an option.

On his way, he'd need to stop off at home, get
hold of those faxed documents on Vincent Naylor,
then—

He stopped walking, took out his mobile and
called Rose Cheney. 'Where are you?'

'I just got home, working late.'

'I need you to do something.' He explained about
Maura Coady, about the danger she might be in.
As he spoke, Cheney made several attempts to cut
in.

'I'm—look, where the hell are you? Can't you—'

'Something's come up—I've got to find someone,
it's—look, please, this is urgent.'

'Shit.'

'And keep your wits about you—this guy, he's a
psycho.'

'Gee, thanks. And I'm doing this—why?'

'Because you know you should.'

Cheney laughed. 'My good deed for the day,
yeah?'

'Something like that.'

59

'I'll be a while—don't go anywhere,' Bob Tidey said.

The taxi driver said, 'Meter's ticking, I'm in no hurry.'

Tidey went upstairs to his apartment and found the file on Vincent Naylor. He sat at the kitchen table, moving from page to page, occasionally scribbling in a notebook.

This was one of the points at which it could go wrong. Finding someone, without being able to use the Garda network, was hit-and-miss. Getting that someone alone, where no one could see, made it harder.

Tidey skipped through the pages on Vincent Naylor, the killing he did for Mickey Kavanagh. He went to the pages of background on Mickey Kavanagh—where he lived, that he lived with a woman with three kids, none of them his. He made notes on Mickey's social habits and hang-outs. The accompanying photo was a poor reproduction, degraded during faxing. Mickey stared at the camera. Bob Tidey stared back.

Kavanagh was a hard-nosed bastard with the power of life and death over his minions—to Tidey, Mickey's sculpted hair and vacant expression gave him the air of a fifth-rate singer from a failed pop band, his mouth half open, ever ready to explain how he never got the breaks.

After about fifteen minutes Tidey went back

down to the taxi and began his search for Mickey Kavanagh.

*   *   *

Vincent Naylor got out of the taxi a couple of hundred yards from Kilcaragh Avenue. When he turned into the street where the bitch nun lived he paused a moment. The whole length of the street, there was just one van parked, the rest were cars. The police preferred vans for snooping. It meant they could have someone watching out the front and someone else watching out the back. They could have a camera peeking—the kind of stuff that you couldn't do from a car without making a circus of it. The van was an old blue Transit, with something on the side about home maintenance. Vincent didn't see it as a cop hideout. Didn't mean they weren't keeping watch from a car, so he walked down the street and back, scoping everything. Nothing to worry about—and he identified number 41. There was a light in the front hall, the rest of the kip in darkness. Could be the bitch was in bed already, maybe she was in the kitchen out back.

Old bitch—no need to let her know why it was happening, just give it to her in the face, on the doorstep.

He pressed the button and heard the bell ring inside. Then he reached into the bag and held the Bernardelli.

Twice more he rang the bell before he decided nothing was going to happen, the bitch wasn't there. OK, maybe in an hour or two. Maybe make a special trip back before leaving Dublin. One way or the other, the bitch is taking it.

As he turned to leave, Vincent Naylor heard an elderly female voice from behind. 'Can I help you, young man?'

*   *   *

At the reception at Jurys Inn, across from Christ Church, Rose Cheney did the talking. Coming through the front doorway, Maura Coady said, 'Is this really necessary?'

'Not to worry, I'll handle the formalities.'

A room for one person, she told the receptionist, two nights, possibly more. She registered Maura Coady as Maura Clark.

When they got to the room, Maura Coady said, 'Very clean, very nice.'

'If you give me your keys, Sergeant Tidey and I will go to your house in the morning—we'll get whatever you need, and bring it here. Is that OK?'

Maura Coady nodded her thanks. 'There are people—I know this—people with real reasons to hate me. But this man—'

'Try to get some sleep.'

'—he doesn't even know me.'

'According to Sergeant Tidey, he's already killed several people. You may not be in danger, but we'd rather not take a chance.'

'How long?'

'I don't know, to be honest—Sergeant Tidey just asked me to make sure you're safe. He'll be in touch.' Cheney handed over a business card. 'My mobile number's on the back—any problem, call me. Really—anything, any time.'

'I will—thank you.'

'We live across the road,' the old woman said. 'Miss Coady's not in. I came over because my husband Phil, he saw her leaving a while ago, with a young woman—probably a relative.'

Vincent Naylor looked behind the old woman, saw a decrepit old man standing at a front door across the road, looking down in the dumps.

'You know where she was going?'

'We knew that other reporter, Anthony—it was on the news tonight, his newspaper says he hasn't been seen. They believe he may have come to some harm. It's unbelievable—Phil is terribly upset. Are you from the same newspaper?'

Vincent nodded. 'Yeah. I need to talk to Miss Coady about something. Did she say where she was going?'

'Phil just saw her leave, he didn't speak to her.'

Vincent said, 'Thanks,' then he began to turn away.

'If you really need to see her, every Sunday morning—she never misses a Sunday—eleven o'clock Mass, the Latin Mass, in the Pro-Cathedral. Do you know where that is?'

'I do,' Vincent Naylor said. 'Eleven o'clock?'

'Every Sunday.'

*   *   *

There was a chance that Mickey Kavanagh was at home. There was a chance the woman he lived with, and her kids, were elsewhere. That would be ideal, to get him alone, at home. Tidey rang the bell of the terraced house in Ballyfermot.

Nothing.

Checking his notebook, Tidey set out for a pub where Mickey Kavanagh was known to drink. When there was no sign of Mickey there he tried a second pub. In the third pub, Mickey Kavanagh was sitting at a window table with four other men, all drinking pints.

Tidey ordered a pint and took it to a corner. He pulled a stool closer and sat down, his drink resting on a narrow ledge. He opened a tabloid, looking towards the page but not at it, his peripheral vision alert to movements at the window table. Every now and then he sipped the pint or turned a page. Almost an hour passed before Mickey Kavanagh stood up and drained his pint. Tidey slid down from his stool, hoping Kavanagh left the pub alone. Instead, on his way to the Gents, Kavanagh ordered more drink. He and his mates obviously intended staying until closing.

In the toilet, Bob Tidey said, 'Gobshite.'

Kavanagh, standing at the urinal, looked over his shoulder. He hurriedly zipped up and turned. 'Do I know you?' He was late thirties, his boy-band hair and pointy-collared shirt giving him a vaguely seventies vibe.

'Gobshite.'

Kavanagh took a step closer. He tried to do it casually, but he couldn't manage it. His face tightened as he psyched himself for the attack.

It wouldn't be a punch or a kick—in too close for that. Just the right set-up, though, to smash his forehead into Tidey's face. The slight backward movement that preceded the lunging head was all the warning Tidey needed. Had the blow hit his nose, possibly breaking it, he'd be blinded by pain, at the mercy of Kavanagh's brawny hands and stomping boots. Instead, he took the blow to the side of the head, jerking back to limit the impact—but it still hurt like fuck.

Tidey had a grip on Kavanagh's shirt front and he allowed himself to fall backwards, pulling Kavanagh off balance, swinging him round, his hands taking Kavanagh's wrist, then twisting his arm behind him, pushing him until Kavanagh's face hit the wall above the urinal. Tidey kicked Kavanagh's feet from under him and watched him slide down, face first into his own piss. It took a few seconds to cuff him and leave him sitting slumped against the wall under the condom machine. Tidey took his notebook out, and jammed it under the door leading back to the bar. When 999 put him through to Command and Control his breathing was heavy. 'Detective Sergeant Robert Tidey, Cavendish Avenue—I've been assaulted.' He gave the address, told them he had his assailant in the Gents toilet in the lounge, and asked them to hurry.

Kavanagh, his face smeared with blood and piss, seemed more indignant than worried. 'What the fuck?' he said.

'Gobshite,' Tidey said.

Eventually, one of Kavanagh's mates arrived at the toilet door, pushing at it and calling his name. Tidey kept a shoulder to the door, his foot holding the notebook in place so it acted as a doorstop. He put a finger to his lips and stared at Kavanagh. The gobshite sat there like a lamb.

Kavanagh's mate went silent, then went walkies in a hurry. There was the sound of a deep country accent. Tidey had his ID ready when he opened the door.

'You OK?' One of the uniforms gestured towards the blood on Tidey's face.

'I'm fine. Be careful with this asshole—I came in here for a piss and he jumped me.'

'Hey—' Kavanagh said.

One of the uniforms leaned over and backhanded his face. 'Be quiet.'

Tidey said, 'Must fancy himself as a big shot. After I cuffed him he told me he's going to have me killed.'

*   *   *

Trixie Dixon was crouched in a foxhole, about to throw a hand grenade at a bunch of Nazi bastards, when the doorbell rang. He paused the PlayStation. In the hallway he said, 'Who is it?'

'Tidey.'

Trixie recognised the voice and opened the door. 'Jesus, what happened to you?'

The policeman's temple was bloody, purple and swollen. Tidey came in and shut the door behind him. 'I need you to do me a favour.'

60

Bob Tidey was up, dressed and ready when two detectives from Turner's Lane came early to take his statement on the arrest of Mickey Kavanagh.

'You're suspended, right?'

'Failure   of   communication—me   and   a

291

superintendent. You know how that goes.'

'You weren't on duty last night?'

'I went for a drink—in fact, I went to a couple of pubs. Quiet night. In need of my own company. Last thing anyone—'

'Let's do this formally.'

'Sure.'

Tidey remained standing, one of the detectives sat at the kitchen table and took notes, the other just stood there looking surly.

'You followed this man into the toilet?'

'I'd no idea anyone was in there—didn't notice the man, never saw him before.'

'And he just attacked you?'

'He said something. He was washing his hands, he looked up when I came in, must have clocked me for a Garda, called me a dirty name—then he went for me, gave me this.' Tidey indicated the damage to his face. 'Headbutt.'

'He says you followed him in there.'

'I told you how it happened.'

'He says you threatened him.'

'I'd no idea who he was.'

The detective standing opposite Tidey said, 'You didn't know it was Mickey Kavanagh?'

'I'd heard the name, but I wouldn't know him from Adam. He's never come up in any case I've been involved with.'

'You didn't threaten him?'

'Why would I?'

'What happened then?'

'I dealt with him, rang it in—you know the rest.'

The detective taking notes said, 'He says he never threatened to kill you.'

Tidey sighed. 'What else would he say? Look—

292

why would I attack a dangerous criminal, someone I've never had reason to investigate? Why would I lie about what he did, what he threatened to do?'

'I've got to put these things to you, you know the drill.'

'Fair enough.'

The detective read his notes back, then spent ten minutes putting Tidey's replies into narrative form. He read the statement aloud.

' "I entered the toilet and a man I now know to be Michael Kavanagh was about to leave. I did not know his identity at the time. He said something that indicated he had identified me as a policeman. I did not at any stage assault Mr Kavanagh or threaten to do so. I did not speak to him. He finished washing his hands and without warning he headbutted me in the face. I subdued my assailant and called for support. While waiting for my colleagues to arrive I did not engage Mr Kavanagh in conversation. At one point he said, 'You have no idea the trouble you are in, you bastard. I'm going to have you wasted.' I did not reply to this. Shortly afterwards, several uniformed members arrived and took Mr Kavanagh away." '

'Anything else?' Tidey said.

'That covers it.'

'Should I keep looking over my shoulder? Is he being bailed?'

'On charges of assaulting a Garda and making a death threat?'

Tidey nodded. 'Good.'

*   *   *

You mow it, and when you've had a few days to

293

admire your handiwork, the grass comes up again. Liam Delaney liked the consistency of nature. But this time of year you had to keep at it or the garden could quickly become a bit of a wilderness. He regretted that the front garden was paved over—done before he bought the place. Right across the city, hundreds of thousands of gardens covered over with brick or cobblelock. And when the heavy rains came there was nowhere for the water to drain away. Then they complain about flooding. Play around with nature, Liam figured, there's a price.

His phone, in the pocket of the denim jacket thrown on a garden chair, made a noise.

The text message said *Meeting*. He and Vincent had agreed to cut out voice calls—safer that way—and keep texts to a minimum. They had the safe house for face-to-face stuff, when something needed sorting. Liam checked his watch, spent another five minutes with the mower, then set off for Rathfillan Terrace, to see what Vincent Naylor wanted.

*   *   *

'My name is William Dixon, they call me Trixie. Christy Dixon is my son.'

Roly Blount said, 'I don't know any Christy Dixon.'

'I need a favour, Mr Blount, and I can do a favour for you.'

Blount didn't answer, just stood there, waiting for Trixie to continue. They were standing in the car park of the Venetian House, a pub out past Cullybawn, in Dublin's western suburbs.

294

Mr Tidey had told him where to find Roly Blount, what to say. Before he got to meet Blount he was taken inside the pub—a flunkey used something that looked like a table tennis bat to check him for weapons or wires. In an alcove on the other side of the pub, eight or ten men including Blount were sitting together, having breakfast, some flicking through the tabloids.

Then Blount took Trixie outside.

Blount's expensive grey suit didn't quite go with a face that seemed to have been chiselled out of weathered concrete. As Frank Tucker's right-hand man, Roly's reputation was as fierce as that of his boss.

'I know you can't say anything, Mr Blount, you have to be careful. Let me tell you the favour I want, then I'll tell you what I can do for you.'

Blount took some chewing gum from a pocket, popped it in his mouth. 'You have a couple of minutes.'

'I know Christy did the odd bit of work for you— that's what has him in jail.'

'Told you, I don't know any Christy.'

'What I want, when he gets out—I know how easy it is, I used to be in the game when I was his age—but I want you to promise me you won't use him, not for anything.'

Blount smiled. 'Look, I don't know any Christy, but if I did, and if he wanted to work for me—I mean, there's a lot of people on the dole who'd jump at the chance of any kind of work.'

'I was talking, last night, to a policeman.'

'Were you now.'

'He was involved in putting Christy in jail.'

'His name?'

'Tidey—he's a sergeant.'

'And?'

'I was having a jar, he came in—he'd already had a few. Said he was celebrating. He was delighted with himself.'

'And?'

'The long and the short of it—there's a little prick named Vincent Naylor, he's been causing trouble for the cops. His solicitor's been negotiating with Tidey. They have a deal.'

'Who's the solicitor?'

'No idea—all Tidey said was they're all patting themselves on the back. This fella Naylor wants to spill his guts.'

'Means nothing to me.'

'You have a fella works for you and Mr Tucker—his name is Mickey Kavanagh—'

'I don't know any Mickey Kavanagh.'

'This cop, he says he's reeling in Vincent Naylor. And, he says, that means he's got the arm on Mickey Kavanagh. He's already got him in a cell.'

Blount was silent for a moment, as though weighing things up. 'We know about that. Mickey got into a fight last night—no big deal, he'll walk.'

'What Tidey says—it came out in bits and pieces—a while back this Vincent Naylor did a job for Mickey Kavanagh, killed someone. Now he's in big trouble—they want him to roll over on Mickey, and he's up for it. Tidey says what they're hoping, they might even get Mickey to roll over and give them Mr Tucker.'

Roly Blount raised his right hand and held Trixie's left cheek, gently. His thumb was half an inch below Trixie's left eye. He moved closer, his face inches away. His touch was so tender he might

296

have been cupping a delicate flower.

'You fuck with me—' Roly said.

'I thought you'd want to know—'

'—you won't see me coming.'

'I swear, Mr Blount.'

'What's the favour?'

'I want you to leave him be. My son Christy—I don't want him involved.'

Roly Blount looked at him for a moment, his hand still on Trixie's cheek, his mouth working on the chewing gum. 'Your boy did us a favour, kept his mouth shut. He gets work from me, all I'm doing is paying him back, that's all.'

'I know that, Mr Blount, and I'm grateful. But now—I've done you a favour, and you can do me a favour. Don't do Christy any more favours.'

Blount let go of Trixie's cheek. He nodded. 'If that's what you want—that's OK by me. As long as you're telling me the truth—this Mickey Kavanagh business.'

'It's what the copper told me.'

'You talk to no one else about this, right?'

'No one.'

'You never came here, right?'

'Never.'

'Now, piss off.'

'Thank you, Mr Blount.'

61

Liam Delaney let himself into the house at Rathfillan Terrace and called out, 'Vincent?'

'In here.'

Vincent was sitting in an armchair facing the living-room door.

'What's the story?'

'I'm heading off tomorrow—I might need a favour.'

'No problem.'

'These people, they've got me flying out from Belfast airport. Bit of a nuisance, but they've done it that way before and they say it's cool. And they've booked a ferry from Larne, just in case.'

Liam smiled. 'Fucking volcanoes—a bit of dust in the air and the airlines take the day off.'

'Either way, I'll need a lift.'

'No problem.'

'You're a star.'

'That other thing you're doing—all done?'

Vincent smiled. 'One last loose end—tomorrow.'

'All this trouble, you sure it's worth the bother?'

'Start something, you have to finish it.'

'That's that, then.'

Vincent said Liam should leave first, that Vincent would wait ten minutes.

Liam said, 'What time you want to set off tomorrow?'

'They'll know tonight if the airports are going to be open—then, eleven o'clock in the morning, I have to go to Mass.'

'Mass?'

'Yeah, in the Pro-Cathedral. After that, I'm free and easy. Let's say we meet here two o'clock.'

*   *   *

Bob Tidey lit a cigarette and after a couple of puffs he noticed he hadn't finished the previous one,

298

perched on the edge of his ashtray. He stubbed them both out and stood up. He'd long seen his apartment as perfectly matching his few needs, but today it seemed as small as a cell. He pulled on a jacket, pocketed his cigarettes and lighter and left the apartment. He'd been walking for ten minutes, going nowhere in particular, his stride a little longer than was comfortable, stretching himself just a little, when he got a text from Holly.

Tonight?

Tidey doubted he'd sleep much tonight, and he wouldn't be up to conversation, or anything much else. He sent a text back, saying he'd be working tonight.

*   *   *

Roly Blount said, 'It looks solid enough. Two people say this Naylor fella did a favour for Mickey Kavanagh—swatted a chancer who was skimming.'

Frank Tucker's suit was better cut than Roly Blount's, his face softer than his lieutenant's.

'You know him?'

'By name. Small-time tosser.'

Roly was chewing gum faster than a football manager in injury time. Frank was as still as a painting.

Frank didn't say anything for a moment. One thumb idly stroking the corner of his lips. 'This whole thing—this Naylor kid, he's in the cop's pocket, and he maybe pulls Mickey in after him. This could go south *very* quickly.'

Roly said, 'Mickey's mouthpiece went in to see him. Mickey says the cop started the fight, set him up for arrest.'

299

'We're working blind. Get on the phone. You and Dermot and Stretch. I want to know where this Naylor fucker lives, who he lives with, who he works with, who his friends are—everything. Where he drinks, who he's screwing on the side, which hand he wipes his arse with. And I want to know all that this evening.'

*   *   *

Vincent Naylor rolled off the bed and spent fifteen minutes washing the whore's perfume away. When he came out of the shower she was still on the bed. He said, 'You still here?'

She said, 'You finished?'

'Where you from? China?' He began dressing.

She said no, and she said where she was from, but Vincent didn't catch it. He'd already paid, but now she asked him for taxi fare and he said, 'Sure,' and gave her a twenty. He asked if he should walk her to the bus but she didn't get the joke and said, 'Not necessary.'

When she was gone he took the magazine out of the Bernardelli. He'd worked his way well into the sixteen shells, so he figured it was best to swap this one for the second magazine. After doing the bitch nun at the Pro-Cathedral he'd lose the Bernardelli—no way he could take it with him on the trip.

*   *   *

James Snead was considering whether it was too late to go out. Go to the pub, it's noisy, crowded— by the time you start to get a buzz the staff are

300

banging glasses on the counter and telling everyone it's time they pissed off home. These days, more often than not, he preferred to have his own four walls around him.

The doorbell rang and when he opened up Detective Sergeant Tidey was standing there, taking a bottle of Jameson out of a paper bag. 'I could do with company,' Tidey said.

*   *   *

They were on their second drink when James said, 'What kind of trouble are you in?'

Tidey just looked at him.

'It's all over your face.'

Tidey thought about saying something, then said, 'Nothing more than usual—it's a pressure job.'

'Maybe you should have stuck with the Simon Community.'

'Maybe.'

*   *   *

An hour later, Tidey was sitting on the floor, his back to the sofa. James Snead was in an armchair, there was a lot of air in the bottle and there were long silences between them.

'This thing,' James said, 'you want to talk about it and you don't want to talk about it, that right?'

'I'd say you've put your finger on it.'

'Something you've done?'

'Something I've started—how it ends, that's something else.'

'Tell me this—can you do anything about it?'

'The wheels are turning.'

301

'That's not what I asked. We know the wheels are turning. Can you stop them? Do you want to?'

'It's too late now.'

'Then, what the hell—you don't have a problem.' James poured some more whiskey into both glasses. 'You've done it, whatever it is. Now, all you have to do is live with it.'

62

Vincent Naylor finished his toast, refilled his coffee cup. It being shortly after ten o'clock on Sunday morning, the Kylemore Cafe on O'Connell Street wasn't too busy. Vincent was sitting at a table beside the large window looking out onto North Earl Street. Outside in the bright sunlight, early-bird tourists were taking photographs of the James Joyce statue. First time he saw it, Vincent thought it was supposed to be Charlie Chaplin.

Take care of business, then meet Liam Delaney at the safe house at Rathfillan Terrace. They'd be out of Dublin shortly after two o'clock, on his way to Belfast—the airports were defying the volcano ash—and by this evening he'd be in Glasgow, just a short step from London and Michelle.

Vincent unfolded a wrinkled front page from the *Irish Daily Record* and flattened it on the table beside his plate. ABUSE NUN IS SHOOT-OUT HERO. Since it was published he'd stared at the photo of Maura Coady several times a day. With her short white hair and her stupid buck teeth, he'd have no bother spotting the bitch nun among the faithful plodding their way to the Pro-Cathedral this

302

morning.

*   *   *

When Rose Cheney asked to be put through to
room 327, the receptionist at Jurys Inn said, 'That's
Miss Clark's room?'

'Yes, please.'

'Oh, she's been gone a few minutes.'

'Sorry?'

'I was speaking to her not five minutes ago. She
wasn't sure of which way to go, so she asked me
for directions. She's on her way to the Pro-
Cathedral—eleven o'clock Mass, she said.'

'Shit.'

*   *   *

His mouth was dry, his hangover tolerable, but
Bob Tidey awoke enveloped in a full-fledged cloud
of dread.

Tidey had slept in James Snead's spare room, the
room that used to belong to James's murdered
grandson. James had long ago stripped the room of
all personal belongings—no sign that Oliver had
ever been there.

'Either that, or turn the place into a shrine,'
James had said. The session ended when James
shook the upturned Jameson bottle, to drain the
last few drops.

Naylor.

There was nothing more to do, no way of
knowing what would happen or when. He felt like
someone who'd bet his life on a horse race run at
some undecided course, on some unspecified day.

Last night's drinking was a bad idea, but it wasn't the only bad idea he'd had lately, and in the circumstances it was fitting. He tried to get his thoughts straight, to ask himself for the thousandth time if it was too late to stop this Mickey Kavanagh thing, if it was too dangerous, too reckless, too wicked—or would stopping it be worse? For the thousandth time, measuring his conscience against the circumstances, he decided there was no going back.

He was getting to his feet when his phone rang. His clothes were in a heap on the floor. He bent and groped in his pockets until he found it.

'Yeah.'

'Maura Coady's on her way into the city centre,' Rose Cheney said. 'She left the hotel. She's off to eleven o'clock Mass at the Pro-Cathedral.'

'Christ sake.'

'She should be OK—I mean, this Naylor guy, what are the chances he's going to spot her on her way to Mass?'

'He's killing people. He's been very good at it.'

'And you want me to—'

Tidey was reaching for his trousers. 'Meet me at the Pro-Cathedral.'

As he left the flat, unshaven and unwashed, he could hear James snoring. He found his car, started the engine and motored away. Five minutes later, at a traffic light, he reached into a pocket and realised he'd left his cigarettes behind.

* * *

After her toast and tea Maura Coady looked at Rose Cheney's business card and thought about

304

ringing her. It seemed over-fussy to bother the policewoman at home on a Sunday morning. Mr Tidey wanted her to stay in the hotel room, but that couldn't include wanting her to miss Sunday Mass. The eleven o'clock Mass, the Latin version, with the high ceiling of the Pro-Cathedral echoing back the sounds coming up from the children of the Palestrina Choir. It wasn't just about fulfilling her devotional duties. The solemn surroundings, the exotic language of the Latin Mass, the splendour of the choir, the beauty of it all, kept her spiritually recharged right through the following week.

Her watch said ten thirty, now—plenty of time, lovely sunny morning, the city looking splendid. She was on her way down along the quays, through a city centre she hadn't seen in a long time. She wondered if there could be any more white stone, marble and glass left in the world, they'd used so much of it in Dublin these past few years.

*   *   *

Vincent Naylor left the Kylemore Cafe, unzipping the top of his shoulder bag. He walked down North Earl Street and turned into narrow, sunless Marlborough Street. He climbed the steps to the raised surround and stood beside the railings at the corner of Cathedral Street. From here, he could keep an eye on all three approaches to the church. If she came down from O'Connell Street, that might be a problem—the sightlines were difficult. But the old bitch—white hair, buck teeth—the queen of the kiddie-fiddlers, shouldn't be too hard to spot. Things have a way of working out.

305

Vincent was aware that his grief for Noel had changed. Not lessened, it was just different. There was still an ache every time he thought of his brother. Sometimes he saw or heard something and thought of telling Noel and there was a moment of dizzying loss—then the aching wave rolled over him, strong as ever.

What was new was the feeling of achievement. Instead of falling to pieces when Noel was murdered, he'd done what needed to be done. He'd rebalanced things. He'd shown his respect— he'd done what Noel would have done. He hoped that, wherever he was—however these things work out—Noel knew that.

And it was almost all done, now.

*　　　*　　　*

Bob Tidey came off the North Circular, driving down Summerhill in sparse traffic. He got through the lights, into Parnell Street, approaching the Asian and African shops. There were barriers across the street, a mechanical digger and a few men in work clothes, two yellow trucks off to one side—a diversion sign pointing towards Cumberland Street, on the left. Tidey wrenched the wheel, turned left and travelled ten yards, then ran the car up onto the pavement.

Tidey was out of his car, locking it—back into Parnell Street running. Less than a minute later he was turning left into Marlborough Street, the Pro-Cathedral in view.

*　　　*　　　*

Vincent stood on tiptoes. Making sure the bitch nun wasn't among the small cluster of old biddies shuffling up the steps of the Pro-Cathedral. His phone vibrated in his pocket. As he thumbed the phone he glanced down Marlborough Street, one way and then the other, then he looked at the text.

Shit.

Ten more minutes, max, he'd have had the bitch nun cooling on the pavement. The temptation was huge—hang on, do the job, then hurry to meet Liam.

Meeting, the text said. Liam needed him at Rathfillan Terrace.

No one called a meeting for piddling reasons, and backing each other was too important to start messing with the drill. You get a text, go to the safe house.

Hurrying away, Vincent was thinking about options. Could be he'd come back to Dublin a month from now, take his time, enjoy showing the bitch the gun before doing her in her own house. Better still, Sunday in the Pro-Cathedral, not just an ordinary Mass—special productions for the Holy Joes. These things drag on. He might be able to deal with Liam's problem and get back here before the Mass ended.

*   *   *

Bob Tidey's breathing was stressed, he slowed to a walking pace. Up ahead, he could see Rose Cheney, one arm linked with Maura Coady's. By the time he reached them he was just about able to talk without coughing.

Cheney was smiling. 'Maura would like to stay,

307

hear Mass, listen to the Palestrina Choir—she wants to know if that's all right.'

'Best not,' Tidey said.

'It's almost started,' Maura said. 'What's the harm?'

'I'll stay with her,' Cheney said. 'I'll leave her back at the hotel.'

'Please,' Maura Coady said.

Tidey sighed. He looked at Cheney. 'Go home— you've got a family, it's Sunday. I'll stay with her.'

Maura Coady took her rosary beads from her pocket.

63

Vincent Naylor closed the front door of the house at Rathfillan Terrace and said, 'Hello?' He went into the living room and there was a stranger sitting upright in the armchair facing the door, his face a mess. Vincent's hand went into his shoulder bag, taking hold of the Bernardelli, and another man, coming in from the kitchen, pointed at Vincent and there was a muzzle flash and something very big hit Vincent in the chest. When his eyes opened he was lying on his back and the room smelled like a whole lot of fireworks had gone off. He didn't know if he'd been out for two seconds or two hours. Apart from the stranger in the armchair, there were two men in the room— the man who'd shot him and a smaller guy, a man in his thirties with a bad case of acne.

Vincent levered himself into a sitting position, his back against the wall. He said, 'There's, look, when—'

Vincent could tell he'd been shot low down in the chest. No sucking sound, his lungs were all right, this was—

Vincent recognised the stranger in the armchair.

Liam Delaney, a piece of silver tape across his mouth, a large bloody mess where his right eye should have been. Liam was sitting upright, his feet tied together, more silver tape, and his hands were tucked behind him. Liam's left eye was wide open, staring, his chest heaving, nose flaring. There was blood leaking from the silver tape across his mouth.

Vincent said, 'This, it's not—'

The taller of the two men picked up Vincent's shoulder bag. He took out the Bernardelli, showed it to the acne man. The acne man took it and shot Liam in the forehead. Then he put the muzzle of the gun under Liam's chin and when he squeezed the trigger the room vibrated with the noise. The taller man was standing over Vincent, leaning down. Vincent looked up into the dark muzzle of the man's small silvery gun.

*   *   *

Maura Coady said, 'The young voices, the ancient music, the beauty of it—if ever I have doubts, I think of that sound. It's a foretaste of something beyond all this.'

They were in her room at Jurys Inn, Maura was sitting on the edge of the bed, drinking tea. Tidey was standing. She seemed thinner than ever, fragile, diminished.

'It was lovely,' Tidey said. 'But I want you to stay

309

here until we know there's no more danger from this man. I know it's boring, cooped up in the room, but this man somehow traced a policeman to his home and tried to kill him.'

Maura looked around the room. 'I spent most of my life in a convent, Sergeant—this might be a little frightening, but it's certainly not boring. Next Sunday morning, though, I'm afraid, I'll insist again on my little choral treat.'

Tidey said, 'Let's take it a day at a time.'

She put her cup aside. 'Thank you for everything.' She stood up. Her face seemed paler, a rawness around the eyes. 'I sometimes wonder— when I think about all the awful things that were done, the lives we destroyed—whether I've a right to ever take pleasure again in beauty and innocence.'

Tidey held her elbow. 'What you did, it's not all you are. And if there's a way of getting through this world without doing something wrong—I don't know about it.'

'There are some wrongs that are worse than others.'

Out in the corridor, a couple of people were arguing loudly—something about a radio show.

Tidey said, 'You confessed—you believe in absolution?'

After a moment, speaking slowly, being careful with her words, Maura said, 'All my life I've believed in the sacrament of Confession, but I've always wondered if it wasn't, well—a little convenient.' Her smile was rueful and brief. 'No one has a right to wipe the slate clean, except the people we harmed. And they're out there somewhere, struggling to get on with their lives—

our guilt is not their problem.'

'There's no redemption?'

'And there shouldn't be. There's just living with it, I think. Owning up, and living with the things we do.'

64

Carefully placing his feet, Detective Inspector Martin Pollard entered the room and paused. He'd dealt with scenes like this in the past and he had a way of coping. He looked down, his eyes closed, and he emptied his mind, let his emotions settle. When he opened his eyes his demeanour was as detached and cold as he could make it. He took out his notebook and first did a rough diagram of the room. Technical had already been over the scene, but Pollard needed his own notes. When the diagram was done he flicked over the page and wrote quickly and neatly. He heard a noise and glanced up and there was a uniform looking into the room. Pollard shook his head and the uniform went away.

A couple of minutes later, Detective Sergeant Joan Tyler came in, stood just inside the doorway. 'Bloody savages,' she said.

Martin Pollard took his time finishing his notes, then he and Sergeant Tyler went outside to talk to Technical.

*   *   *

When they were finished eating, they lingered over

what was left of the wine and Holly said, 'You want the good news first, or the bad news?'

'Christ,' Bob Tidey said, 'set me up, then knock me down.'

The restaurant was five minutes' walk from Holly's home. It was all it had to recommend it.

'It's about Grace.'

'Pregnant?'

'The good news is she's got a job. Starts Monday week. The bad news—it's in Leeds.'

A friend of Grace's from UCD had a fledgling business there, funded by an uncle. She imported second-hand Japanese cars. Things were going well and she needed a bookkeeper.

Tidey said, 'At least it's not Australia or Canada.'

'All the same, with Dylan in London—I always took it for granted the kids would live in their own country. Instead, it's like the 1980s.'

'It's a hop and a skip to Leeds, and back.'

'I suppose,' Holly said. 'There's not much money in it, she says, but it's work. She's out celebrating tonight.'

'Good for her.'

'She'll need help, she'll have expenses starting off—rent, things like that.'

'That's what money's for.'

They were halfway back to Holly's place when Tidey's phone rang.

'Yeah?'

Martin Pollard said, 'You heard about the shooting in Santry?'

'It was on the radio—no names so far.'

'Both victims shot twice in the head. One of them's our lad. Naylor was done cleanly, the other guy looks like someone's been using him for butchery practice.'

'Jesus.'

Tidey stopped walking, stood in the street with the phone down by his side. He took a long breath.

Holly grabbed his arm and he shook his head. When he put the phone back to his ear, Pollard was in mid-sentence.

'Sorry, I missed that.'

'The second victim—his name's Liam Delaney. We went to his place this evening. His sister was there, says she was visiting this morning and two men came for Delaney. He told her everything was fine, that he'd be back in a few hours. Told her she shouldn't call the police.'

'You got suspects?'

'Naylor never worried much about who he pissed off. He might have been on anyone's list.'

Tidey said, 'Yeah.'

'You'll tell that old nun, let her know everything's over, there's nothing to worry about?'

'I will, I will. Listen, thanks for calling.'

Holly said, 'What is it?'

'Work,' he said, 'just something at work.'

*   *   *

Bob Tidey leaned on the kitchen counter. He took the salt cellar and moved it a few inches to stand alongside the pepper grinder. He straightened the lid on the butter dish.

After the phone call, there had been no conversation on the walk back to Holly's place. Now, she put an arm around his waist and pressed her face against his shoulder. 'Talk when you can—or let it be, whichever.'

313

His voice was barely audible. 'Later.'

* * *

'I've done something.'

'Can you say?'

'No.'

They were in bed. He was lying on his back, her head resting on his arm. The sex had been brisk, and over quickly.

'How bad?'

'I've put people away for less.'

'Is it a case?'

'Just the way things came together.'

'Bob—'

'There was no right thing to do. But something had to be done.' He said it like it was a mathematical formula he'd worked out.

'It wasn't—did you take something? What I mean is, was it crooked?'

'I've never taken anything.'

'Are you in trouble?'

He thought about that for a moment, then said, 'No one can connect me to anything.'

'Then—'

Tidey said nothing for a long time. Then he said, 'I'm not who I set out to be—not any longer. And I don't know where it goes from here.'

* * *

He came out of sleep abruptly, his breathing fast. He'd felt himself stepping off a cliff—plummeting feet first, then his upper body weight taking him over into a wild tumble, unable to get a fix on the

314

sky or the earth, no control—then he was awake, Holly was sleeping beside him, the house was silent and Bob Tidey's fingernails were digging into his palms.

He sat up, feet on the floor, poised on the edge of the bed, and heard again Martin Pollard's words.

Naylor was done cleanly, the other guy looks like someone's been using him for butchery practice.

Tidey took a long, deep breath, held it and let it out slowly.

This was one of those extreme events that fills the mind. It takes time for things like that to find their proper size, to become one more piece in a messy, never-finished jigsaw. Hang on long enough to get perspective, Bob Tidey told himself, and anything can be endured.

'Bob?' Holly's head was raised from the pillow.

'It's OK,' Tidey said.

Holly turned, looked at the clock. 'Nearly one o'clock.'

Tidey said, 'I'd better go—is Grace—'

Holly moved in the bed, reached up and put a hand on his shoulder.

'You can have a chat with her in the morning.'

'Are we—' Tidey said, and he stopped because he wasn't sure he wanted to know the answer.

Holly's voice was drowsy. 'Go to sleep,' she said.

ACKNOWLEDGEMENTS

Julie Lordan, as always, was my first reader and advisor. She and Cathleen Kerrigan were supportive through the lost weekends and preoccupied holidays.

Publishing Director Liz Foley's commentary on the first draft and Briony Everroad's editing greatly improved the novel. Katherine Fry did the meticulous copy-edit. Thanks to all and special thanks, as always, to my friends Pat Brennan and Evelyn Bracken, for their fast and thorough appraisal and advice.